℗ TO LIVE

TO LIVE AMONG WOLVES

TO LIVE AMONG WOLVES

Book One of
The Legends of Arcadia Series

Morgan Hubbard

Wistful Publishing
Visit the author's website at morganhubbardauthor.com

Cover design by Maria Spada
Formatting by Evenstar Books

ISBN 979-8-9863981-2-9

To those of wild spirits and daydreams.
May you find peace among trees.

Author's Note

The following is a fantasy story, one I'd like to believe. The locations are based on fact, though I've tweaked them just a bit here and there for the purpose of my story. Please do not use this map or the contents of this book as any sort of guide, or else you'll be hopelessly lost in the Smoky Mountains. And unfortunately, I doubt a king from some ancient wolf pack will come to your rescue. He's far too busy with a human girl and his two siblings and all his other Alpha responsibilities.

That being said, the locations of places such as the Great Mountain (also known as Mt. Leconte) and Feru Falls (also known as Grotto Falls) are approximated for the purpose of this story. The rivers mentioned are not, in fact, the Little River and the Tennessee River as that would put Arcadia somewhere south of Knoxville and northeast of Maryville. Instead, the Little River that causes Eden so much trouble is fictional as is the Great River that Silas loves.

I would also like to point out three very real facts about the Smokies and the Appalachian Mountains:

1. Blue Ghost Beetles (also known as blue ghost fireflies) are real! They are unusual and rare, but they typically make an appearance during the synchronous lightning bug season in June.

2. Wolves really did exist in the Appalachian Mountains. Red wolves (*canis rufus*) had a historic range stretching from Pennsylvania to south Florida and all the way west to San Antonio, Texas. Way back in the early 1700s, there were bounties for wolves in North Carolina. Later, in the 1800s, the red wolf was distinguished as a separate species from gray wolves. By the 1920s, the red wolf was considered eradicated from most states. Today, it's estimated there are 50 red wolves living in a reserve on the east coast of North Carolina thanks to captive breeding programs with red wolves taken from south Texas. Not much is being done to bring them back out of endangered status like their gray cousins out west. One day, I'd like to do a special edition set of the Legends of Arcadia trilogy where a percentage of the money I receive will go to funding the protection of these red wolves. They've come to mean a lot to me over the course of researching for this trilogy, and I'd hate to see them disappear on account of no one caring enough to help.

3. Silas makes a comment about people going missing in the Appalachian Mountains. It's rumored that around 400 people go missing in Tennessee each year, and the Great Smoky Mountains National Park is considered one of the more dangerous National Parks. While no one quite knows how many people disappear each year in the Appalachian Mountains (including the Great Smoky Mountains), it's a regular enough occurrence that a solo hiker disappearing wouldn't necessarily be uncommon.

And if at any point you think to yourself, "that's unrealistic," please remind yourself that this is a fantasy book, however convincing it may be.

May you find peace among the trees,

Morgan Hubbard

P.S. - I would also like to say that with the growing concerns of AI books and art and everything else, I wrote every word of this without the use of AI. I started drafting it in September of 2022 and finished somewhere in July of 2023, almost a full year of drafting! And then I edited SEVERAL times and finally have this official version you're reading today! It's taken nearly two full years from conception to publication. There were many days and nights that dishes went undone, laundry unfolded, floors unswept, and food uncooked. I'm mostly a beverage goblin when drafting which makes for very frequent bathroom trips and not a lot else getting done besides poorly written scenes, Spotify playlists, and Pinterest boards.

P.P.S. - You can find links to said Spotify playlists, Pinterest boards, and wolfish things on my website at morganhubbardauthor.com, if you're at all interested.

Pronunciation Guide

Characters and Creatures

- Lycaon (*lie-KAY-ohn*) - Ancient king of Arcadia/swear word
- Macon (*MAY-kohn*) - current Elder of Arcadia
- Micca (*MEEK-ah*) - race of forest dwellers who tend to nature
- Micc (*MEEK*) - singular of Micca
- Ugal (*OO-guhl*) - lizard-like amphibious creature
- Kuslar (*KOOS-lahr*) - nocturnal pixie-like creatures that hibernate in the winter
- Kusla (*KOOS-lah*) - singular of Kuslar

Proper Nouns and Places

- Joulo (*YAOO-loh*) - winter solstice/Yule
- Lo Sain e lo Feru (*LOH SAH-een ay loh FAY-roo*) - The Legend of the Wild
- Sarva (*SAHR-vah*) - autumn equinox/Festival of Kings
- Arcadia (*ahr-CAY-dee-ah*) - Home of the *virlukos*
- The Yard - "foyer" of Arcadia
- Guardian's Glade - throne room
- Mender's Heath - Healer's quarters
- The Boneyard - Hunter's hangout area/Sparring Arena
- The Sage Brush - Seer's quarters
- Rauha (*RAOO-hah*) - peace; the trio's place of peace
- Feru Falls (*FAY-roo*) - Wild Falls; the gateway to Arcadia
- Kulas (*KOO-lahs*) - a mead-like beverage brewed by *virlukos*; names for its golden hue and the brewing process which includes the hard work of volunteer kuslar

THE RIVER

MAGIC HAPPENED WHEN HUMANS and nature collided.

The little girl, no more than four years of age, squealed while the wind whipped through her dark curls. A storm bit at the edges of my friends, the Great Mountains. The black clouds approached, knocking tree branches down in their wake.

On my north bank, familiar friends approached, the ancient language drifting to me along with the scent of wet dog.

"Ellie, it's alright. There are only five of them. And one is small." An alpha wolf sniffed the air, his ears alert.

"How can you tell?" Ellie tucked her tail low between her back paws.

The couple's eyes focused on my southern bank, where the child squatted and played in the shallows of my Spirit.

"Iain, the children." Fear lingered in the mother's quickening heartbeat.

Under the ground cover, three pups studied their parents.

"Do you think this is a lesson in stealth?" The brown-eyed and golden-furred Caroline wondered.

"No way." Her steel-eyed and dark-furred brother, Nash, shook his shoulders and head. "Maybe the humans are lost and need our help."

"I don't think it's either of those things." The green-eyed and gray-furred Silas snuck out from the bushes, away from his family and closer to my north bank.

Wolves didn't often visit my waters after the red wolf population dwindled so many years ago, but the *virlukos* had their ways.

Silas treaded away from his siblings, coming level with the human girl across the river. She collected a few stones, moving to place them with her stone circle in the damp grass of my south bank.

"She isn't lost." Silas mused to himself.

He stepped closer.

Still oblivious, the human child perked up, scanning my darkening waters.

"She isn't scared, nor is she threatening." He inched closer, snapping a twig under his small paw. In a moment, his mother circled him.

"Silas, what were you thinking? You could've been spotted!" She nipped at his neck scruff.

"But she didn't see me!" Silas toppled away over his front feet. "See?"

They turned towards the human.

"What is she doing?" His mother's ears perked up. "Where is her family?"

"They're farther up the river." Iain nudged Silas with his nose. "Go find your siblings and bring them over here."

"Yes, Father." Silas trotted away, disappearing under the ground cover.

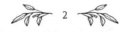

"Iain." Ellie's eyes didn't leave the girl. "There's something about this child."

"For the last time, she's harmless."

"It's not that."

Ellie's Spirit shifted. Something moved.

"What is it, El?" Iain rubbed his shoulder against hers, perking his ears at the sound of thunder in the distance.

Ellie lowered her head. "I'm not sure. There's something... Something I can't quite place about her. It's like she's—"

Then, the child balanced on a stone, talking to herself about a fossil she believed had been buried on my northern bank. Preparing to cross, she leapt for a moss-blanketed rock near the middle of my waters.

With a terrified scream, she slipped and sank under my current like a stone.

Her panic coursed through her veins like the water between my banks, her fear magnetic and palpable. She attempted to scream but only managed to take some of me with her. The child tumbled deeper into my current. She submerged into a kind of dark that only the stars and I know.

Farther down my north bank, Iain sprang into the water. He paddled upstream, waiting to catch the girl and carry her to safety once the current brought her his way. Grabbing the back of her shirt like the scruff on his pups' necks, Iain dragged her onto my silty northern shore.

Thunder rumbled, causing the leaves on the surrounding trees to shiver while the young girl coughed up my water from her lungs. She wiped tears away from her mud-colored eyes as Iain watched from a respectable distance.

Ellie observed from the tree line. Something settled over her Spirit that hadn't been there when the family first arrived. Something...

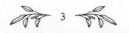

Iain's ears pinned back as he glanced up at the darkening skies. His reddish fur melted to gray around the muzzle, and my water clung to his thick fur in droplets. His steel eyes turned towards the young girl again.

Ellie howled low, causing the child to startle. The three pups responded in shrill, answering howls.

The girl tucked her sopping wet hair behind her ear and gazed up at the wolf. With tentative movements, she reached her hand up to Iain, who pressed his damp muzzle to her small palm.

She giggled, and the sound harmonized with my gurgling current, a melody like none other. Nature and humanity together.

Iain stepped back, shaking the water out of his coat. His fur slipped away like the waterfalls tumbling farther north, revealing human skin beneath. The shape of a middle-aged man appeared, the skin by his eyes crinkled from consistent mirth. His hands were large, and his hair reached his shoulders. Wet curls framed his face, a face I'd seen many times.

Iain knelt next to the child, and I marveled at the contrast between his bronze bare skin and her own paleness decorated with freckles.

"Your family will be looking for you, child." Soft around the edges, Iain's voice ran across my waters, rippling like stone against a placid pond.

"My name is Eden." The human child straightened.

A deep laugh bubbled out of Iain's chest. "Wonderful to meet you, Eden." He smiled. "My name is Iain."

"Iain," she repeated, her curious voice sounding out the name.

He tilted his head to the side. "Are you not afraid, child?"

As Eden's lips parted, words on the tip of her tongue, the three pups tumbled out of the ground cover onto my silty northern shore. Silas rolled upside down, phased, and landed flat on his back. Nash pinned his shoulders down and shifted. They both had a mess of dark hair.

Caroline regarded Eden, shaking her coat to reveal long, golden hair like the sun hiding behind the storm clouds overhead.

Eden observed them with a frowning face, no doubt noting the biggest difference between her and them. *They* were naked. *She* was clothed.

"Who is she?" Caroline asked her father.

"A friend." Iain smiled. "Children, meet Eden."

Silas and Nash stood, dusting themselves off and began bickering again.

Caroline stepped forward and introduced herself. She gave Eden a tight smile.

"Boys." Iain raised an eyebrow.

"I'm Nash." He flashed a grin at the young girl.

Rolling his eyes, Silas elbowed his brother. "I'm Silas. It's nice to meet you, Eden."

"It's nice to meet you, too." Eden's eyebrows furrowed, thunder rumbling closer now.

Ellie called slightly from the cover of the forest, pulling her family's attention to her. I could sense her unease lingering.

Iain turned back to Eden, smiling once again. "While I would love to stay awhile, we have important business elsewhere. Can you find your family alright, Eden?"

Caroline grabbed her father's arm. "There are more of *them*?"

Iain tucked a piece of her blonde hair behind her ear, and she relaxed at his gentle touch.

Eden nodded. "I can walk back up the river until I find them."

"Good." Iain beamed. "Run along now, Eden." He turned to his sons. "Silas, go follow and make sure she makes it back up the river."

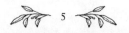

Silas's eyebrows raised. "But—"

"It is our duty to take care of the lost and help those in need." Iain straightened, eyebrows knitting together.

Silas bowed his head with a sigh. "Yes, Father."

I would've done my best to cradle the child and keep her safe. But I was only a river, nothing more.

With a stretch, Silas's fur grew back and his siblings followed suit, all three different shades: Nash, a grayish black; Silas, an ashy gray; and Caroline, a sandy beige.

Nash and Caroline bounded up the bank and into the darkening forest.

Iain nudged Eden forward with his hand.

"Will I see you again?" Eden turned, squinting up at him.

He smiled. "*Veime, myt, au dumahn,* Eden. Only time will tell. Now, run along."

The human girl stepped forward before turning around again. "And he'll stay with me?" She pointed at Silas's gray form.

"He'll be with you the whole way back. I promise." Iain's eyes sparkled. He stretched his body along my sand, red fur replacing tanned skin.

Satisfied with Iain's word, Eden made her way back up my shores. Nash and Caroline tucked under their mother, sticking their muzzles between her teeth with affection.

Meanwhile, Iain stood watch at the edge of my north bank, gazing at the oncoming storm while Eden returned to her family. Silas shrunk in her wake, a silent shadow only a few feet away but unseen by the girl.

"This girl is much different than the other humans I've seen." Silas mused, ducking under a fallen tree. His ears perked up when he came within reach of her family's heartbeats. They drummed along with the sound of my current, but they were unbothered by Eden's absence.

"Has no one noticed that she's been gone?" Silas snapped his head

6

towards the girl.

Eden stopped, craning her neck to gaze into the trees. She seemed disappointed that she couldn't see Silas protecting her from the shadows of the forest.

Back with the rest of the family, Ellie nudged Iain with her nose. "I think we'll see Eden again."

"What makes you say that?" Iain tilted his head to the side, gazing at his mate.

"There's something lingering in the wind."

And she was right.

The electricity pulsing through my waters.

A dark magic crackled somewhere up in the hollers of the Great Mountain, in the folds of *Shaconage*.

The winds changed as a lightning bolt cracked the sky in half. Caroline and Nash scrambled for safety under their parents when Silas came bounding back.

"She's back with her family." Silas panted. "They hadn't noticed she'd gone."

"You did well, son." Ellie licked behind his ears, sticking his fur at an odd angle.

"Will she be okay?" Silas pawed at his face.

Ellie straightened, staring off in the direction that Eden had gone. "I think she'll be more than okay, Silas."

As the thunder rolled, her howl fell across my banks and downstream, a call to the future. She wondered and waited for it to reveal itself in its ambling, flowing way, unsure if it would remain hidden under the depths of my currents, obscured like time itself.

Ever-changing.

Transient.

Ephemeral.

1

SILAS

FOURTEEN YEARS LATER

I KNEW SOMETHING WAS AMISS when I returned to Arcadia after a routine patrol around our territory. The Yard remained empty save a few of this year's pups, still bumbling around on lanky legs. I phased back to human form and strode through the trees, the young ones nipping at my bare feet.

"Where have you been?" My sister rushed over to me, wrapping her arms around my shoulders.

"Caroline?"

I heard her heart thrashing.

She pushed back, searching my eyes. "You were gone. We've done the best we could, but–" Her voice caught in her throat as tears spilled down her cheeks.

I noticed how her smooth and pale skin had become puffy and blotchy under her eyes, her stoic expression replaced with fear.

"Has Nash come home?" I bit down on my tongue, holding back words that I wanted to say, wondering if my reckless brother had returned after a month of no contact. He'd left us without notice again like he'd done for four years since humans killed our mother. The last I'd seen Nash, he sulked around the Aisle of Kings after dinner.

Maybe it had been my fault he disappeared like he did. Maybe I turned him away. Maybe he wanted to avoid being a spare part. That caused countless arguments between him and me about who would be crowned King and who would be left behind after our father's passing. Caroline hadn't cared about titles, which upset Nash even more.

But despite our fights, I wanted—*needed*—him here. *We* needed him here. He still belonged in Arcadia.

Caroline shook her head, tears running down her face.

If not Nash...

"No," I said, shaking my head, realization hitting me. My father and Caroline were the only things that kept me going anymore. "He's smarter than that. He—He wouldn't."

Caroline's hands trembled when she covered her lips, eyebrows pinched tight.

A sharp ache settled in my chest as I pushed past her, sprinting down the old stone path that led to Guardian's Glade. Caroline moved behind me as I came to a halt at the wooden double doors shielding the way, hedges high around the outskirts of the glade.

What will I find inside? Desperation and terror filled my veins.

Caroline pulled the silver robe off my hook, passing it to me. It matched hers, though I noticed the red staining the edges of her sleeves. My heart dropped in my chest at the crimson color. I turned and noticed Nash's hook, still laden with his robe, meaning he still hadn't returned home, not even for *Joulo.*

He always loved feasts and festivals. Endless food, dancing, and

merriment. He hadn't returned for *Sarva*—the Festival of Kings—but I figured he would at least return for *Joulo* since it had always been his favorite.

Slipping the robe over my shoulders, I tied and buttoned it.

"What should I expect?" I asked, my back to my sister.

"He's not going to make it," Caroline breathed.

My eyes fluttered closed and my heart caved. The forest around me, usually teeming with life, stood frozen like the waterfall gate marking the boundaries of our forest. The life that thrived in the safety of our woods paused, knowing that something historic occurred among the trees.

Knowing that there would be a shift in the days to come.

With a deep breath, I rested my hands on the smooth wood of the door, attempting to calm my racing heart. I could hear how fast mine thrummed, matching Caroline's tempo. But I couldn't hear past the enchantments over the throne room. I didn't know what lay behind those doors. And something about the unknown terrified me.

I pushed the door open, a muffled scream reaching my ears. A chill ran down the length of my spine. I crossed the room in a few strides, heading for his bedroom hidden behind the throne.

"Father," I ran to his side, where several Healers backed away, giving me space.

"Silas," he coughed, blood running down his chin. "My son."

My eyes searched for his wounds. He had several scratches, which weren't uncommon on a normal day. But the mangled mess where his left foot should have been drew my eyes along with the hole in his side.

"Father," I said, tears running down my face.

He grimaced and turned to me, sputtering. "Keep following our commands, and uphold our secrecy. Do as I trained you. Always be kind."

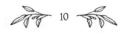

"No, Father, please." I held his face in my hands, his scruffy, graying beard rough against my smooth palms, his curly hair stuck to his cheeks with sweat. "I can't do this. I can't do this without you. My training—"

"You're ready," he said. The Healers came closer, tending to his wounds the best they could. "Nash?"

My heart sank with his half-spoken question. "I'll find him."

"He has a place in this pack with you and your sister." My father coughed until he spit up blood again, phasing half between *virlukos* and human. It took him longer to speak after he settled back into his human state. "I am proud of you, my son. My King."

I held back a sob as I laid my head on his chest. His hand rested on my head, his blood-stained fingers touching my dark roots, holding me close.

This isn't how I wanted this to happen. This isn't how I wanted to become King.

No. This is a dream.

This has to be a dream.

I can't lose my father, too.

"Caroline," my father called.

"Father." She threw her arms around his neck, body trembling from grief, her frame wracked with sobs. I wondered how long she'd been there by his side, suffering alone in my absence while I patrolled the surrounding mountains.

I held them both for a moment, not wanting things to change. I thought of our childhood running in the woods with our mother and father, being one with the forest. When we recovered our mother's body, we buried her in the Aisle of Kings. The dark days following had lightened as the sun rose on our family. But that place, that graveyard... My stomach dropped when I thought of burying my father, stacking his stones to hold onto his spirit. And Nash wouldn't be there to help.

My father, my King.

"Silas," my father said, voice hoarse. "Promise me that you'll find Nash."

I lifted my head, wiping away tears. "I promise, Father. I'll find him. I'll bring him home."

He smiled. "I can die in peace, knowing my kingdom lies in capable hands. I can finally see my bride. My Ellie."

The thought of him and my mother together comforted me, the only comfort I could find. They would finally dance again. No human would be able to touch them. They would be without pain. *Free.*

With effort, my father pulled me closer and kissed my forehead. He settled back down in his bed with a low moan.

I squeezed his hand and sat up straight as he sucked in a labored breath.

"I love all three of you very much. May you always find peace among trees. *Rauha ussen, lyco au lyce.*"

His hand slipped from mine, and I watched the light leave his eyes.

His heart stopped.

"No." I shook my head. "No, that's—"

This can't be happening. This isn't real.

Something in my chest caved, an ache replacing the spot my father held in my heart.

The entire throne room paused, no one willing to break the silence of such a somber moment. Tears ran down my face, too hot for the winter. I pulled Caroline to me, wrapping her in a tight hug, our father's blood staining our silver robes. She shook against me and cried into my shoulder.

Everything I'd ever known—everything I loved in this world—it meant nothing without him here. He had been my rock, a safe place when fear attacked. He'd taught me everything I knew, and now he had left me in a single heartbeat.

Why live when there was no one to live for? But of course, there were many people to live for. An entire kingdom needed me. They needed a king, not me.

I held Caroline for a long while, but time meant nothing with my father gone. When she pulled away, her sunken eyes stared right through me, face void of emotion.

Clearing my throat, I turned to the head Healer. "Asa, I need you to take Caroline and make sure she's tended to, whatever she needs."

"Of course, my king."

I opened my mouth to correct him, but the words stayed lodged in my throat.

He was right, after all.

I was the new King of Arcadia.

2

EDEN

ONE YEAR LATER

I LOVED TREES.

I could be happy in the forest.

Through some incredible circumstances, I accepted a part-time job for the autumn and winter seasons where I helped manage trails for the park services. I studied what grew and dwelled there.

My History of Art professor had noticed my consistent concentration on all things forests and trees and wolves. She had a former graduate student who worked for the National Park Service who knew about all sorts of positions around our local area related to wildlife and fisheries.

And that's how I ended up being paid to be in the forest doing a study on ferns. I didn't earn much, but it kept me out of my parents' hair and helped me avoid socializing.

My close acquaintances in my freshman college classes would always say that normal college girls didn't isolate themselves and that socializing benefitted my mental health, contrary to my belief.

The joke was on them because I wasn't isolated.

I preferred the term *independent*.

Big difference.

But the forest felt alive today. The autumn breeze sent gusts through the tops of the spruce and cedars. The melody deafened birdsong. Something had awoken the forest. Nature stirred with excitement, the leaves swirling in eddies along the ground, whipping the hair that had escaped my curly ponytail.

Freedom.

The study page I worked on had a roughly sketched fern with the scientific name for this particular plant.

Asplenium montanum

It was once thought that these specific ferns were helpful in healing ailments of the spleen due to the shape and design of the leaves and fronds. Hence their name 'spleenwort'. However, not much validity has been found in that wives' tale.

It's not that I didn't like ferns, only they weren't my main fascination.

I'd really been drawing a coyote track not too far from the spleenwort, so I squatted to copy the roundness of the pad in contrast to the sharp claws. They were smaller than wolves but sort of cousins. Like the cattle dog of the woods. So they counted at least for something in my book.

While I labeled my drawing, something cracked behind me. Not the kind of sound that birds and squirrels made.

A deer maybe.

After a cursory glance around, I packed up my bag of journaling supplies and snacks.

I retied my hiking boots, tightened my ponytail of messy curls,

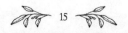

and pulled my oversized sweatshirt out of my bag, slipping it on over my long-sleeved shirt. The air had dropped several degrees since I sat down half an hour ago. Winter made its way to Tennessee, elbowing autumn out of the picture.

I stood and tugged my leggings up.

Turning to head back down the trail, another loud snapping of branches caught my attention. A mass of rustling leaves followed in its wake.

Bobcats wouldn't be out in the open right now. And it sounds too big to be a deer.

I crouched as I walked, and my neck prickled like someone or something watched me. I stepped off the trail and surveyed my surroundings. Nothing moved. I knew I could spook a coyote or a bear if necessary. Worst case scenario, I'd lose my backpack if I had to throw it as a distraction with my snacks. I briefly lamented the potential loss of all my wolf studies, specifically the ancient history of the red wolves in my region. I tugged my journal out of my bag while I climbed further on the trail and up a switchback.

The crack and rustle from before had disappeared, leaving me once again alone in the woods.

In a way, the silence seemed scarier. The wind died. After the trees were so loud for so long, the silence now enveloped my senses. My ears ached to hear something, *anything*. The forest had gone deadly still, pausing for a breath in anticipation of... *something*.

Maybe it's waiting for whatever woke it up.

I started to turn around when something caught my eye under a group of saplings. Crouching lower, I pulled the sapling's leaves to the side.

"No way," I whispered to the trees.

Forgetting my nerves and pulling out a pencil, I sketched the track etched into the dirt. It was large—larger than any other print I had ever seen in those parts. Bigger than a grown man's hand, maybe nine inches long and six or seven inches wide. And it had claws that I imagined would be thick and sharp from the straight marks in the dirt at the end of each digit. Maybe worst or *best* of all...

A wolf print.

It can't be.

But it is.

I made frantic notes along the side of my quick drawing.

Could this be what made the loud crack and rustling noises? My heart quickened at the thought. Wolves don't give up their prey so easily, but a creature of that magnitude had to be impossible to miss. It had to be twice the size of a juvenile black bear.

But there hadn't been wolves in these parts in centuries. The red wolves were eradicated long before I had been born, and there were only a couple dozen in existence out on the coast of North Carolina. And even those were small, forty to eighty pounds at most.

None of this makes any sense. Have I found another werewolf after all these years?

Whatever creature had made that print was big. Bigger than big. And I began to feel like the forest wanted to be left alone for the day.

Shoving my journal and pencils back into my backpack, I zipped it shut, ready to head back to my car.

A snap behind me accompanied a low reverberating growl. The sound crawled up my spine, the creature's hot breath making my body tremble with chills.

Stay calm.

I slowly turned to catch a glimpse, thinking that if the creature's curiosity took over, it might investigate and go away. Or smell my bag and want a snack. Both were viable options, and I could be patient if it meant surviving.

Out of my peripheral, I saw a wall of fur.

Bear.

And then a tail swished behind it.

My heart sank as I connected the track in front of me to the beast behind. I used all my self control to not run out of pure terror. I angled my head up until I could see the top of the creature's head.

Big wolf. Massive gray wolf.

The beast, larger than a brown bear, bared its teeth and snarled at me. The growl rattled in my chest. Its green eyes were unblinking, a sign of dominance and intense focus.

I turned my body, and the wolf snapped at the air, more a warning than an actual attack. I froze, my backpack slung over one arm. I kicked myself for not spotting it in the first place. At the same time, I wondered how a beast that big could sneak right by me.

The wolf stepped forward, and I swear the ground shook. Breath erratic and heart racing, I thought of the bear spray on the seat of my car and blamed my complacency.

I glanced back. The bank pitched down for a decent length.

It would hurt, but I could tumble backwards down the bank and potentially escape.

If I was honest with myself, I would've chosen a broken limb and escape by evasion rather than get chewed by the creature staring me down. I loved wolves, but I had a healthy respect for them.

They were still wild.

Unless it's a werewolf.

Since I'd grown up, I'd seen many more stories and movies of predatory werewolves, but nothing like the ones I had encountered as a young child. Iain had been gentle, human even. And he had rescued me when I could have died.

Could this be Iain? Had his red fur grayed with age?

"Do you remember me?" I said as calmly as possible.

The wolf opened its mouth wider, showing sharp teeth and curling its tongue outward. I stepped back, the ground shifting beneath my feet.

"Iain—"

My words cut off as I slipped down the embankment, hitting branches and leaves as I tumbled. My face burned. I cursed.

Through the dizziness of the tumble, a dark shadow bounded after me. I flailed for a grip on anything my hands could find.

My heart drummed in my ears, and I tried to slow my descent without breaking a limb. I leaned my body sideways and rolled over a log, falling headlong towards a collection of stones.

Everything disappeared, but the shadow of a wolf remained ingrained in my mind.

3

SILAS

SHE WAS AN IMBECILE like all other nettle-brained humans. I skidded to a stop next to her still form, wondering if she had killed herself from the fall. Humans were notoriously fragile.

Why did she think that was a good idea?

Sure, my wolf form loomed larger than most animals she had seen in the wild, but I wouldn't actually eat her. No sense in throwing yourself down a hill into Lycaon knows what.

But her last word—it had sounded like she'd said my father's name. But that was impossible. He'd been dead for nearly a year. And how could a human mistake me for him when we looked nothing alike?

Phasing back to my human form, I rolled the girl's body over, her head lolling in my hands. I brushed her curly dark hair out of her eyes. They remained closed, even at my touch.

Her face rested so peacefully she could have been sleeping.

Blood trickled down her forehead from a wound, probably from bashing her head into the ground, and she had a slight cut across her cheek. I checked her arms, where a few red spots had already begun forming.

Those will definitely bruise.

But she breathed deep, heart beating steadily in her ribcage.

My father's words echoed in my thoughts.

Always rescue those in need. Always be kind.

It was, after all, what he had lived for, what I *still* lived for.

What Arcadia lives for.

I searched and found waybread growing nearby. Plucking off a few of the broad leaves, I stuck them in my mouth, chewing until the leaves were squishy. Brushing the girl's hair aside again, I arranged the poultice over the bigger wound, pressing it down to cover the cut.

Licking my thumb, I rubbed the blood away from her cheek, leaving behind a puffy scratch mark that would disappear in a day or so. Or minutes if she could see my Healers.

She seemed familiar, yet I couldn't place where I'd seen her before. Most humans existed outside of the forest, driving mechanical beasts, voluntarily locking themselves in stone buildings for daylight hours, and boxing up their feet in shoes. It's no wonder that most of them couldn't survive in the wild. They'd pampered themselves to the point of taming their wild spirits.

I glanced around, finding her backpack. Digging past plastic-wrapped food and miscellaneous art supplies, I found what had piqued my curiosity.

I'd stumbled upon her when she leaned over the ferns, sketching them in her book. At first, I wondered if she might need my help, thus fulfilling the ancient duties of my people. Protecting humans and leading them back to civilization when they found themselves lost or injured.

But then she'd studied the ground with more intensity, her heart rate increasing tremendously. The sound of it jumping piqued my attention.

So absorbed in her notes, she didn't see me coming up over the embankment. Of course, that's when I made noise, purposely trying to scare her away. Instead, I had only made her more curious.

Precisely what made her an imbecile.

Curiosity.

And then she found my print. I realized my own mistake: she wasn't lost.

And maybe I wasn't her first *virlukos*. Maybe she *had* met my father.

Granted, she probably called us *werewolves*.

Again, imbecile.

And she *had* to throw herself down that hill. And me—being King of Arcadia—I *had* to protect the human. But that didn't mean I couldn't at least erase the notes she'd written down about me.

Opening the journal, I leafed through the book. Page after page, case studies were documented on all different types of creatures and plants native to the area and some other non-native species. Pieces of newspapers and magazines haphazardly stuck to a few of the pages, some corners sticking out of the sides, no rhyme or reason for the setup.

Dogwood.

Elderberry.

Synchronous Lightning Bugs.

Black Bear.

Solomon's Seal.

Most were diagrams, artistic renditions, and lists of facts about the different creatures or plants. Then the entries became interesting.

Red Wolf.

Smoke Wolf.

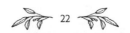

Timber Wolf.

Gray Wolf.

Werewolf.

I flipped back to Smoke Wolf, reading the entry. The drawing showed a black dog in a cloud of smoke, a soft red glow replacing the eyes.

Said to be pure evil and kill for fun. Only the sound of rattling chains will deter the Smoke Wolf.

I scoffed out loud. "Nothing deters *him*. He's a parasite."

I flipped to the Werewolf entry.

"*Virlukos*," I corrected, shaking my head.

Noted as one of the more common myths to circle the globe, werewolves date back for centuries. Occasionally known as wolf-men or lycanthrope, these creatures are known to shift between wolf and human form. Greatly disputed, some say they phase involuntarily when there's a full moon. Others say that they shift for seven years at a time, only becoming human again if they survive the seven-year period.

Potentially growing up to ten feet tall, bipedal werewolves are the stuff of nightmares, wreaking havoc on rural towns. Though there are lesser-known myths suggesting some werewolves are meant to be protectors for children and lost travelers.

Under the written entry, she had drawn several different depictions of werewolves. Some looked ridiculous while others were fairly accurate. Most of them, however, captured the fear most people had for werewolves of legend and fairytale.

I flipped to the page she'd been working on, moments before I startled her, and critiqued her sketch of my print. Decent, except she'd gotten the shape of my palmar pad wrong. Next to the drawing, she'd guessed at the size of my paw.

9" by 6 or 7"?

"Nine by seven and a half," I muttered, shaking my head again.

This was serious information to consider.

For one, most people believed that werewolves were fantastical creatures from ghost stories and legends. Or at least that's what my history lessons had led me to believe as they delved into the centuries of wolf folklore and fairytales. On the other hand, this human had lots of *real* information. Sure, it had been mixed in with a bunch of fox spit, but real nonetheless.

I could leave her here. She'd wake up and think she'd passed out and hurt herself.

I glanced up where the path waited. Would she remember where she'd fallen from?

You could wait for her to rouse.

I observed the girl again, face soft and undisturbed.

Do I take her in? She seems so familiar.

My father's words again rang clear in my mind. What would he do? What would my father have done had he been alive?

But I knew what he would do.

What he always did.

He would take her in, ensure she survived the fall, and then assess if the situation with her journal warranted action.

I flipped through the journal again, not even reading the pages anymore. My mind shifted between duties as protector of my people and duties as leader of the *virlukos*. They usually coincided on a regular basis, but this could be an issue. Bringing a human home was unprecedented.

"*Lo vaara e feru*," I said to myself.

Replacing the journal in the bag, I sat it to the side and stood to my full height, stretching my limbs, fur replacing skin, claws replacing fingernails. I landed on all fours with a thud against the dirt.

I shook out my fur, then rolled the girl onto my back, her limp body draped over my shoulders. I threw my head back in a low and long howl. I paused to listen and picked up the backpack with my mouth.

A few moments later, another echoed my call.

With a huff, I took off.

4

EDEN

"YOUR FAMILY WILL BE *looking for you, child.*"

"*My name is Eden,*" I corrected him.

"*I know you, Eden.*" He smiled, his parted lips displaying rows of white teeth.

"*Iain.*" The name sounded familiar on my tongue despite how little I spoke it.

The wolf-man smiled again. Tilting his head to the side, human hair shifted across his shoulders. "*You are afraid?*"

The same question I had been asking myself. Why was I afraid this time? What changed in the past fifteen years? This encounter in the forest had been a different wolf. It hadn't been Iain with his dusty red coat. Maybe it was one of the wolf pups I had met that day. What were their names?

The scent of moss and tree sap woke me from my fuzzy dreams... or were they memories?

The sound of birdsong drifted through branches.

Myehh. Myehh. Chek-chek-chek.

Gray Catbird.

I opened my eyes, shielding them from the bright afternoon light streaming through the live branches that made up a roof-like covering. Everything faded to orange from the mix of leaves and pine straw, casting the world in a golden glow. The forest seemed different, like winter and autumn had backed up several steps, allowing the end of summer to take over once again.

Am I dead?

I pushed myself to my elbows, the action causing my stomach to turn. Pain radiated from my head, sending nauseating waves through my body.

Not dead.

Bringing a hand up to my hairline, I hissed in pain. Something crusted, crumbly, and green fell in my hands. I rolled it between my fingers, eyebrows furrowing.

Even sitting, I felt lightheaded and dizzy. Pressure built up on the right side of my forehead, causing a sharp ache behind my eye. Injured at the least and concussed at the worst.

But decidedly not dead.

So where am I?

I sat on an odd, cot-like thing in a room with thick hedges for walls and living tree branches for the ceiling. A wooden wardrobe stood to the left, covered in a leafy pattern. To my right, a nightstand hosted a wooden mug. I picked it up. After an experimental sniff and sip, I guess it would most likely be water. And I was parched.

I drained the mug in a few gulps and noticed a small table with two chairs sitting further to the right. Fresh wildflowers in a clay vase decorated the table, like columbine and bluebells.

My mind flitted to Wendy living with the Lost Boys, her home and

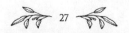

clearing decorated with bluebells and lilies. Magical, and completely impossible.

Spring wildflowers in late autumn? This is like Neverland.

Stumbling, I made my way over to the wardrobe. The soft wood felt warm to the touch, even the intricate carvings. It reminded me of things I'd read in books as a child. A cursory glance revealed that there would be no lamppost or lions.

Pulling open the door, I found silk robes in several colors, faded dresses, a pair of pants, and a matching plain brown shirt.

What is this place?

I closed the door and turned around, surveying the room—if you could even call it that. The structure consisted of plants, and I couldn't spot a single bit of metal or plastic. I noticed a wooden door tucked inside of the hedges, hidden among the branches.

Still dizzy, I stumbled towards it. I placed my ear against it, trying to hear any kind of sound. Warmth radiated from the wood like the wardrobe, soothing against my sore skin. I'd been bruised in several places, but that wasn't my main concern. I was alive in a strange forest room, and I needed to find my way out.

I tried the handle. Locked.

My heart pounded as I observed the plants that made up the walls. They were too thick to see through, and thorns were threaded through them, like a rose bush.

This is a prison cell.

I inhaled several measured breaths. Losing my head and breaking down wouldn't help the situation.

My mind flashed back to the massive wolf that I'd run from, tumbling down the hill.

Is that why I dreamt of Iain?

Did I finally find them again?

The rattling of keys caught my attention when the door handle jiggled. I took three steps back to be a safe distance from whatever stood on the other side of that door. I grabbed the empty mug from the table, the only thing within sight I could use in self defense.

As if I could bludgeon a wolf to death with a wooden cup.

Gliding into my cell, a dark-skinned man swished towards me, draped in a light blue robe in a similar style to the ones hung in the wardrobe.

"Welcome, young one, to Arcadia!" The man smiled, arms outstretched to me. "My name is Bennett. How did you sleep?"

I hesitated, unsure what Arcadia was or what this guy could be capable of. If my suspicions were correct, he probably wasn't as tame as he seemed.

"Fine," I said.

He tucked his hands back into a prayer position. "Excellent. I've come to retrieve you for your council with the King. You'll need a robe, of course."

"I'm sorry, did you say *king*?" I shook my head, knowing I must've hit my head way harder than I thought.

Bennett's smile faltered. "Are you not the researcher?"

My heart sank when I turned. I lost my backpack full of my studies. My journal full of drawings and observations... gone. All my research, all my sketches, everything I did in my spare time had disappeared.

And someone else had it.

"Ahem." Bennett drew my attention back. "You must be wanting your things. You may have them back *after* the council with the King."

I ran my fingers through my tangled curls with my free hand, trying to quell the anxiety building in my chest.

"Your robe, young one." Bennett stepped over to the wardrobe and pulled out a beige robe.

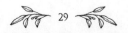

I dropped the empty mug onto the bed and took the robe from him, sliding it off the wooden hanger. Wrapping it over my shoulders, I tied it once on the inside by my right hip over my leggings and once again on the outside by my left hip. The bell sleeves hung low and wide, and I instantly felt like someone from all the fantasy movies I loved so much.

"Your, um... shoes?" He stared at my feet.

"What about them?"

He motioned to them. "You're walking on sacred ground. It is imperative you connect with Arcadia through the soil. We respect Arcadia in that way."

With a sigh, I unlaced my boots, setting them next to the wardrobe with my socks. The mossy floor cooled my bare skin.

"Thank you. Follow me!" the man commanded, leading me through the door out of my prison cell.

I wasn't sure what I had expected, since I'd only been awake for a few minutes, but a sunlit path of rocks and pine straw between walls of trees surprised me, like stepping into a dream. A few people stood around, watching us. They were dressed in similar robes, all different kinds of colors. Beige like mine, deep violet, various hues of forest greens, forget-me-not blue, cardinal red, pale ivory, and everything in between. Among them walked a handful of massive wolves like the one I had seen, but none of them looked familiar.

None of them were Iain.

"This way, young one." Bennett moved his arm in front of him, leading me down a less populated path, less pine straw as well.

Not that I deserved any special treatment, but his calling me by the title *young one* didn't make me like him. And his graceful gliding didn't help either. I, the picture of an absolute fool, stumbled around on sensitive, bare feet.

We arrived at a crossroads of sorts where a few paths diverged.

He chose the most narrow but well-maintained path, lined with stone instead of pine needles. My feet ached on the chilled rock.

The trees growing around weren't a planned forest; rather, they looked ancient and mystical, dressed in moss and lichen. Something like an old-growth forest. It smelled like springtime, reminding me of the fresh flowers in my prison cell.

How impossible.

After a few more twists and turns, we approached the end of the path and a set of wooden double doors, like the wardrobe. A silver-colored robe hung from a hook next to them, but there wasn't anything else of note nearby. A thick wall of the same thorny plants guarded whatever lay behind them.

Exactly like my prison cell.

Is this entire place a prison of the forest?

At the doors, Bennett stopped, inhaling deeply. He whispered something under his breath only for the wind to know before opening the wide doors.

A rush of summery air blew my hair over my shoulders as light blinded me from the clearing. Blinking a few times, I made out several rows of people—maybe thirty or forty in total, young and old with all shades of skin and robes of many colors—watching me with sharp eyes. At the farthest wall of the forest glade, a throne of moss and wood sat, like it had been carved out of a large, old tree stump. And a young man perched in the chair, twisted vines sitting on his head like a crown, a stark contrast to his silver robes.

He seemed so familiar that it stopped me in my tracks. Something in my memories vied for attention, trying to uncover an image from my dreams after being woken from a deep sleep. The recall felt groggy, like trudging through a mud-covered trail.

The young man—somewhere around my age—squinted at me, his

lips quirking up on the left side. The way he sat unmoving in his seat made my skin crawl. He had all the self-confidence and no friendliness.

Some king.

Bennett nudged me forward until I stood before the foot of the wooden throne. The stiff king gazed down at me.

"You will kneel before the King of Arcadia," my guide commanded.

Glancing up at the king through my lashes, I knelt. I prayed that all the princess movies I had watched growing up helped me seem at least somewhat less ignorant than I was.

What an embarrassment.

The king tilted his head to the side like a curious dog, furrowing his eyebrows. In the process, he stepped down from the throne and circled me. I kept my eyes down and body still, noticing how the floor wasn't grass like I thought, but stone hiding under a layer of forest. I also watched his bare feet, dirty and calloused. His toes were long and straight, remarkably different from mine.

Who were these forest people? And what was this kingdom, Arcadia?

The king knelt before me with speed, striking green eyes boring into mine. Something almost tangible burned inside of him. It took effort to hold his gaze for long. I turned my head down again, swallowing my fear. I'd never been in a situation where I had no control, and it humbled me.

Terrified me.

"Eden." His rough tenor voice broke the dead silence of the glade.

Heart pounding, I glanced up at him. His face revealed nothing.

How does he know my name?

My mind raced with questions, but now wasn't the time to ask.

The king's eyes roamed over my features, causing the hair on my neck to stand on end. I couldn't tell if he assessed me or merely observed.

"How have you liked your room?" he asked, his voice startling me once again. I swear it reverberated between my ribs.

I met his gaze. "It's been acceptable, your highness."

I'd be the first to admit that I've never been one to stand up to speak in front of a crowd. Having any attention had always been unwanted. But having someone's undivided attention unnerved me. A flash of something wild shifted behind his eyes, and I regretted glancing back up. Almost like it rested under his skin, begging to come out.

"The lock was precautionary. We didn't need you getting lost in these unfamiliar woods, seeing as you took a tumble yesterday."

"Yesterday?" I repeated.

He nodded. His dark hair had been swept back and held by his crown, but pieces had slipped out, dangling in front of his eyes. I had the strangest desire to tuck them back into place, and I cursed myself for it.

"You were rescued yesterday afternoon." He shifted his jaw. "Our head Healer, Asa, began working to staunch the bleeding and try to limit your symptoms from the trauma your head received."

I lifted a hand to the right side of my head where the green, crumbly substance stuck to my hair.

"You'll probably be lightheaded for a day or so," he said, a hint of disdain in his voice, "so I'll try not to interrogate you too much."

"Interrogate me?"

Maybe I'd hit my head harder than I thought, but I had trouble keeping up. As the king stood, Bennett pulled me to my feet.

"This human," the king addressed the crowd now in a commanding voice, "has information that poses a potential threat for the exposure of Arcadia to the outside world."

"What?" The accusation stunned me.

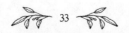

Am I being sentenced to prison? Or to death?

Murmurs of assent rippled among the crowd.

Bennett stepped back, and a man and a woman grabbed hold of each of my wrists.

"You can't do this!" I said while they pulled my hands behind my back. I shook my shoulders, trying to yank them free. "There are laws."

"Your laws mean nothing here." The king growled, and his eyes grew dark.

"That's what *you* think, *your majesty*," I said.

He stepped towards me. "Will your people come searching for you? Will they break through our centuries-old defenses? Will they be relentless and overturn every rock, attempting every possible solution, including magic and wildcraft and brute force? Won't they give up long before that moment, believing your body to be lost to the great Appalachian Mountains, *Shaconage*? Won't they add your name to a long list of missing faces from years past that the Great Mountain swallowed?"

His words weighed my stomach like a millstone in the sea. All of my hope of rescue or returning to normal civilization was dashed to the stones all at once. People went missing in these hills and hollers nearly every year. What made me any different?

The king came within an inch or so, close enough for me to catch the scent of some tree or plant on his skin. His eyes roamed my face before settling on my eyes. "Or wouldn't you rather stay here in this place you've searched for all these years? It is, after all, a *wild* place."

He must have my journal.

The thought of this man rifling through my studies made my face hot. There weren't sensitive topics, but I had put my heart and soul into creating this encyclopedia of sorts. It meant so much to me, this search for werewolves. It had become my identity.

And he saw all of it.

When I said nothing, he mumbled, "I thought so."

He started to turn away, but I didn't know where I stood. I didn't know what crime he charged me for, and I worried that my silence would seal my fate.

"Please," I called out.

"Please what?" he bit back, turning his head to face me.

"I don't understand what's going on."

"You have too much valuable information. It's important that this place remains a secret, and you know too much. And you wouldn't be of much use to me."

"Try me."

I saw a light flash in the king's eyes. Then he turned to face me, raising his eyebrows. "Is that a challenge?"

A jolt of fear rippled over my skin, goose flesh covering my limbs. It must've been some primal reaction to a threat. He stepped back, rubbing his thumb over his bottom lip, eyeing me and sizing me up.

A young woman with honey-blonde hair stepped forward, her robe matching the king's silvery one. "Are you sure this is wise?"

The king threw her a sharp glance. "Caroline, I think she underestimates us."

"I don't believe–" The young woman stopped mid-sentence, gaze turning to the opening doors.

I craned my neck to see past the people holding onto me. A very naked man waltzed in the room, pulling on the silver robe I'd seen hanging by the door, one matching the king and this woman. The newcomer's loose curls hung past his chin, an image I had seen before, one I'd dreamed of for years, desperate not to forget. For a moment, my mind flashed to that day on the riverbank with Iain, my guardian werewolf.

But the man coming down the aisle now wasn't Iain. He looked too young.

"Nash," the king breathed.

Realization dawned on me.

Caroline . . . Nash. These are Iain's pups.

My gaze flew to the king's, and my heart skipped a beat. *Silas.* The cold-hearted king standing before me was the one who had ensured I returned to my family all those years ago.

"Wonderful! A welcoming committee! What did I miss?" Nash finished buttoning his robe and clapped his hands, rubbing them together. The crowd murmured, and Nash noticed me for the first time, still held back by the two guards. "And who might you be?"

He came altogether too close for my liking, breath tickling the hairs on the side of my neck. He looked me up and down, taking a deep, measured breath. Tilting his head sideways, he stared at me through his eyelashes.

Without turning his face away, he asked, "Brother, why is it that you have a human in Arcadia?"

The king—*Silas*—huffed. "I'm afraid you've missed quite a lot in the time you've been gone."

That flash of wild I had seen in Silas had been replaced with white-hot emotion, boiling under the surface. Anger emanated from him, and many of the crowd reflected it as well.

And the thought occurred to me, if Silas wore the crown, what happened to Iain? Surely he would still be king unless something terrible happened.

"Where is Father?" Nash asked, moving away from me. "I'd like to speak with him. And why are you wearing his crown?" Nash craned his neck around the throne as if Iain would be hiding behind it.

Something is wrong. Something strange is going on here.

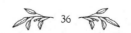

"Nash." Caroline stepped forward, laying a hand on his shoulder. She lowered her voice to a murmur that I could barely hear. "Can we talk in private, please?"

Nash glanced between his siblings.

Silas swallowed, never taking his eyes off of Nash, but addressed the crowd. "Council adjourned. We will decide the human's fate tomorrow." Turning back towards me, he said, "Bennett, take her to Mender's Heath. Check her wounds again. Feed her. I'm sure she's hungry."

With that, Bennett led me back down the path. The double doors closed behind me, cutting off my view of Silas as he sank back down on his throne, shoulders weighed by something immensely heavy.

Whatever I stumbled upon, I wasn't welcome, and I had a bad feeling about all of it.

5

SILAS

I TRIED TO WORK out the tension behind my eyes, but nothing stopped the throbbing that lived there whenever Nash stood in my presence. Especially now.

Now, of all times when I'm dealing with a potential threat to the kingdom.

"Does someone want to explain what's going on here?" Nash threw his hand in the air at me, looking at Caroline. "Why is he wearing Father's crown?"

"Why don't we sit down?" Caroline stepped towards our brother.

"Where is he?" Nash's shoulders tensed.

"Nash–" Caroline said.

I can't handle gentleness.

Not now.

Not after what we went through without him.

"He's dead," I snapped.

Caroline froze, clenching her hands into fists.

"Dead?" Nash furrowed his brow. "How did he... How did—"

"Out searching for you." I stood from my throne and stepped closer to him. "He died, trying to see if you'd been caught in the city."

A wounded expression passed over his eyes, his resolve faltering. "No, I told him... Why would he—"

"Because at that point, you hadn't bothered coming back in a month, Nash!" I shouted in his face. "We were planning the *Joulo* feast, and the waterfall had frozen, and you hadn't bothered to return."

"I planned to come back. I was in the *Washita* mountains." He seemed fragile, like this might break him. He'd always been the tougher one, but the roles reversed.

I was the Alpha.

He was the Omega.

"And now, you've been gone for a year. You decided to show up unannounced and without remorse. You are reckless and irresponsible. And it's your fault our father is dead."

"Silas," Caroline gasped.

Nash shook his head, eyes dazed.

"Enough, Caroline," I snapped. "Stop treating him like a pup. He chose his place in this pack. You're both dismissed."

I pushed through them, leaving Guardian's Glade and heading Lycaon knows where. I needed out.

I found myself walking on the route through the residential court. I smiled at my people as I passed, headed to Eden's room.

I hadn't recognized her at first when she'd slipped and rolled down that hill. Only after flipping through her journal did I find her name, and that's when faded and foggy memories from my childhood drifted back into focus.

Father.

The riverbank.

Virlukos lessons.

Arcadia existed as a place for legends, creatures to save the day when humans failed. When people became lost or cold or starving, we rescued them. Only the trained Guardians ventured into the towns to resupply rarer items that we couldn't salvage in the forest. Most of our job occurred in the mountains, where idiot humans became lost.

And it was safer to be a wolf in the forest.

But I hadn't thought of Eden since that day. She was a human—a lesson—in my young mind. Though she must've remembered that encounter to adulthood. She had done extensive research on wolves. Other things, too. But there were pages upon pages of facts and drawings of wolves, tracks, food, dens, pups, and even legends.

In a way, it fascinated me. This human met my father once and never forgot. How many times had I seen that humans could be reckless and ruthless? And yet, she'd been drawing portraits of my father along with little floral patterns and fairytales.

Danger would follow her for knowing so much. And I needed to know how much the other humans knew. If they knew and believed the *virlukos* existed, it was only a matter of time before they hunted us down or trapped us to discover our secrets.

I had to protect my pack above all. Arcadia meant more than following rules to save a human. Even if it meant breaking one of my father's rules for the sake of my people. Eliminating one problem all for the greater good.

Even if she reminds me of my father?

The memories of him rushed back like they never left. So many happy memories with my father, so many things he taught me. Though now, they were almost unwelcome, making me second-guess my decisions as king.

Had it only been less than a year since his passing? My father was forty when he died, young for a shapeshifting king.

The truth of the matter, my short time as king had been tumultuous. I hadn't been trained. I had never assisted with most duties of the king. I had mixed emotions about taking his place back then. Unworthy, untrained, and grappling with grief at the loss of my hero, and not much changed in a year.

My reminiscing thoughts stilled when I found myself lingering in front of Eden's door. It wasn't that she was special to me, only that she brought back so many of those memories. Memories I cherished.

But she didn't know that. She didn't know that she meant something to me, no matter how small that *something* was. And a part of me hated her for hanging onto my father's memory. Why would a nettle-brained human remember his legacy?

Another part of me hated myself for bringing her here. If I had left her there, I could've taken her journal and waited until she regained consciousness. It would have minimized the threat of exposure while also saving a human like we had been designed to do. And I wouldn't be so... *frustrated*.

Pulling the keys from a hook on the door frame, I unlocked the door.

I knocked, hesitant at what proper manners were between a wolf king and a human prisoner. Because this had never happened before now. No human had ever stepped foot on Arcadian soil before Eden.

"Come in?" her voice questioned, muffled by the door and the hedges grown by Seer and *micca* magic. No doubt the Seers watched me from the shadows.

I slipped the keys in the pocket of my robe when I entered her room, simple, like the rest of the residential court. Wolves didn't need much to entertain them indoors when they had the world at their claws.

Clearing my throat, I held my hands behind my back, focusing on everything else but her.

Always rescue those in need.

Always be kind.

I repeated my father's words over and over like a chant in my head before speaking up, resisting the urge to ask about what she knew. That could wait until tomorrow.

"I wanted to make sure they fed you." I tried to keep my voice conversational.

Eden sat in one of the chairs at the small table eating a piece of spruce bread. I sat across from her. The wood squeaked, my ears hyper-aware of the sound. I folded my hands on the table, attempting to smile, but it fell flat on my lips. I refocused my attention on her heartbeat.

Eden swallowed her bite of bread. "The healer checked me out and said I should be fine tomorrow. He put more of that stuff on my head."

"Good." I nodded. "Waybread should help you heal."

We sat in awkward silence for a moment.

"So how–"

"I wanted–"

We both paused mid-sentence.

I motioned for her to speak. "You go first."

"How did you find me?" she asked. "You remembered me."

I cleared my throat again. "I had forgotten about that day by the river until I read your journal. It all rushed back to me, like a dream."

I surprised myself with the truth, but something about missing my father and Nash returning and Eden mixed up in all of it. My heart ached for simple days. Running through our mountains. My father's laugh bubbling up from his chest, rushing like a waterfall.

I missed those days.

I missed *him*.

"I never forgot you," Eden whispered. "Or Caroline and Nash."

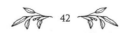

A worried expression passed over her face for a moment, then she glanced up at me. "What happened to Iain, your father?"

My chest ached, hearing his name again.

She remembered him, his name.

Iain.

Not *your majesty* or *King of Arcadia.*

Iain.

Familiar with a man she'd met only once.

Pushing my dark hair up and out of my eyes, I sighed, breath catching in my throat. "He died... ten months ago. And I assumed the role of King of Arcadia."

The truth made my eyebrows furrow, eliciting an emotion I couldn't quite name or pin down. I wrestled with the idea, rolling it around in my mind.

Is this regret?

A foreign emotion.

Would things have been different if Nash had been there when our father died?

"That must've been pretty difficult for someone so young." She took another bite of spruce bread.

Pity from a human? She cares.

Why do I care that she cares?

I shook my head, the wolf side of me warring for control with the human side. Thoughts overlapped each other, making my head all fuzzy. I didn't want to give this human an upper hand on me when she already knew so much. "I shouldn't be here."

"I'm sorry, I didn't mean–"

I stood, cutting her off. I needed to do the best for my people regardless of what this human meant to me or what my father had meant to her. "Be ready tomorrow."

When I reached for the door, she jumped to her feet. "Be ready for what?"

I half turned, gazing at her sidelong. "My people have been restless and scared since their King died. Helping is our purpose *and* our downfall. They will not release you with the knowledge you possess. I suggest you make a case if you wish to leave."

She swallowed, face tense and unsure. "You know, I thought you all might be cruel when I found you."

I turned to face her, irritation bristling under my skin. Something about how she said the word *cruel* rubbed me the wrong way since it was *her* kind that killed my mother and father. But it wouldn't do to take my grief and frustration out on her. I pushed the emotion away like a wolf pup nipping at my heels.

Eden brushed her mess of curly hair behind her ear. "I told myself that I must have imagined a wolf that rescued me from the river. But I've searched for you all for so many years."

I raised an eyebrow.

Always be kind.

After my father's words fluttered through my thoughts, an image of Nash overpowered them. He snapped at me for caring, for stooping so low as gentleness when humans brought death with them.

She blushed. "I can't believe I've found you."

"*You* didn't find us. You were brought here." The words tumbled out before I could stop, bitterness lacing every syllable.

Her smile faltered, and she shrugged. "What's the difference? I'm here, aren't I?"

"You arrogant humans think you're so important. That the world revolves around you."

"No, that's not—"

My emotions hit a rolling boil. "You think you *found* Arcadia? You

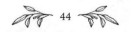

44

think you weren't being followed that day? You think that you're so brilliant that you discovered the best-kept secret in *Shaconage*?"

"No, I only meant that I'm grateful to be here. This is all I ever wanted."

"This?" I sighed. "You wanted to be a prisoner on trial?"

"That's not what I meant, and you know it. Stop twisting my words." She moved away from the table. "You're being so unfair. Just because I'm human doesn't mean I think like the ones you've dealt with."

"All humans are the same." I tilted my head from side to side, failing to keep a level head. "You're weak, powerless, thick-headed, and arrogant. You care so little about the impact you're having on the greater world. You take and take and take and never give. And you've lost the wildness you were born with."

"You're cold, you know that?" She shook her head, and I noticed her pale features growing splotchy. "Unfeeling and unkind."

"Any feeling I had left when I lost my father," I growled.

I stepped to her with purpose. She backed up against the hedges but stepped forward to avoid the thorns, bumping into me. I grabbed her arm with enough force that her head shot up, frantic and cornered. I noticed the bruising on her arm had turned a slight blue-ish gray.

My heart jumped inside my chest as I stared into her eyes. She seemed so small at that moment, so *human*. I could almost taste her fear in the air. I ran my tongue over the sharp edge of my teeth, leaning down close to her right ear. Her pulse beat faster.

"I am wild at heart, a wolf at the core. I could rip your throat in seconds," I whispered, voice rough around the edges. "Don't for one second think that I've forgotten the wild. Or that it has forgotten me."

I pulled back to look her in the eyes.

Fear.

Paralyzing fear.

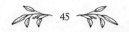

Good.

Fear is good.

Much better than familiarity.

I felt her breath on my cheek, her skin against my hand cold despite the warmth emanating from Arcadia's life source.

She shuddered in my grasp, and I released her, backing up.

She didn't move.

I swallowed down whatever emotions had lodged in my throat, heat running through my body. Turning away, I headed for the door, pulling out the keys.

"Be ready," I barked, slamming the door behind me.

I ignored the strange looks from the few people still mingling in the residential court as I locked Eden's door.

I headed back to Guardian's Glade. Nash and Caroline had gone, leaving the throne room empty and soulless.

How did this kingdom crumble in a single day?

The day after my father died, I buried him in the Aisle of Kings next to my mother. I stacked his stones. I wept. The tears of grief had since dried into burning anger. Yet all of these raw emotions kept bubbling to the surface.

I wasn't ready to be a king.

My father realized that Nash would be an Omega. His destiny was to be at the mercy of the pack.

But that didn't mean I was ready to be the Alpha.

I slipped out of my robe, hanging it on the hook.

I needed space.

I needed air rushing past me.

I needed the oxygen rising in and out of my lungs, heart racing, blood pumping through my veins.

Freedom.

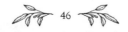

I quickened my pace through the Yard past the pups. I phased as I slipped around the rock formation concealing our forest. With a quick trot, I maneuvered the masked hallway, light calling me further onward.

At the end of the hall, I slipped through the opening and launched into the cold water of the cascade. The mountain water ran over my head, wetting my gray coat.

Feru Falls meant safety. It meant *home*.

I'm not going to allow my home to fall apart.

6

EDEN

I RESORTED TO PACING.

My limbs were itching to move, to hike, to swim—something, anything other than sitting motionless in my prison cell.

Silas—*King* Silas—unsettled me.

I thought maybe his memory of me would make things different, like we were old friends or something.

Enemies, more like.

I fought the urge to scream. Being cooped up drove me crazy, but what if all the other werewolves were like Silas? Sweet at first, then they turn around to rip your throat out.

I shuddered at the thought and the passing memory of his breath against my cheek, my neck... pulse thrumming beneath my skin.

He had meant it, too.

That flash of wild I had seen in his eyes at the council meeting rippled underneath the surface, like it lived in his ribcage nestled under his heart. Maybe it's what made his heart beat.

Regardless of what or where that wild lived, it had unnerved me. He'd switched so fast that it seemed almost like he had two personalities inside of him: one, kind and caring with a playful spirit; the other, untamed and angry and broken.

He's still hurting from losing his father. I can give him a little grace for being broken.

I hated how logical I could be.

Morning had slipped into afternoon now, liquid gold spreading through the leaves of the bright green trees above me despite it being late autumn. I wondered how they had maintained their color with the growing cold. Then again, everything felt warmer here, like the place teemed with magic. And maybe it *was* magical.

Wherever it is.

I'd been informed I'd been here for a whole day. I wondered if everyone whispered about the intruder, wondering if my presence meant danger. Silas said in the Council that I threatened the exposure of Arcadia, but I wasn't like some humans who would want to hunt them. I wanted to know them and learn from them.

Will they understand that?

I threw myself onto the soft bed, gazing up at the foliage.

I thought of all those years, all the ridicule I'd faced for believing in something beyond comprehension. I remembered the insults so vividly and the hatred for being stuck between the two things: my beliefs and my immediate reality.

I had wanted this.

I wanted to find the truth, proof that magic existed somewhere in the world. I had searched for countless hours on computers and paid careful attention to plants, fungi, creatures, and anything else I thought provided some answers.

And here I sat, in the den of an ancient race of shapeshifters, right

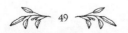

under my nose for fifteen-odd years, facing a trial I didn't think I could win against a king who was equal parts aggravating and fascinating. Here I lay, contemplating how I could convince him to let me stay.

It was a crazy idea.

I was crazy for even thinking it.

But I belonged here. Or at least, I didn't belong with humans mocking what I knew to be true. Or maybe they would understand if they only knew.

I doubted myself countless times over the years, but I always found my way back to what I knew in the deepest parts of me. Shapeshifters roamed the Appalachian Mountains.

And I found them again.

The sound of keys caught my attention. Sitting up, I wondered if Silas had either come back to rip my throat out or apologize for his behavior.

Unlikely.

Instead, golden hair slipped through the doorway, a graceful body robed in silver.

"Hello, Eden." Caroline smiled, warm, hot chocolate eyes watching me. "You seem relieved."

I sighed. "I thought you were Silas."

Caroline's lips quirked downwards. "Is he causing you trouble?"

Shrugging, I tucked my hair behind my ear. "I don't think he wants me here."

"He *brought* you here, Eden."

I stared at the woman in front of me. "*He* brought me here?"

Caroline tilted her head. "He thought it was the wisest decision… at the time."

"So why does he bring me here and then turn around to be uncaring and unfeeling?"

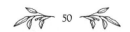

TO LIVE AMONG WOLVES

"Silas is still not sure where he stands as Alpha. He wasn't ready when our father passed." A far-off expression clouded her gaze. "None of us were. Our people, they're still healing. They're scared. It takes time to heal from a wound so deep, losing your King when his heirs are still pups."

I wondered over the social structure of their kingdom. If Silas was king now at a young age, he must've been barely an adult when he was crowned. That would be difficult for anyone, let alone dealing with the grief that comes with losing someone so close to you.

"I came to talk about your council tomorrow." Caroline stepped over to the wardrobe. "You should wear this robe. It will communicate that you are here to learn and not to destroy."

She handed me a light green robe, soft to the touch, like cool water running through my hands.

"When you speak with them, speak from your heart. Don't try to be like us. And don't try to be eloquent." Caroline shook her head. "They want to watch you fall. Don't allow them to succeed."

She turned back to the table and picked up my plate.

"Caroline." I set the robe aside. "Why are you helping me?"

The young woman paused near the door. A vague sadness passed over her face. But it left as soon as it had arrived. Instead, a smile lit up her features.

"My father always said that we should be kind to all we come across. The *virlukos* were created to be kind. We were created to help the earth and all that inhabit it. It's in our blood."

"*Virlukos*?" I asked, stumbling over the pronunciation.

"Our race. Our people."

"What does it mean?"

"Men of wolves. Or, as your people call us, *werewolves*." She chuckled, leaving me alone in my prison cell.

My mind wondered if the werewolves—*virlukos*—would even be willing to hear my case. Maybe they would refuse my hearing in the morning and refuse my plea. I hoped they would come with kindness, with whatever Caroline claimed rested in their blood.

Their loss of King Iain saddened me. It was obvious that their grief stayed back, dammed up right under the surface.

I stood and draped the light green robe over one of the chairs by the table.

I began to pace again, this time working out what I would say to the *virlukos*.

"Citizens of Arcadia," I muttered to myself. "Sounds like a superhero comic."

I walked another circle around the moss-covered floor before trying again. "Good afternoon, people of Arcadia." I groaned in exasperation. "No, definitely not that."

I made another round in the room.

"Hello. My name is Eden," I started. I shrugged to myself and continued. "When I was four, I nearly died. I slipped into the Little River, its water swallowing me whole."

I shivered. The memory of the icy waters choking my lungs burned in my memory. The phantom fire lingered in my chest. Since then, I'd never been quite comfortable in the water.

With a deep breath, I continued my speech to the empty room. "In a daze, I was dragged onto shore. That's when I first met Iain, the moment I discovered that magic was real. The day I met the *virlukos*."

I stopped pacing, and an ache worked its way into my chest where the fire had been.

Iain.

Countless times I'd dreamed of him. He would race through the trees, a younger version of myself clinging to his back. I heard his laugh, smelled the pine on his fur. He went with me wherever I went. He had been my imaginary friend growing up, only I knew that he wasn't imaginary.

But now he was gone, and I would never see him again.

7

SILAS

TROTTING BACK INTO THE Yard, I kept my form until I arrived at Guardian's Glade. My people nodded in a slight bow when I passed, but no one stopped to talk to me.

That had been the most difficult transition aside from losing my father—people who I once talked to daily now stood in the shadows, afraid to speak with their king. An invisible barrier stood between me and the public.

Or maybe they were as unsure as I was, everyone shifting into new roles, and no one prepared for their new place.

After phasing by the double doors of Guardian's Glade, I slipped into my silver robe, buttoning it tight. Only one place existed where I could go and be myself—to be Silas.

In the Aisle of Kings.

In the blue light of dusk, I walked down the dirt path, flanked on both sides by heath pearlwort, a million white blooms peeking out of the green. The tall, thin pines mixed in with beeches and maples dotted my surroundings. I walked a well-worn path, one that every wolf journeyed several times a year.

I was a weekly regular.

Walking through the arch, I ran my hands along its branches. Twisted and woven, its bark had been worn smooth over the years. Laying my hands on its magic-warmed body was almost my way of knocking before entering the sacred space, littered with lavender and lemon balm.

I stepped past years of ancient kings, the ones who came before us. Their graves were marked by balanced stones, a good mix of big and small stacks. Sometimes you could tell which stacks were balanced by the same king.

I had to balance my father's stones.

I remember my hands shaking so much that I struggled with the last few pieces. I had my sister to help me, but it took time to center the stones. After a long and difficult struggle, I balanced the last stone and knelt forward, crying with my forehead in the freshly dug dirt. My tears watered the earth.

Lycaon, how I miss him.

I turned around the bend in the path now, to the more recent kings and family graves, surprised to find someone at my father's graveside.

I kept my voice low. "Nash?"

Taking careful steps, I moved towards my brother. Nash's arms wrapped around his knees, head bent low between his legs. I noticed the tremor in his shoulders. Nash's head shot up at my voice, eyes red and puffy. He wiped his nose with the back of his hand. "What do you want?" he asked, voice raw.

He didn't turn away.

I thought for a moment about him. There was a quiet strength in keeping his head up despite the hot tears running down his cheeks, the momentary reflection of a prince buried inside somewhere.

I sat down a foot or so away, not wanting to scare him off. He'd come back, and no matter how angry he made me, he was still my brother. Nothing would ever change that.

And as angry as he made me, I wanted to understand. I wanted to know why he had left, where he had gone, why he'd decided to return, and what he expected from me.

Nash kept silent, turning back to stare at the cairn. The stone at the top still stood strong, its tip balanced carefully on a smaller one.

Nash should have been there to help us.

"Remember when he used to make us fight?" Nash sniffled, breaking the silence. He shifted, one knee lying to the side, arms gripping the other tight.

I cleared my throat. "Yeah, I do."

Of course I remembered wrestling matches with my brother every day as a child. I came home with bruises and scratches from rolling around in the underbrush. I ate dirt more times than I could count or remember. But things had changed when Nash started disappearing every day or so. I ate his meals. I doubled my training. I took my role seriously.

I had earned it.

"And Caroline would always beg to join in." Nash chuckled. "She's all bark and no bite though."

I laughed. "Still is."

A comfortable type of silence fell on us. I listened to the breeze that rustled through the trees and lavender. A whistling emitted from our father's grave, but I knew it would be another twenty-four hours until I saw him again. The stones, on occasion, caused an eerie whistling sound, like the ghosts of the ancients wanted to join the conversations of the living. But it would never bring them back, not fully.

Not yet.

"What do we do now?" Nash said.

I blinked a few times. Rarely was my brother vulnerable, especially with me. Our relationship had always been physical, where he'd wrestle me to the ground or beat me in a hunt. We'd never had much of a chance to talk about losing our mother before he started disappearing all the time. And now, Nash finally began processing the loss of our father and asking *me* for advice.

"Well," I half shrugged. "We keep going. We do what he trained us to do since we were pups. And we make him proud."

Nash turned to me. His eyes were sunken in his face, like he had not eaten in quite some time. "Do you think he would have been proud of you?" he asked.

I didn't expect the question. And I didn't know how to answer.

"What do you mean? Like being king?"

"With Eden." Nash shook his head. "Do you think he would've been proud of how you've handled all this?"

"I–" I stuttered. "How I've handled this? It's a less-than-ideal situation."

"It's only that you have a human held prisoner, and as much as I don't like humans knowing we exist... Does this not go against what he trained us to do? His mantra was to always be kind, and right now, this isn't being kind to Eden."

I opened my mouth to answer, but no words poured out. I had been asking myself that same question for twenty-four hours.

I shook my head. "I'm doing the best I can, Nash."

"It's not good enough."

I turned back, searching my brother's face for any sign of jest. He was stone-faced and serious, an unusual thing for him.

"Do you think I wanted this?" I motioned to our father's grave. "Do

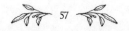

you think I wanted to balance our father's stones at such a young age?"

"No, but–"

I stood up, dusting the soil off of my robe. "Do you think I wanted to have to choose the safety of Arcadia over the values of the *virlukos*?"

Nash scrambled to his feet. "No! I just–"

"Do you think I wanted to lose my brother, thinking he'd been killed? Promise our dying father that I would find you? Spend months serving and helping and ruling all the while worried sick that I would fail my father's last wish?"

Nash's face fell. "I didn't know."

"No, you didn't, Nash. Because you weren't here." I clenched my jaw tight. "You only ever think of yourself."

I moved to walk away, but Nash grabbed my arm. "Maybe before." His face contorted, regret lining every crease. "But I'm back now. Give me a chance."

I couldn't face him. I turned to the trees above us.

"Silas," he begged.

It drew my attention, if only for the fact that very few people called me that anymore. Always "my king" or "*je kunan*", but never Silas. The desperation hung in his voice.

"Silas, please." He squeezed my arm. "I have nowhere else to go."

Taking a deep breath and blowing it away in the breeze, I held up a finger. Nash paused for a moment, staring.

"One chance, Nash."

His face lit up as he wrapped me in a hug, nearly throwing me off balance. "Thank you," he mumbled before backing up. He brushed his long hair out of his eyes, and in the blue dusk, he looked so much like our father.

"So," I said. "You think I'm not doing a good enough job. What do we do about Eden? Do you think she's a threat?" I crossed my arms.

"She's—"

"Talented. Caroline showed me her research journal. She's cataloged so many things."

"But she's—"

"Intelligent, too. Caroline said she followed your tracks and measured them before you scared her into bashing her head into a rock."

I scoffed. "I did not scare her. She slipped. Not my fault."

Nash grinned. "Okay, *fine*. What were you thinking about her then?"

I thought of the first time she truly saw me, both of us kneeling in Guardian's Glade. The world had shrunk to nothing besides her, like she snared me in some trap with her gaze.

"She has bear cub eyes."

Nash raised his eyebrows.

Lycaon, help me.

I shrugged. "The color reminds me of a bear cub."

"A bear cub? Silas, that can't be a compliment. Please do not tell her that."

"An observation, *not* a compliment. And why would I tell her?" Nash laughed, but I kept going, frustration building. "When would I ever compliment her? Besides, when I was in her room, I *did* scare her. I doubt she'd listen to anything I had to say right about now."

Nash ran his hand over his chin. "You were in her room. Alone?"

"Stop it." I shook my head. "I only wanted to make sure that... that she had... that I—"

"You like her." Nash smiled.

"No, Nash. No. I mean it." I pointed at him. "I do not like her. I *can't* like her. Even if I did, you know that's not how this works for me."

Nash's smile faded. "Yeah, I know. That's soon, right?"

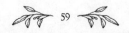

59

He gazed around at the trees and the balanced stone markers. The blue ghost beetles started their evening, instinct preparing them for the magic they would make the next evening. I inhaled, wanting to savor this moment. My control had been limited as King. These moments away from the responsibility felt more like Silas and less like the King of Arcadia. And I had precious few of those moments left.

"Tomorrow," I managed to mutter.

"Are you nervous?"

Rolling my eyes, I sighed. "Would you like to ask an intelligent question?"

Nash growled. "It's a better question than 'Hey! I know I just came home, but how are you feeling about losing your freedom and betrothal and being a king and having responsibility for an entire kingdom?'"

"Nervous," I mumbled, frustrated that I couldn't come up with anything better. "You try being told you can't marry for love when it's all you've ever wanted. And yet, I can't even think about the woman I'll call my wife because the festivities and winter preparations have distracted me, and now I have a human on my hands."

"Have you thought about inviting Archer and Andra?"

I swore under my breath. I'd forgotten. They were the closest things we had to friends from another pack.

Hurried footsteps stole my attention and my moment of peace. Turning, I spotted Eden's night guard running towards us, robed in light blue.

I stepped forward. "Kane, what's wrong?"

"Your majesty." He tilted his head to me in a short bow. "He's here."

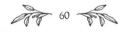

8

EDEN

I AIN AND I RAN through the woods. This time, I rode with Silas, watching Iain match our pace. His paws pounded against the earth, the ground shaking with each footfall.

A wolf howled in the distance, and we slowed to a walking pace. I slipped off Silas's back, running my fingers through his thick fur, and began walking between him and Iain.

This was peace.

I was born to be here, to live among wolves.

The smell of snow hung in the air, the moss floor cold under my bare feet. I stared up at the trees, limbs bare and lifeless. Soon, they would freeze until the spring, slipping into their winter slumber. And then Life would begin anew.

A low growl startled me. I tensed. Silas circled me now, and for a moment, I thought I had become his prey. But he gazed out into the woods. I glanced at Iain, who sniffed the air, ears pinned back and eyes squinting.

Danger.

Something approached.

The air shifted, warmer than it should have been as a dense fog shrouded the forest. Iain growled low when something emerged from the mist.

A wolf, darker than night, approached. His eyes blazed like the sun. He walked towards us, shoulders shifting his muscles with each step.

"You have the heart of a wolf, young one," the dark wolf spoke in my head. "The mind of a huntress. The spirit of the wild."

"Eden," Iain whispered gently. "You are safe here in Arcadia."

The strange wolf laughed, the sound of it rumbling in my chest even from a distance. Power thrummed in his veins, emanating from him in the fog.

"Eden," he mused. "My name is Nyx. I have a feeling we'll become good friends."

Silas and Iain both moved to stand in front of me in protective stances.

"Or perhaps not." Nyx growled. "I wouldn't mind being the one to kill the King of Arcadia."

"No, please." I shot my eyes to Iain. "You can't die like this."

Nyx licked his teeth. "I've already killed him once. I'll gladly do it again. Didn't they warn you about the big, bad wolf?"

With a lunge, Nyx's teeth dug into Iain's shoulder. If I screamed, I couldn't hear it. My heartbeat rushed into my ears as everything moved in slow motion.

Nyx pulled at Iain's flesh, ripping a yelp from Iain.

"Eden, run!" he grunted. "Silas!"

I watched Nyx rip Iain's left foot clean off. The king phased between his human form and his wolf form when he tumbled to the ground. He gasped for air like he was drowning.

"Father!" Silas shouted, frozen in terror.

"Leave now, Silas," Iain hissed while Nyx loomed over him. "You're ready."

Nyx shifted like the smoke, a towering dark figure of a man. He ripped a branch from one of the dormant trees with too much ease for normal human strength. He lifted it high above Iain's body.

"No!" I shouted. I turned away while Nyx finished off the King of Arcadia. Silas tugged me onto his back and charged away from the gruesome scene, his flight response kicking in.

Tears stung my face while the brutal wind whipped past us.

Iain had been murdered.

Behind us, Nyx gained ground like he was flying, heavy paws attacking the earth. I clutched Silas's fur tight, praying that we would make it back to the safety of Arcadia.

I turned around once more. The terrible, dark wolf disappeared.

As I righted myself, Silas fell from beneath me, shifting direction. For a moment, I soared until I rolled and tumbled on the ground, the wind knocked out of me.

This was all some horrible nightmare. It had to be.

A paw crushed my chest in an instant, pinning my back to the ground and threatening to snap my collarbone. Claws dug into the thin layer of skin over my bones. Nyx, covered in Iain's blood, breathed in my face. The smell of iron turned my stomach.

"You should know better than to run from wolves, Eden."

"Please, I don't understand," I cried. Tears streamed down my cheeks, sliding past my ears. Every part of me grew sticky with sweat. A drop of Iain's blood dripped on my cheek from Nyx's snarling lips, and the sound of rattling keys sent chills up my spine.

"You will. In time." Nyx bared his bloody teeth.

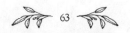

I screamed, but nothing came.

"Eden?" Silas shook my shoulders, awakening the aches in my body from the dream. "Eden, wake up. Can you hear me?"

I blinked. The chilly, shrouded forest no longer surrounded me, but my prison cell. No longer crushed by the weight of a wolf, but safe and sound in my bed.

Darkness had seeped over the forest as dusk fell. Shadows danced across Silas's face. He leaned over me, knees on either side of my stomach, one hand slipped under my neck the other on my arm.

I raised a hand to my cheeks and felt real tears. "Nyx," I whispered.

"Oh, Lycaon," a voice said.

A moment passed before I realized that Nash stood in the doorway.

"Silas." Caroline stepped into view, hand on the king's shoulder.

"Eden, what happened?" he asked, voice breaking.

I didn't know kings could be scared.

I didn't know wolves could be scared.

I swallowed, my throat raw from screaming. *Real* screaming.

How much of that was actually a nightmare?

"I dreamt that you and I were running with Iain in the woods. He said I'd be safe in Arcadia, but then—" My eyesight glazed over while I tried to remember what I had seen.

Blood.

Blazing red eyes.

Iain's face when he died.

"A wolf calling himself Nyx killed Iain. He killed your father. I watched it happen. Iain's leg—" My voice broke off with the vision repeating itself behind my eyelids.

The room fell silent, Silas's hand still supporting my head. His muscles tensed. I felt his eyes on me, but I kept my gaze away.

"She's a human. It could be just a dream, right?" Nash asked.

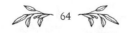

"He..." Nash didn't finish his sentence.

"He'd lost a lot of blood, Nash," Caroline whispered. "His left foot was gone. And he never said what he'd encountered that day."

"Was no one with him?" Nash sounded incredulous.

Neither of his siblings answered him.

With a thumb, Silas brushed a drop of blood off my cheek, examining it.

Iain's blood in my dream.

"You brought Nyx into Arcadia," Silas muttered to me in defeat.

Nash flinched.

"But I didn't. It was a dream, right?" Silas sat up straight as I pushed myself up on my arm. "Dreams aren't real."

Caroline shook her head. "Dreams are weighty but fickle. Once, Nyx had the Sight. That magic may still be in his blood, giving him power. It's possible but rare to manifest in dreams. So if you dreamt of him..." She shrugged like that answered all of my questions.

But Iain's blood on Silas's thumb told the rest of the story.

Whatever it was, at least part of it had been real. Nyx had been real. And what scared me the most now was the expression of pure anger in Silas's gaze. I searched for any sign of hope. But the wild overpowered his green eyes.

I didn't know if that wild anger was for Nyx or for me.

9

SILAS

I KEPT A RELENTLESS pace, her wrist gripped in my hand. I drug the traitor all the way to the Boneyard before throwing her to the ground, her mess of curly hair flying in her face.

Stupid, beautifully wild hair.

Nash pulled my shoulder. "What in the *silva* are you doing?"

"Silas, please be rational." Caroline stopped on the other side of me.

"Enough!" I growled, turning to Eden. "I made a mistake bringing you here. I let myself be blinded by the past, and now you've put my entire pack in danger. And it's my fault."

My hands trembled at my side.

How could I be so stupid?

She stared up at me with those bear cub eyes, shaking her head. "I didn't– I would never– I didn't think–"

"That's because you *humans* never think!" I shouted, stepping away before I made any poor decisions.

I could hear my heartbeat loud and clear, *thump-thump, thump-thump, thump-thump.*

Control. Control. Control.

I sucked in a few breaths, trying to slow my heart.

Slow down.

Breathe.

Come back to yourself.

"Silas," Nash muttered as he stepped closer, skin pale. "She's a human. They don't know anything. She can't be connected to Nyx. You can't blame her for this."

"His image is in the journal, Nash. I saw it."

And you brought her into your home. Stupid Silas.

Stupid Eden being where she doesn't belong.

Stupid Caroline for not trusting my leadership.

Stupid Nash trying to take Eden's side.

"The journal doesn't mean anything, Si." Nash grabbed my shoulders, ducking into my vision. "Maybe she was in the wrong place at the wrong time. You know how Nyx is. Maybe someone else–"

With my left arm, I pushed his hands off my shoulders. With the other, I sent a fist into his stomach. The blow caught him off guard. He doubled over.

An inkling of remorse niggled at the back of my mind. I hadn't intended to harm him. I only wanted him to shut up.

"You don't have an opinion, *brother*." I spit out the word like an insult and stepped back towards Eden, who still sat on the mossy floor. "Get up."

She stood but kept her distance from me.

Not nearly far enough.

The adrenaline coursing through my veins woke the wild in me. It howled in my head, feet pounding in my chest. Its teeth were bared,

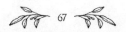

ready to defend.

I did this.

I have to fix this.

How do I fix this?

"Silas, stop this." Nash threw an arm around my neck, pulling me into a headlock. One arm braced my head, and the other wrapped around my throat.

Reaching up, I grabbed his elbow and pulled it forward. Feeling his grasp around my neck falter, I twisted myself backwards and to his right, throwing him into a side headlock.

"It's been a while since we've wrestled, Nash," I taunted, using minimal strength to hold him in place. He'd lost a lot of weight since I'd seen him last. "I've gotten better."

Pulling my left arm and pinning it behind my back, he pressed his other hand to the side of my face, keeping me at arm's length.

"I can see you've been practicing," Nash grunted. "Did Caroline finally let you win?"

A growl escaped my lips. I pulled my leg around his and knocked us both to the ground. In the fall, Nash had loosened his grip enough for me to roll out, moving on top of him to keep his shoulders down.

"Stop fighting me!" I growled, pushing my forearm down on his neck.

"I will fight you until you see reason," Nash hissed back.

He hooked a leg around mine and rolled, landing on top, forcing all of his weight on my chest. These were no longer sarcastic jabs, and the realization shook me.

"Give it up, Si," he panted. "You can't protect everyone."

"I have to try." I gasped, fighting for a grip on his body. Rotating myself onto my stomach under his chest, I wrestled him over my shoulder, standing with a struggle.

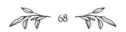 68

Wrapping his arms around my neck, he leaned his weight all the way forward, rolling us into the trees. We broke apart, and I was on my feet in an instant, ready for the next attack.

"Silas," he breathed, standing much slower than I expected. "I'm done. I wish that you could see that the human world is not against you."

He turned his back on me and trudged back to the Boneyard to stand next to Caroline, who had an arm wrapped around Eden's shoulders.

That girl has turned my whole family against me.

Shaking my head, I moved to follow Nash. "That's rich coming from you. You've hated humans since Mother died. You just can't accept that I finally won, Nash." I rolled out my neck, stretching the parts that were already sore.

"No, Silas," he said, turning to me with more aggression than I expected. "You can win if that's what you really want."

I took a few breaths, my brain fumbling for a response.

"Do you want a fractured family? So be it. Do you want a disloyal or terrified pack? So be it." He threw a hand at Eden. "Do you want to alienate us from humans even more than we are now? So be it."

Caroline reached a hand up to his shoulder but said nothing. How come she supported him when he'd been absent for so long? When he'd left us?

Shaking his head, Nash continued, "I know Nyx is dangerous. I know you're scared. I know you're doing your best, Si." His eyes met mine, our conversation from the Aisle of Kings flashing in my mind. "But I don't think blaming Eden for our father's death is right. *She* didn't lead Nyx here." He roughed his hand over his jaw, shaking his head. "But what do I know? I'm just the Omega."

He shrugged Caroline's hand off of his shoulder and started the

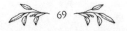

trek back to the residential court alone.

"I'm going to check on him," Caroline whispered, glancing from me to Eden. Without waiting for an answer, she jogged back up the path to catch up with our brother, robes rippling behind her.

I refused to look at the human in front of me. Instead, my eyes found the antler sheds mounted on the trees around the clearing, the ghost beetles flickering from their beds in the high grass, the mostly full moon illuminating the forest. When Eden sniffled, the sound pulled my gaze. It startled me, but I remembered the scream that had come from her room while we fought to unlock it.

Whatever she'd witnessed must have been terrifying.

She had seen my father's death, and Nyx himself. Not even a *virlukos* of Arcadia would say that was a trot in the woods.

I thought over Nash's words. He had never been the logical one in an argument. This had to be a first.

"I'm sorry for overreacting," I murmured.

For a moment, I thought she hadn't heard me, so I glanced up. Tears slipped down her face, reflecting the pale light of the moon.

"Eden?" I reached for her, but she stumbled two steps back, arms crossed tight over her midsection. A breath escaped her, and she turned her face away.

No wonder she's scared of me. I'm a complete mess. What have I done?

10
EDEN

I TRIED TO TAMP down my emotions, but the anxiety only grew. It seemed silly to cry now after so much had happened. I hadn't cried when I'd been brought in front of the Council. I hadn't cried when Silas had threatened to rip out my throat. And I hadn't processed my dream until that moment.

Nyx.

Exactly the entry in my journal for the Smoke Wolf.

Folklore.

Or so I thought.

The reality of such a creature being real and knowing my name... It broke whatever dam I had built that held back my tears.

And then there was Silas.

He watched me, head tilted.

What did I do to deserve his wrath aside from being born a human?

"Eden," he said. "Can I–" Silas closed his mouth, something at war in his mind. "Would you like a hug?"

"What?" I wiped away some of the tears on my face.

It wasn't that I didn't understand the question, only that I couldn't have heard him. A moment ago, he blamed me for things and fought with his brother, and now... I wasn't sure.

Silas gazed at the branches far above us, muttering something under his breath before turning back at me. "Would you like a hug? Is that something that would comfort you?"

I couldn't help but laugh.

He's dead serious.

Silas turned away, mumbling something about humans.

"A hug won't fix it." Apologies wouldn't fix it either, but something had shifted in him after that argument with Nash. An unseen war raged inside of his head, one I would never understand. He struggled as much as I did to understand everything going on. And if a hug is what kept this version of Silas around, I would take it. "A hug is as good of a peace offering as I'll get from you."

His eyes slid up to mine, questions swirling in their dark green forests. "If I gave you a hug, would that make you not flinch when I'm near you?"

I paused, remembering the flash of wildness in his eyes while he dragged me through the woods. I remembered his breath against my cheek and the flutter in my heart any time his eyes met mine.

I found myself *seeing* him maybe for the first time. Caroline said he hadn't been ready, that they had thrust the title of king on him in a time of grief and pain. I saw the broken pieces and his attempts to glue them back together. I saw his eyes, searching. I thought of being a friend. I thought of knowing him.

And I thought about being held by him.

Curse attractive werewolves.

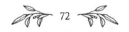

I nodded.

With uneasy movements, Silas stepped toward me and wrapped his arms around my shoulders. I hugged him back. His strong muscles shifted under his robe, the scent of the mountains after it rains overwhelming my senses. The moment felt warm, like cozying up by a campfire.

When I could no longer breathe from sheer closeness to this king, he stepped back, running his fingers through his loose curls.

He avoided my gaze as he cleared his throat. "So, I can take you back to your room. Or if…"

His voice trailed off when he met my eyes in the dark. At that moment, I became aware of how alone we were. There were so many words on my lips waiting to finish that sentence.

"Silas," I swallowed. "You have to understand, I never intended for this to happen. I have only ever wanted to find you again. If I had known…"

"I know." He straightened himself, messing with the buttons on his robe.

"I know it's not much to offer, but if there's anything I can do to help…"

He rubbed his eyes. "What could you do for me?" It sounded like a rhetorical question.

"I don't know."

After a moment, he turned on his heel and headed back up the path waving me onward.

I followed in silence until we arrived at my room. "Um, goodnight," I whispered, gazing up at him.

"Goodnight, Eden." His voice sounded rough and uneven.

He turned around and left, not glancing back.

Not even to lock me in my room.

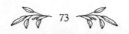

The next morning, I woke up much too exhausted to worry about Silas. I had a sneaking feeling that the cause of my headache was lack of caffeine in addition to the healing head wound.

You would think an advanced race of shapeshifters would figure out some way to have coffee, even in the woods.

While I lay there staring at the branches above me, I wondered about the world outside of Arcadia. They'd probably found my car parked in its usual spot in the State Park's lot. They probably found the bear spray I'd left there and my school bag with some textbooks. They'd probably interviewed people I worked with and asked if anyone had seen me.

My last known location would be my car or the trail I'd been assigned to that day, but they wouldn't find anything. A bit of blood, maybe. But how far was Arcadia from that trail? How far had Silas brought me?

And did I want them to find me?

Strange enough, my answer would be no. I wanted to research the wild, this was it. No job application or internship could ever afford me this experience. How could I turn back now when there were so many new things to discover?

Not knowing the time, I went ahead and changed into the light green robe per Caroline's recommendation. I had been worried about being accepted at the Council, but the nightmare about Nyx left me shaken.

I fussed with the robe, thinking about what I would say. Everything felt like my fault. And while I cherished the fact that I could witness the very thing I'd desired most, I hadn't asked to be brought here. And I didn't think I deserved to be tried for threatening the exposure of

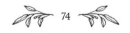

Arcadia because I had doodles of cartoon werewolves in my journal. Betraying the people who had rescued me as a little girl was something I would never do.

Humans often destroyed the things that made them curious. I would die before I let that happen to Arcadia.

Soon, Bennett guided me to the same large room. This time I knew what to do and knelt low before Silas.

The same smirk rested on his face, but something besides wildness rested behind those eyes. Something soft. He seemed well rested after the night we'd had.

I didn't have time to unravel any mysteries Silas held as he addressed his people and pulled me to my feet. He turned me to face the crowd.

"As you all know, yesterday this human was to be tried for threatening exposure of our kingdom."

I watched him out of the corner of my eyes. He stood tall and regal in his silvery robe, a crown of willow tucked over his mess of dark hair. He gleamed in the early morning sun, the epitome of some forest god or spirit.

Maybe that's what virlukos are.

"Yesterday, in addition to this woman, we received two other guests." Silas swallowed. "My dear brother, Nash, son of King Iain. May his spirit find peace among trees."

The crowd of people repeated Silas's words, paying homage to their former king.

Nash ducked his head where he stood in the front row of the crowd with Caroline.

Silas waited for them to grow quiet before continuing. "And last night, our safe haven of Arcadia was breached by Nyx through a nightmare."

Murmurs of disbelief rippled over the council. Gratitude rushed through me realizing he hadn't said whose nightmare it had been. Silas held up a single hand and silenced them all at once. The people waited, all watching their king.

Despite what Caroline had said and the interactions I had seen with my own eyes, Silas was a good king. They respected him even when they were scared.

Dropping his hand, Silas glanced at me.

"As you all know, dreams are fickle, but I believe it best to treat it as reality. In lieu of the circumstances at hand, I have decided to pardon this woman for the intrusion if she agrees to assist us. I believe she has valuable insight on Nyx and the outside world. And I grant her honorary Historian authority until the Winter Equinox."

Another rumble of murmurs from the crowd.

Caroline stepped onto the dais of wood, passing me a deep blue robe. In the light of the sun, the robe flickered like starlight. It, like the other robes, felt like water in my hands.

Silas quieted the crowd once more. "She is to be treated like any other human we have served in the past. But she is of equal status to any one of the pack. I'll need to talk to the Branches immediately. Council meeting dismissed."

While the people filed out of the hall casting backward glances at me, Caroline pulled me aside. "Welcome to the pack."

I shook my head. "I don't understand. You said they were scared."

Caroline nodded. "And they still are. But they are more afraid of Nyx."

Nash meandered over while Silas conferred with a group of six or seven people, a rainbow of robes. I watched while he spoke with each of them, delegating responsibilities.

"So what valuable insight do you have on Nyx?" Nash asked, hands in the pockets of his robe. "Last I checked, you didn't know who he was until last night."

"I *still* don't know who he is. And I'm not aware of any information that I have to help you. But I would give it in a heartbeat if I could. I told Silas as much last night."

Caroline shrugged. "The fact that you had a dream about Nyx makes you pretty important. You may have access to things we don't know."

Silas now stood with three men in violet and one man in light blue, the guard who had stood outside my door and led me to the throne room with Bennett.

I motioned my head to him. "Is he giving orders?"

Caroline and Nash followed my gaze.

"He's giving them the information they need to talk one-on-one with whoever has questions," Caroline said. "But I have your pack orders."

"I already have orders?" My brow furrowed. "But I still don't know what it is I'm supposed to be doing."

"You're first wanted in the kitchen."

"Historians work in the kitchen?"

She laughed, a sound like songbirds. "No, not at all. But *Sarva* is tonight, and we need all the help we can get for preparation."

"*Sarva*? What is that?"

"Kind of like your version of Thanksgiving or Christmas, but different. *Sarva* is one of many feasts and festivals we celebrate, but this one is where our ancestors come back for an evening to give advice, reminisce, and visit Arcadia again."

"Wolves have holidays?" I brushed my hair back over my shoulder. "I guess I didn't expect it to be so..."

"So what?" Caroline grinned.

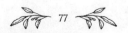

I shrugged. "So human?"

"What?" Nash scoffed. "You think we don't know how to let loose and get wild?" He smiled and ran his tongue over his teeth.

Caroline rolled her eyes as she grabbed my hand. "Ignore him. I usually do." She pulled me after her.

The cooks had me making the delicious spruce bread I'd been given the morning before, along with preparing the dough for an apple and berry tart. Someone had begun to roast deer meat over a fire, and it elicited a grumble from my stomach.

Caroline set down her copy of the *virlukos* history of law she'd been reading from for the past hour or so. I had learned a lot about why they existed, the values they stood for, pack hierarchy laws, and so many little things I hadn't even considered. It all made my head spin.

Caroline closed the book. "If you've had enough of making bread and cooking, we'll take lunch in Guardian's Glade and discuss your plans for tonight."

On our path back to the throne room, a young man in a violet robe stopped us.

"Caroline, I–" He froze, staring at her.

"Is everything all right, Markus?" Caroline tilted her head.

The man called Markus moved his lips, but no sound came out. A slight chuckle escaped him. I bit my tongue to stop from laughing.

A blush crept up his ears as he ducked his head down. "Sorry, I'm– *Vanni*."

He slipped past us, keeping his head down.

"Oh, Markus." Caroline shook her head with a smile as we continued our walk.

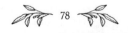

"What was that about?" I glanced back to watch Markus trip through a group of pups playing in the pathway.

"No, it's stupid."

"Come on! *Something* happened back there."

Caroline sighed. "I keep feeling like he's going to, I don't know, ask me to eat with him? Or help with his Seer stuff. It's not like a Historian like myself would have much to add."

"Maybe he's scared."

"It's not like I'm Queen. And I never wanted to be, by the way." She clarified, one finger in the air. "Is it something I put off? Or am I imagining whatever this is?"

"It's like he wants to talk but can't find the words. Maybe you make the first move. A nudge in the right direction and see where it takes you."

She smiled and walked on. I followed her back to where we had the council meeting. When we entered, Silas was in his wolf form. From what I gathered, he and Nash were walking through their responsibilities for the evening while Caroline would manage the rest of the festivities. She told me that custom called for the sons of the late King to lead the Spirits of the past back to their burial spots as an end to the festivities, and there were certain processes they had to follow.

Everyone bristled with energy. I heard whispers about people excited to see certain people again and talk of music and dance.

But the conversations I wanted to hear only lasted a few seconds. People would whisper about the king and share an expression ranging somewhere between amused and concerned. But I never caught on to what they were suggesting.

Now, while the men walked through with Elder Macon what they were supposed to say and do, I wondered if we might be hosting another wolf pack.

"Caroline." I turned away from the brothers. "You never told me why you all celebrate the equinox. I know a little about the history and why you protect humans. But why is this night so important to you all?"

Caroline closed the book she had brought along with her. "It's one of our most sacred events and has been for centuries. But this year is special."

"Why this year?"

Caroline frowned. "It's the first *Sarva* since the Passing of Kings. Kind of a post-coronation ceremony. And Silas is twenty."

"And that's a special age?" I turned back to Silas, who had phased, bare back facing me as he put on his robe. I saw his shoulder muscles tense when he moved to slide his arms in the sleeves.

I turned to Caroline, face burning. My face had to be scarlet like the cover of her book.

"Silas is the new King of Arcadia, so he and our father share a heart-to-heart. It's a moment where the new king or queen can ask questions of the predecessor. King Iain will return in Spirit as well as our people, along with all of the other ancestral kings and queens of old," Caroline continued, oblivious to my abashed state. "As for Silas's age, tonight his life mate will be assigned."

I swallowed. "So it's a wedding feast."

"You could say that." Caroline shrugged as the boys headed our way. "Each Branch has a representative that votes on which heir is first in line when the heirs are between the ages of fifteen and twenty. Usually the decision is made when the heirs reach twenty, but under the circumstances, they voted early. Nash had disappeared, and I'd grown numb the years after our mother had died, so Silas was the natural choice. And now, our father will decide who will be our new queen."

"So Iain is coming back to life?"

Caroline shook her head, thumbing through the book in front of her. "Not exactly. His Spirit will return for the evening. But as far as I know, they are sentient and responsive, like they're truly living without having full bodies."

I bit my lip as I traced the grain of the table. "And Iain chooses the queen based on merit?"

Caroline shrugged. "I've never really thought about it, never something I had to consider. Maybe he knows something we don't now that he's passed. Or maybe it's knowledge passed to him from the Elder. But by midnight, we'll have a chosen queen and the ceremony will take place during *Joulo*."

Why does the thought of Silas marrying some wild wolf girl make my stomach hurt?

I chided myself, upset for allowing my emotions to twist into whatever this mess was. Silas made it very clear that he disliked humans. And he'd been so moody that I had trouble keeping up with him.

Then I remembered the hug.

The smell of rain.

His strength despite his circumstance.

I had to admit the attraction, but that didn't mean I had to hold onto it. Nor could I.

It'll all be over tonight.

"Glad you ladies could join us for a meal." Nash flopped down next to me. "Seems like I'll be accompanying you tonight, since you're the guest of honor. Kind of like a weird body guard."

"Guest of honor? All I've done is have nightmares and bake bread." I chuckled, trying to ease the growing tension I felt near Silas. The image of his back flashed in my mind, and I ducked my head to my bowl of stew.

"But bread is a delicious food," Nash reasoned, picking up his bowl. "Speaking of, I hope we're having apple berry tart tonight. It was Mother's favorite."

Caroline smiled. "You always tried to take mine!"

"And I always had the nasty job of keeping the peace." Silas chuckled.

I ate my stew in silence, listening to them reminisce about the past. The thought of their childhood spoiled by the loss of both their mother and their father made my appetite go sour. I pushed my bowl away from me on the table.

"You don't look so good." Nash touched my shoulder. "Please don't tell me you're one of those humans who eats only vegetables. Because that stew has a ton of meat in it."

I shook my head, managing a smile. "So much has changed, and I wish I could go back to the Little River where we all met and start again. Do you still go out there?"

Silas and Caroline stopped eating and exchanged a glance.

"Eden," Silas began, "if Nyx is able to infiltrate your dreams, it means he's near. I had a discussion with the Elder and our top Seers this morning, and they all agree that we can't allow you to leave Arcadia until we sort this out. With the threat of danger..."

My mind brought up memories of the nightmare intermingled with the brief history of the Arcadian pack of *virlukos* Caroline had shared while we baked.

I looked down at my hands in my lap. If Nyx was real and prowling around the Appalachian Mountains, I didn't want to be alone either. But the words *until we sort this out* echoed in my thoughts.

Will I be allowed to stay when this is all over?

Maybe I could work in the kitchens and help cook or babysit the pups.

The thought disappeared as Silas began asking me questions about

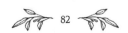

my research journal. I told him the basics of my job for the National Park Service and talked about my own personal studies.

"After meeting y'all, I grew obsessed with wolves and all things folklore. I journaled about it. If I had my journal now, I would show you."

Silas stood and walked over to a door that I hadn't noticed before, hidden behind his throne in the hedge. After a moment and the slight squeaking of wood on wood, he returned with my journal in hand.

"I kept it in my room," he mumbled, passing me the journal. "For safekeeping."

The idea of him reading my journal brought heat to my cheeks. I had assumed he'd read through it, but the confession felt like he'd read the pages of my soul.

I leafed through the entries with memory more than intent. My fingers opened the pages of the Smoke Wolf. A very fuzzy and blended drawing of a dark wolf and red eyes nearly jumped from the page.

"I got the idea of him from *the Hound of the Baskervilles* by Arthur Conan Doyle," I murmured, remembering the haunting mystery. "The only things I could find out about the Smoke Wolf cryptid are here, from some page about Appalachian folklore and how to protect yourself. Most of it was sasquatch or whatever, but there were small sections about werewolves, wendigos, raven mockers, and the Smoke Wolf."

Caroline rolled her eyes at the word *werewolf*, but the boys sat at full attention.

"So the first time you'd ever encountered Nyx was in your dream last night?" Silas asked.

I nodded, not wanting to look at him. Between his constant mood swings and how much he dealt with, I walked on eggshells around him. And for whatever reason, my mind kept falling back to the purpose of tonight's festivities. I couldn't help but wonder if Silas felt nervous.

His engagement feast is tonight, but instead of worrying about his future with his wife, he's having to worry about an outside threat.

All because he's the king. Or because of me.

But he cared for his people.

And that should be his biggest priority, right?

I hoped for his sake that I dreamt of nothing that night. He deserved at least one moment of happiness.

11

SILAS

ROBE.

Hair.

Ceremonial paint.

Honeysuckle crown.

I kept my eyes closed, taking in the moment while my pack prepared me for the evening. Many times, I watched my father undergo the same treatment.

Robe.

Braided hair.

Equinox paint.

Ceremonial crown.

He had longer hair, like Nash, so his had to be styled. He and my mother had been paired before he became king, so he never had this ceremonial paint while I grew up. And he'd opted not to remarry when my mother passed.

This was all new for me.

My eyes had been shadowed by the paint. The dark line cut across my face from cheekbone to cheekbone. The royal lineage painted straight across my face. My heart drummed as a purple-robed Seer painted a rune on my forehead, a vertical line with five crossbars.

The Yew tree.

Grief.

Ancestral memory.

The Seer painted another rune on my chin. A vertical line with a single horizontal line right through the center.

The Spruce tree.

Divine Light.

Happiness.

He then added smaller decorative lines, dots, and symbols to my pale face.

When they finished my ceremonial paint, they placed a crown of honeysuckle on my head, nestled like every other crown I'd worn. It held my hair out of my face and carried so much meaning.

Pure happiness and tenderness.

It was time for *Sarva*, the ancestral Festival of Kings.

"Are you nervous?" Caroline whispered, the solemnity of the evening weighing heavy in her words as she straightened my robe around the neckline. Her hair had been braided, a dainty crown of willow adorning her head, and a single stripe had been painted across her face like mine. She looped her arm through mine as we stood before the wooden door leading out of my room and into Guardian's Glade.

I nodded but didn't reply.

I didn't trust my voice.

I knew this day would come for me. The day my father died, this became my role. I mourned the loss of *Silas*, of the previous me, and put on the robe of a king.

This was who I became: King of Arcadia.

And kings were assigned their life mate, a partner to share in the grief of losing the previous king and the responsibilities of running a kingdom.

I walked through my mind, lining up all the eligible women in our pack. Which one my father would choose for me, I couldn't say. I hadn't been close with any of them in particular. And even if I had been before my father died, people stopped coming around after I assumed his role as king.

In Arcadia, my closest friends were Caroline, Elder Macon, and Markus. No one else really called on me anymore.

I thought of our two friends, Andra and Archer, in Lukosan, wondering if they would've attended had I thought to send for them. Nash had mentioned them, but with everything else tumbling through my thoughts, I'd forgotten. Maybe Father would have chosen Andra for me to marry, uniting two packs.

The door opened and Caroline accompanied me out of my room into Guardian's Glade where my people awaited my arrival. Lanterns flickered around the walls, illuminating the throne room with a warm yellow glow. Elder Macon addressed the crowd from the aisle, his staff by his side, blue ghost beetles lighting the top of it. He turned to smile at us before returning to the telling of history. I saw the elder tree rune painted on his forehead.

The symbol itself resembled the yew tree symbol on my forehead, but the crossbars on the Elder's forehead were slanted.

Life and death.

Transition.

Lines of men and women and children stood in a crowd listening to the Elder, split down the middle by an aisle of stone. Nash stood at the front of the crowd, a smaller, barren crown of branches adorning his head and a single stripe of paint across his eyes matching mine and Caroline's.

And next to him, Eden.

She was dazzling—despite the darkening hue of the evening—in her new historian robe, a deep blue gilded with magic, like a galaxy of stars and her face painted with delicate black markings. In the center of her forehead, a single vertical line with a small curl connected to the center on the right side of the line.

Honeysuckle.

Pure happiness.

Tenderness.

I bit my tongue and turned away. Several other of the young women had the mark of the honeysuckle.

The realization of the marking hit me like a rushing waterfall: The Seers included Eden in the pairing ceremony.

Never in my lifetime, nor at any point in the *virlukos* history had a human been present for the Festival of Kings. Which meant that never, in all of our history, had a human participated in the matching ceremony.

I inhaled, holding the breath in my throat. I bit my tongue in the attempt to keep myself calm.

Surely, it's for show. To put her at ease.

But Seers didn't follow logic. They followed their inner eye, a gift from the Other Realm where the Spirits slept.

What do they know that they aren't telling me?

I turned back to Eden, noticing her curly hair pulled back in a braided crown, bits of spruce tucked between the plaits. A few strands fell to frame her face, which positively beamed. She watched me, and I stared back.

"What do you see in her?" Caroline whispered.

"Nothing," I replied a little too fast.

"Liar." I could hear the smugness in her voice.

I cleared my throat. "Truth be told, I see that they've included her in the matching."

"Markus came by this afternoon and asked if she wanted to be included. Eden said yes. Are you upset?"

I tore my eyes away from Eden, turning to face Caroline. A small frown hid at the corner of her lips.

"I'm confused... and nervous."

"Out of our pack, is there someone you'd pick for yourself?" Her brow furrowed as she turned only her eyes to scan the crowd.

I licked my lips, my mouth dry. "I've never allowed myself to dream like that. I would've only experienced heartbreak."

Caroline smiled, pity evident in her expression. "Not even in other packs? Not even Lukosan?"

I hesitated. At one point, I might've thought of Andra that way, a potential partner in this duty as Alpha, as King. But I shook my head. "I did wonder why I hadn't invited Andra and Archer tonight. Nash asked me, too. I guess it wasn't in the stars."

She sighed. "No point in lamenting now. You'll know your mate soon."

"*Too* soon." I straightened my shoulders. "Remind me what I'm supposed to do again. My brain has gone blank."

Caroline chuckled. "Go sit. You'll remember what to do."

With a small bow, Caroline left the dais and joined my brother and our human guest among the crowd. I assumed my seat on the throne.

Watching Eden stare up at the Elder in wonder, I imagined what it would be like if things weren't so tense between us. We'd started off on the wrong paw. She'd proven to be helpful and hardworking while prepping for *Sarva*. She had a certain courage about her that I didn't

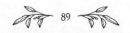

expect. And I found myself struggling to look away from her bear cub eyes.

Lycaon, help me. This girl has messed with my head.

I straightened again, willing myself to focus.

The Elder stepped onto the dais with all the grace of someone who had lived for so long, his violet robe swooping behind him. My father had been King for the changing of Elders, and I was a pup. I remembered the ceremony taking place, though I'm sure I was bored with the ritual side of things.

This Elder, Elder Macon, had been like a second father to me the past year, like a grandfather all the other years before that.

"Rise, young King." His brittle voice boomed over the utter silence enveloping the glade.

I stood, staring straight ahead while Elder Macon addressed the crowd. "In accordance with our centuries-old custom, the first autumnal equinox after the heir apparent is twenty years of age, a pairing is made. This *Sarva* is a bit different from tradition since we lost our noble King nigh on a year ago. May his spirit find peace among trees." He bowed his head, and each person repeated the solemn words, then he gestured to me. "But before the celebrations commence, our good King Silas will lead us to the Aisle of Kings, where King Iain and those who preceded will rise for the evening." Elder Macon smiled, drawing his hands together, clasped at his midsection. "I ask for your silence while we enter this momentous time in our people's history." He turned to me again. "My king?"

I stepped down onto the stone path leading out of Guardian's Glade. Every eye followed me, then footsteps beginning with the Elder and the front row where the royal family stood.

I led my people through our forest to the Aisle of Kings. The blue-lit beetles were already awake, all of them spread out amongst the balanced stone graves. I walked down the long aisle to my father's stones.

Turning back to Elder Macon, I caught his eye. With a nod, he turned to our people, raising his arms high above his head, his long sleeves sliding down his arm. People spread out around the forest and among the graves in earnest silence. Nash stood between Caroline and Eden, the latter of which looked enamored by the sacred space.

A smile crept to my lips.

Humans, so fascinated by the little things.

The smile faded from my lips.

A human.

I wondered if Eden knew her attending this ceremony meant she'd been included in the pack. That there was a chance that she could become Queen of Arcadia, however small that possibility may be.

I turned to the Elder, who lowered his hands.

He muttered words from the Ancient Tongue before we adopted the common speech of this region. The blue beetles lifted high into the air, lighting up the glade in a fierce azure, casting everyone in a dim glow.

I only caught a few of the Elder's words.

Cara... Friend.

Veime... Long past.

Bene... Thank you.

Vanni... Goodbye.

The beetles rose and drifted down the path to the entrance of the Aisle of Kings where the very first balanced stones stood, marking the deaths of the ancient *virlukos* from centuries past. The light grew as wolves from the Other Realm trod down the path, glimmers of history breathing our air again.

Something moved from my father's grave, the beetles buzzing

around the balancing stones—the stones I balanced. The light from the insects and Spirits cast a moody blue over the forest, an ethereal atmosphere sliding into my lungs as I breathed the same air of our kings.

I held my breath when a form emerged from the precarious stack over my parents' grave, swirling to life in front of me. Though cast in the Spirit shades of cerulean, I knew my father's eyes anywhere.

Steel.

Like the frosty grass in the winter.

The sky when it rained.

Fish scales slipping through the rivers.

Father.

I took a deep, shuddered breath as my throat tightened with emotion. My vision swam, and his gaze pierced mine. Those eyes captivated me, frozen.

"*My son.*"

His voice wasn't audible, but it stirred in my memory like someone speaking through the pack connection.

He bowed to me. He seemed proud.

Beside him, another glimmer emerged from the standing stones next to my father's. A female alpha shook herself into being, blinking in the darkness. With an affection I could only dream of, she nuzzled my father.

Mother.

With a soft nudge, my father moved past me and meandered through the crowd with my mother and other countless Spirits. I sidled up to Elder Macon, who put an arm around my shoulder.

My father—King Iain—slipped under my sister's arm and circled Nash, nudging his other son with his muzzle. Nash's tears reflected in the bright blue hue of our father.

My heart pinched. I hadn't thought of how difficult it would be for him, seeing our father like this. Nash had missed so much when he'd been gone. His grief was fresh, palpable, heavy.

Next to Nash, Eden held her arms close to her. Her lip trembled, and tears slid down her cheek.

Countless faces among the crowd smiled and sniffled in the peaceful night. The forest knew a momentous thing occurred, the near-constant breeze dying down to a rustle. I noticed many of my people wiping away tears while their beloved King made his way through the crowd, greeting his people one at a time.

Oh Lycaon, how could I be so blind to their pain?

After an eternity of praying that he'd look at me again, he turned his head back. Those steel eyes caught mine, a glint of something unrecognizable in them.

One day, I'd join him. I'd return to my grieving people, a Spirit from the stones. I would walk among my people to comfort their hurting souls.

But today was my pairing.

Today, it was me being comforted.

Mother circled Father and sat next to him. She seemed so content, different from the past celebration of kings when she'd seemed dim and lonely. Her life partner had gone home to her, crossed to the Other Realm, and sat with her forevermore in peaceful rest.

I wondered if the person my father chose to be my partner would ever love me with that much ferocity.

Father turned, eyes scanning over the crowd. Not nervous or sad, he gazed over the many painted faces. He moved seemingly without purpose between people and trees. He circled around, coming back to my mother who nuzzled him again. With a determined stance, my father moved closer and bowed low in front of Eden.

Elder Macon's arm slipped from my shoulder, eyes catching my own. Nash went pale, snapping his head to Caroline, who clutched Eden's hand.

Holy silva.

A human.

Elder Macon cleared his throat, swallowing hard. "My child," he murmured, waving Eden over with his right hand, left hand still clutching the blue-lit staff.

Eden hesitated, eye's finding my father, who had righted himself once again. "Iain," she whispered.

"Welcome to the pack, daughter," he said, though his lips did not move.

In that instant, something shifted. Eden's face froze, lips parted. She had to have heard him in her head, the pack communication.

Lycaon, no.

This was all a huge misunderstanding, and it would clear up as soon as I could speak to my father alone.

All around me, howls erupted from the ancient kings, causing chills to run down my spine. The howls resounded and echoed in the still forest. The night felt colder than it should have, given the warmth of magic in our forest.

A human.

Eden's eyes lifted to mine.

She must be terrified. Does she know what just happened?

Memories of the day before sprouted in my head. I remembered her tension, her fear coursing through her veins. I had *felt* it in her pulse.

She stepped forward, dropping Caroline's hand and taking the Elder's outstretched one. He smiled like this was normal, drawing her to his right side as I stood on his left. But my body went numb.

Shocked. Trapped in disbelief.

"Wolves of Arcadia," he said, "your new Queen."

Another resounding howl from the Spirits, this time accompanied by calls from the stunned people of my kingdom.

Elder Macon patted Eden's hand with his own. "May you reign with a wolf spirit and the mind of a protector."

Eden paled and wavered where she stood as my people dropped their robes, phasing into their wolf forms.

The Elder placed her left hand in my right and stepped back.

"May *Sarva* commence!"

12

EDEN

EVERYTHING EXPLODED WITH MOTION.

The Spirit Wolves began to run back down the path that led to the Yard, along with the people of Arcadia. The people who had been serene and silent moments ago were phasing and sprinting through the forest, paws hitting the earth with unparalleled force.

Light fell away as the warmth of the Spirits disappeared between the trees. Caroline and Nash left, turning to watch Silas and I as they returned the way we had come. I couldn't imagine how it would feel to see a deceased loved one again, let alone your King. It must've been bittersweet.

The only ones remaining were King Iain and his deceased wife, along with the wizardly man and Silas.

"I'll leave you four alone to talk." The wizard man bowed and began walking down the path.

When the old man disappeared, my resolve gave out, and I fell to my knees. Silas scrambled to hold onto me. A ringing started in my ears, and my vision swam, growing dark around the edges.

"Eden," Silas said, voice distant and fuzzy like my ears were stuffed with cotton. He knelt beside me, arms holding me up.

Iain's form moved towards us, the same steel eyes boring into my soul.

"I don't understand." I didn't know if I had said it aloud, if my lips succeeded in forming words. My voice seemed disembodied.

When Markus had asked me if I wanted to be a part of the celebrations, I thought he meant an invitation to the party. But I had been named the new Queen of Arcadia.

Me. A *human*.

Iain sat in front of me, tilting his head to the side. *"It's not our job to understand. We trust and follow."*

The voice in my head bothered me the most. After nineteen years of only hearing my voice in my head, it terrified me to hear a man's voice instead.

"Father." Silas tensed. "This can't be right. She's—"

"As much a spirit of the trees as you, my son." Iain's voice sounded from nowhere and everywhere all at once.

"What does this mean?" I asked, eyes flicking between Silas and Iain, wondering if either of them would explain why I could hear Iain's voice in my mind. Why not before? Why now?

"We're—" Silas swallowed, eyes flicking around. "I think we're bound."

"But what does that mean?" I turned to Iain for answers.

He smiled in a wolfish way.

The female wolf spoke up, stepping forward, her voice clear like a river in my thoughts. *"You are to be the next Queen of Arcadia when winter arrives."*

My heart jumped in my chest.

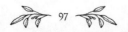

Winter.

Three months.

My chest caved in on itself, sharp pain after every inhale. My vision blurred, leaving everything a fuzzy blue.

"Father, she's human," Silas protested.

I didn't blame him. I'd been nothing but trouble for him. I was human and practically responsible for Nyx.

"*Always rescue those in need,*" Iain answered. "*Always be kind.*"

Silas groaned beside me. "But why this? Why now? You think a human can rule Arcadia despite not being raised in our culture? Or even attempt to keep up on a hunt? She's not one of *us.*"

He was right: I wasn't one of them. But those words from Silas caused the tightness in my chest to increase. It stung coming from him, even if he spoke the truth.

Iain lifted his head again. "*The winds are changing, son. She will be a valuable asset for all of Arcadia when the times shift their current like the river.*"

"Nyx has returned," Silas started. "He came for *her.*"

"*Your father is right, Si.*" His mother shifted on her feet, glowing bright. I imagined she looked a lot like Caroline when she walked with the living. Her voice, soft and feathery, lifted again in my mind. "*She will be a valuable asset to you in the coming months.*"

"Mother," Silas started. "Our enemy has targeted this *human.*"

"*Then it is your duty to protect her.*" His mother raised her eyebrows. "*I figured you of all wolves would understand that. Do you not care for her already?*"

"I do." He sounded pained. "I care for her. Of course I do."

My face flushed from his words, cheeks warm. The idea of Silas caring for me was laughable. He'd made it quite clear that he didn't appreciate humans, nor did he like me, and he'd said I didn't belong.

Tolerant? Sure. But caring? I didn't see it.

"*Son.*" Iain shifted his paws. "*Our time is short here. I will not change my decision. Eden will be the next Queen of Arcadia. She will be your life partner, and you will be hers.*"

I felt Iain's eyes on me, but I could only watch the blue beetles drifting among the sprigs of lavender. "That's it then?" I murmured.

Silas's mother tilted her head. "*You have the option to say no. As much as we hope you'll choose to stay, you are still your own.*"

"Eden," Silas whispered.

When I didn't respond, Silas wrapped an arm under each of my own, pulling me to my feet. My vision shifted back into focus. His eyes had no hint of the wild or even frustration. He stared at me like I puzzled him.

"Do you want to stay?" he muttered.

"I have cherished every moment here, even despite being a prisoner for most of it."

A smirk brightened his face. "Think about it then."

"But I'm human," I started to protest, echoing his own worries from moments ago.

"I'd be nettle-brained not to notice." He ran a hand through his hair. "But I have to trust my father and my mother."

How could I say no?

"*Think about it.*" Silas's mother moved to stand next to her husband. "*Whatever choice you make will be honored.*"

"Eden." Silas's voice sounded rougher than before. "We have to join the others. There's a feast waiting. I have responsibilities as king. And you..."

He inhaled but held onto it instead of saying anything further.

I bit the inside of my cheek, understanding despite his silence. "What do I need to do?"

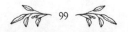

Silas turned to his mother, who bowed her head, and he cleared his throat to speak. "Well, you'll sit next to me, where the queen sits."

Nodding, I exhaled. "Lead the way."

Slipping his hand in mine, Silas led the way down the darkening path towards a huge fire in the center of the Yard. I kept my head held high despite my growing desire to disappear. Pups wrestled and people mingled in wolf and human form. Some of the Spirits sat around the fire observing their legacy while others wrestled with each other or their families still living.

Never had I been to a party like this one. Wolves chatted with the kings of the past, and food and drink were abundant. Music played somewhere in the bustling crowd over the yaps and whines from different groups.

Silas led me over to a table decorated to perfection. Great boughs of spruce had been tucked and twisted with honeysuckle vines, pinecones dotting it here and there. Lanterns had been lit, casting the table in a warm glow.

Silas guided me to a seat near the middle like I was bound to break. As soon as I sat, Nash pulled his brother to the side and Caroline followed, leaving me alone in such an unknown place.

Not that I hadn't spent time alone in Arcadia. My first two nights had felt a little strange, staring up at the tree branches covering the hedged room. But here, after being named a queen, I felt helpless. I knew nothing.

Deep breaths.

I watched the conversation between the three siblings. Nash seemed tense, Caroline even more so. Silas bristled with frustration.

I can't imagine how they feel. I've infiltrated their safe haven.

Silas motioned with his hands, quick and choppy.

Is he angry that I'd been chosen for him?

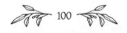

Nash nodded. Caroline turned away.

Silas stalked back over to me, dropping into his chair.

"Everything okay?" I asked, my voice a whisper.

"Fine," he grumbled.

"Because I won't blame you if you hate this. I've caused so much trouble. I understand if you're upset."

"You're right, I'm upset," he growled, not looking at me. His eyes flicked around the celebration. "I have a right to be very upset. I am a king, yet I have no control. My siblings doubt our father's judgment. I don't pretend to understand any more than they do. Yet my bound mate is unrightfully judged for being human." He shook his head, the muscles in his jaw twitching.

"*You* judged me for being human." I didn't plan to say it, but the words were out.

Silas looked like I'd elbowed him in the stomach. And I didn't want to hear his response. "I didn't ask for this, Silas."

He turned to me, something like vulnerability swirling in his eyes. "You don't want it?"

I blinked a few times, his image blurring as my brows furrowed. "Want it?"

His hand slid to his sternum. "Can you not feel it?"

"Feel what?" I moved my hand up to my own chest.

Yes, there was an ache there. Yes, the anxious thought nagged at me that I couldn't do this, that whatever *this* was it couldn't be real. Yes, a piece of me wanted to know the king, the *real* version of him.

But what *should* I have felt when I'd bound to a wolf king against my will?

Markus had asked if I wanted to be a part of the ceremony. I'd thought he meant the celebration as a whole. I hadn't thought he meant the matching ceremony. I'd never even considered it.

Silas held my hand now and moved it to his chest. His heart thrummed beneath my fingertips, the heat from his body burning my skin. He gazed at me with such intensity that I had to turn away. I didn't need tension to make my cheeks red. My face had grown hot enough from the bonfire.

"Can you feel it?" Silas breathed.

Emotion overcame him, rippling through his body. It pulled my eyes back to his, but he wasn't watching me. I followed his gaze to his father, who sat by the fireside watching.

"Would you join me for a dance?" Silas muttered.

I thought I had misheard when he pulled me to my feet. No sooner had we stepped down by the fire when a low howl crooned from Iain. The crowds shifted and moved to the outside of the clearing away from the fire. Flutes were brought to a few Seers, who began to play and sing a haunting melody.

Following his lead as best as I could, Silas spun us around the fire and between other dancing couples. His eyes were always on mine, mine on my feet. I was never a very good dancer, not when dozens of eyes were watching me.

"Silas?" I asked, glancing up at him.

"Yes?"

"We're bound. But what does that call for in the meantime? Am I to stay with you or..." I swallowed, glanced away, and tried to push the embarrassment aside. "What happens if we find that I'm wretched at this, being queen?"

"Eden, it's not a simple thing. Our problems are not solved in a single dance. But we still take them a single step at a time."

"And what if I can't dance? What if I stumble?"

Passion swirled in his eyes. "I'll be right here with you. I promise to catch you when you stumble and guide you when you lose your way."

I paused, mouth open. "Silas, I–"

"My King." The old man from before laid a hand on Silas's shoulder, stopping our dance. Silas stepped back, giving my hand a light kiss, and followed the man to the side where Nash stood waiting.

The fires were lower now. *How long had we been dancing?*

Iain and his wife approached me as regal as ever.

"*Daughter*," Iain's voice rumbled in my head.

I didn't know how much one word could affect me. Tears welled in my eyes, and I blinked them away.

"*You will be a great queen.*" He smiled with pride. "*Do not let them look down on you for who you are. You are destined to do much, things you don't even realize.*"

I nodded, not knowing if I could squeak out any words. Not knowing if I had any words to say after fifteen years of trying to find him again.

"*Every Queen of Arcadia from the past is behind you,*" Silas's mother spoke with tenderness. "*You have the Spirits of hundreds of generations supporting you. I believe you're going to do great things, daughter. Take care of our son.*"

With short bows of their heads, the former King and Queen of Arcadia joined their sons and the Elder. Together, the brothers ducked into the dark, with Iain and their mother trailing behind.

I turned in a circle searching for anything familiar.

My eyes found the safety of the table where Caroline sat picking at a piece of deer meat. I held up the bottom of my robe like a grand duchess in some old animated film and made my way over to my seat.

Caroline glanced my way and wiped her hands. "I need to apologize for my behavior earlier," she swallowed. "It was unjust of me. It's only that..."

While she searched for words, I sat beside her.

"Nothing like this has ever happened. Ever. In all of our history.

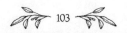

And I know our history like it happened yesterday. It's just—"

"Frustrating?" I offered.

"Infuriating!" Caroline sighed. "Not you of course, but the deviation from tradition. I don't understand it. I asked Silas for an explanation, but he couldn't offer one. Even our own father could only tell us that you would be a valuable asset as the seasons change, whatever that means." She huffed and laid her head in her hands. Her voice was muffled when she continued. "It's not like we haven't existed fine with the past three season changes without him."

"I understand, Caroline." I laid a hand on her shoulder. "I didn't expect this. A week ago, I wasn't sure you all existed. And now I'm supposed to be your queen with no experience and vastly underprepared for the position."

She laughed and met my eyes. "Does that mean you'll forgive me then?"

"There's nothing to forgive. But if it makes you feel better, then yes. I forgive you."

Caroline placed a hand on my own and offered a smile. "Then officially, welcome to the pack."

The welcome that she meant as kindness daunted me. I now lived with an ancient wolf pack.

I am running with the wolves.

It did beg the question...

Will I choose to stay?

13

SILAS

I FOLLOWED ELDER MACON down the path to the Aisle of Kings. Nash and our parents trailed behind me, speaking in hurried, hushed tones. I wanted to know what they discussed, but I kept my head held forward.

I had the chance to say goodbye to our father. Nash never had that chance.

"Elder," I muttered.

He turned his head back to glance at me, stepping forward with his staff in hand.

"If I am to be bound to Eden... If we are to have–"

I stopped myself. It felt strange to talk about Eden like this, like she and I had known each other before this week. But I had to know. What did this union mean for the future of Arcadia?

"Yes." Elder Macon started. "I understand your concern. However, the law is law. Your father has a reason, whatever it might be. He is a part of the roots of Arcadia now. You, as the trunk of Arcadia, have to trust that. We, as the branches of Arcadia, have to trust that."

He stopped and placed a hand on my shoulder when we passed the archway that marked the entrance. "Trust your father, your *king*."

I nodded, then turned back to my family. Nash's skin was tinted by the blue light from our parents' Spirits. Tears reflected on his cheeks, but he didn't move to wipe them away.

I pulled off my robe, passing it to the Elder. Nash did the same. As I knelt before my father, I phased, coming to rest at eye level with his Spirit.

"*Father.*" I trembled, this moment weighing on me. Time rushed by, and I couldn't stop it or slow it down.

"*Son.*" He smiled with such affection that I had to turn my face away.

"*You thought I was ready. I'm not ready for this.*"

He nuzzled my neck. "*You welcomed your brother back home. You've kept our people safe these past months. You found Eden.*"

"*I don't understand. Are we to have no heirs? Is this the end of Arcadia?*"

"*Trust me, Silas.*"

I met his eyes, hoping he couldn't tell how *little* I trusted the wisdom of this union. I wanted to be brave, to be bold. I wanted to make him proud.

Nash moved, rubbing his head against my shoulder.

"*Your path lies straight in front of you, son.*" My mother lowered her head.

"*And if I fail?*"

Nash straightened. "*I'll be right next to you this time.*"

"*The time is coming when you will need to depend on each other.*" My father's eyes shimmered. "*You have to trust each other with your lives. Arcadia depends on you two and Caroline and Eden.*"

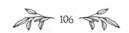

"It's time," Elder Macon spoke up. He motioned us onward into the eerie quiet of the Aisle of Kings.

Not yet. Please, five more minutes.

I needed them here.

Reluctantly, I took the lead, with my parents behind me and Nash taking the rear, leaving Elder Macon behind to wait at the entrance.

Sucking in a breath, I stopped to the right of my parents' graves, leaving space for Nash to stand to the left of the stones like we practiced.

Guardians of their graves.

"*Sons.*" My father watched us. "*I am so proud of you both. I expect great things when I visit next autumn. And I want all the details about the binding celebration for the King.*"

I turned my eyes down.

"*Silas.*" My father shifted his paws in the dirt, his blue glow casting strange shadows through the standing stones. "*Make room. Your future is bright.*"

He howled, echoing lonesome amongst the trees. For a moment, nothing happened. Then, all at once, the forest burst to life again, azure Spirits running through the trees, a chorus of yaps and barks joining them. The ghost beetles drifted nearer, swirling around myself, Nash, our mother, and our father like a windstorm.

The Spirits each began diving back into their individual resting places like lanterns going out, the forest growing darker by the second.

"*Please don't leave.*" I met my father's steel eyes.

My mother's Spirit ran through her stones and disappeared.

"*It's never goodbye, son.*" My father stepped backward. "*You'll feel me in the autumn breeze.*"

Another wolf Spirit disappeared.

"*You'll hear me in the rumbling of the Great River after the melting of the winter snow.*"

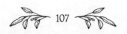

And another.

"You'll smell me after the spring rain. You'll see me in the setting of the summer sun."

"Please don't leave me again." A familiar ache settled in my chest. His Spirit remained, a solitary light in the darkness.

"I'll be back before you know it."

And with one last step, he launched himself towards the stones I'd balanced last winter, disappearing in a rush of blue and the buzzing of wings.

The night met me with deafening silence. *"Don't leave."*

The dark swallowed my heart, leaving me cold and empty. I phased, pulling at the soil of their grave. My tears hit the dirt one after the other, and I wondered what my father had done after his king, his *father,* had passed.

I had so many questions for him, questions he should have answered during my training that had never come.

Loneliness encompassed me, swallowing me whole.

"Si?"

I looked up as Nash stood on bare feet. He tucked the loose strands of his hair behind his ear, taking deep breaths.

"Come on," he said, jerking his head back towards the archway where the Elder waited for us. His splotchy face revealed none of the emotions he'd hidden inside. "You need to get back to the feast. They'll be missing you."

I pushed myself to my feet, head still hanging low. I rubbed the tears away with the backs of my thumbs.

With one hand on my shoulder, he pulled me into a hug, short but tight like he was afraid to lose me.

"We'll get through this," he mumbled.

"But Nyx–"

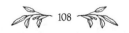

"Will come whenever he comes." Nash held both of my shoulders at arm's length now. "And we'll be ready for him."

I nodded. "And Eden?"

Nash's lips quirked into a grin. "She'll learn to hold her own. We can train her."

Nyx was one of the legends of Arcadia, this dark force that swore to bring the kingdom to ruins. He had been a Seer once, and a good one at that. But the story said that they banished him for treason, the details lost to history.

Whispers of his return swirled around every few decades, some sort of dark magic that could hide him in the rivers, his essence seeping deep into the foundations of *Shaconage*. The Great Mountain sheltered us all, good and evil and everything in between.

My jaw tightened as I thought of Eden fighting against the massive dark wolf. If she happened to wander outside of Arcadia's protected borders, he could reach her. And she stood no chance against him. Lycaon forbid it ever reached that point.

No matter what it costs, I will keep her safe.

My thoughts surprised me, something about the inevitability of it all. If I had no say in the matter, if it was chosen for me, it would only hurt if I fought it harder. Yet, in only a few hours, I'd grown so protective of a mere human.

What emotions will grow in the coming months?

Attempting to swallow my mixed emotions, I patted my brother's arm and headed towards the Elder.

Elder Macon passed us our robes and we returned to the celebration. The fire still burned, though smaller than before, surrounded by wolves and robed figures, the Spirits long since gone. The rest of the group danced like branches in the wind, flutes punctuating the crackle of the fire and drifting along the breeze that brought me to the table.

Some people sat in small groups discussing our visit with the Spirits. Some of them seemed grieved. Others looked joyful. Everyone had mixed emotions.

My eyes found Eden, now wearing a single bloom of lavender tucked into her braided crown behind her ear. Eden spoke with two of the Seers, a woman with long dark hair named Aubrey and her husband, tall and blond-headed with spooky gray eyes. The skin on my neck chilled.

One of my least favorite people has cornered my mate.

Unacceptable.

I excused myself from Nash and walked up behind Eden, sliding my hand to the small of her back, a movement so foreign yet so familiar. She turned her face up, surprised.

"Silas." She smiled. "I wondered how long you'd be. Aubrey and Ransom were explaining the um..." She turned to the Seers in front of us.

Ransom flashed an arrogant smile.

Silva, I did not like him.

"The ceremonial runes," Aubrey supplied.

"Yes!" Eden said. "It's beautiful, the way that everything here has meaning. Even the flowers." She ran her fingers along the lavender.

Lavender.

Devotion.

Purity.

Calm.

This is what the Seers foresaw in our future, or at least Eden's.

Will she be devoted to me as a wolf or as a human? How loyal can humans be?

Ransom caught my eye. Speaking to him always felt like he read my soul, the way it shifted and bent away from the life I chose to live. He could see my doubts, my shortcomings. Perhaps that's what irritated me about him.

Or maybe his face bothered me. And how many times he had bet on Nash instead of me over the years.

"Cedar." He handed me a sprig with three tiny cones attached. "When burned, it purifies, leaving protection and positivity in its wake. A worthy sacrifice, don't you think?"

"Immortality," I whispered, running my thumb along the green sprig.

I met Ransom's eyes. My brow furrowed as something shifted in his face. I didn't trust him. Aubrey, maybe. But something about Ransom bothered me. Like he knew everything, which of course, he did.

But why cedar?

"My love, we must be going." He turned his head towards Aubrey, but his gaze remained fixed on my face. "We don't want to overstay our welcome. We should leave these two alone to celebrate this night while they can."

A sense of doom settled in my spirit as they glided away.

Cursed seers. Spouting flowery fox spit while the rest of us deal with the real world.

Clearing my throat, I turned to Eden, offering her a smile. "Will you take a walk with me?"

I tucked the sprig of cedar into a pocket of my robe, holding my other arm out for her. She took it, sliding her arm around mine.

Leading us past the fire, I brought her through the residential loop, passing the empty rooms and dens. Most of my pack still celebrated out in the Yard.

It's our pack now.

"Eden," I started before I could grasp my thoughts. "I know this has been a bit fast for you."

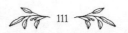

She turned her face away, watching the beetles light up the forest around us, away from the orange glow of the fire.

"While I can't allow you to venture out of our borders alone, maybe I can work out a way for us to leave together with a few Guardians so you don't feel so trapped. That way I can protect you if..." I held both of her hands into my own. I inhaled before speaking again, knowing I would need to say it well. "The thing is, Eden, I want this to work out. Against all possibility, I trust my father."

Dropping one of her hands, I brushed her cheek, cupping her face. The motion felt strange, like my fingers had wanted to touch her skin since they'd first met this beautiful human.

And since when did I think she was beautiful?

Or have I always?

The emotions that bubbled inside of my stomach were unusual and strong. She opened her mouth but hesitated. I could hear the war in her heart. I felt it raging within myself.

Words slipped out of my mouth despite my better judgment. "It's okay. I want you to choose this. You don't have to decide now."

The relief that flooded her face cinched my chest.

Lycaon, I want her to stay.

She slipped her hands around my torso and tucked her head under my chin. The motion brought a strange flutter to my chest. I held her tight.

"Thank you," she whispered.

Nodding, I glanced up, her room two doors down. I walked her to her door, swallowing any pessimistic or doubting thoughts.

She could say no. But she could say yes.

She will decide later.

"Thank you again for..." she said, voice trailing off when she met my eyes.

"Of course," I mumbled, caught up in the softness of her bear cub eyes.

"Goodnight, Si," she whispered, using my family nickname.

"Goodnight, Eden."

Her hand slipped from mine when she ducked into her room, the door shutting with a soft click. The sound of finality.

I fell hard and fast.

Lycaon, help me if she decides to leave.

If Eden left... The thought alone broke me.

14

EDEN

I LEANED BACK AGAINST the doorframe, breathing deep.

Breathe. Don't panic.

I slid to the ground, holding my legs to my chest like they could protect me from the chaos of my life.

"This is what you get, searching for trouble," I mumbled to myself, leaning my forehead against my knees. "This is what you get for being curious."

If only I hadn't met Iain and Silas on the bank of the Little River.

If only I hadn't accepted the wildlife job.

If only I hadn't been out researching ferns on that trail.

If only, if only, if only...

I crawled to my bed and under the blankets, taking the lavender and spruce sprigs out of my braided hair. I thought a lot about this little world hidden from humans. I thought about their kitchenware, their robes, their bedding... all of it strange and beautiful.

Human, yet not.

I wouldn't take any of it back.

The thought surprised me. If given the chance, I would live all of this again and again and again despite the weight of responsibility.

Silas's face kept interrupting my thoughts.

Silas, Silas, Silas.

My future husband.

A groan escaped my lips as I flipped over, face in the feather pillow. This couldn't be real. Even if I didn't regret what had happened to bring me here, the whole thing was absurd.

Two and a half days ago, I was a girl—a college student—who liked wildlife. Tonight, I was a researcher in a magical, ancient wolf pack in the forest who had gotten herself engaged to a King.

A wild fairytale.

But that's what I wanted, right? To live among wolves?

My heart fluttered in my chest as I allowed myself to dream for a moment.

Me, being a queen.

Me, having a tight-knit family.

Me, discovering the magic of Arcadia.

But Silas had offered me a way out, an option where I could choose to leave it behind and go back to live a normal human life. All the books I had read of children finding themselves in extraordinary situations, they always went back to the human world. Not once did one choose to stay.

Will I choose to stay now?

Now that I have responsibilities?

A yawn forced its way out when I flipped over again, curling my body into a tight ball.

Hadn't I always dreamt of being here in this place? I'd dreamt of this since I'd been dragged out of that cold mountain water. I had imagined a future where wolves were my playmates, my friends, my family. And before tonight, I'd even considered asking to stay. Now, I'd been *chosen*.

I wondered what good I could do for Arcadia, or even Silas. How might I aid them when I was merely a human? And how could I possibly live up to the legacy that preceded me?

I walked familiar paths. The light filtered through the green leaves, unusual for autumn. The packed dirt thudded under my boots while I made my way up the winding trail.

Hiking was exhilarating. My leg muscles ached, but the journey and the view were worth it.

A raven swooped into my path, watching from its perch in a dead tree. Odd, seeing a raven here when crows were more common.

Coming around the bend, a rustling noise caught my attention. I scanned the forest around me. Trees and bushes, logs and stumps that tricked my brain into thinking an animal watched me.

Another rustle from behind.

I whipped around only to find the raven, fluttering its wings, now standing in the dirt.

Laughing nervously to myself, thinking I'd gone paranoid, I turned back to the path only to be met with a wall of fur.

"Glad you could make it back, daughter of Arcadia," Nyx growled, almost smirking at me.

"What do you want?" I stepped back, creating space between us.

"So brave in her dreams." He tilted his head to the side. "I wonder what it'll be like to smell you in person."

The dark wolf began to circle me, but I turned to face him.

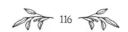

"You didn't answer my question." I tried to sound confident, but my voice wavered.

Nyx stopped in the trail, stretching his body. *"Only what I've wanted for centuries: the downfall of Arcadia. Surely you, a human, would help me with my life's quest to end their tyranny?"* *Tilting his head, he paused only for a moment.* *"No? Well, that's a shame. Maybe Silas or Caroline would stand up for you, spurred by revenge for their father's death."*

"Don't go near them," I hissed.

Nyx laughed, the rumble resounding in my ribcage. *"You don't have much to bargain with, dearest. Maybe if you met me in your woods. You know the place. Where your story began."*

"I–" *My voice cut out. I wanted to move my feet, but my legs wouldn't obey.*

"You could bring Nash. It'd be nice to have a reunion." *He grinned, incisor and canine teeth a bright white against his dark fur. His amber eyes flashed at me.*

Nyx crouched, lips curling to reveal even more teeth ready to tear me apart. I could only watch as he pounced, knocking me to the ground, breath escaping my lungs.

"Big, bad wolf!" I opened my eyes to see the trees hanging above my head, dark in the deep of the night.

A dream.

A nightmare.

I struggled to pull air into my lungs as I pushed myself off the ground. The blankets were in disarray, and I gathered that I must've thrown myself off of my bed.

Thank God for that, I thought. I could only imagine how long the nightmare would have held me in its clutches otherwise.

But what in the world had the dream meant? There had been the

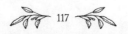

raven and Nyx, and he'd mentioned a reunion with Nash.

What happens when I fall back asleep again? Another meeting? Another attack?

I shook my head and adjusted my robe. I needed to move. The door was unlocked, so I slipped through it, bare feet silent on the pine straw. Making my way through the residential court, I noticed a lot of the doors were open and the rooms empty.

I knew wolves were nocturnal, but I wondered how human they were with their life patterns. So far, they had fed me like humans. And they operated during the day as far as I could tell.

I caught a flash of tails as two wolves trotted down a winding path to my right. They barely looked up when I passed behind them.

At night, the Yard seemed ominous without the light from the bonfire, ancestral ghosts, or blue beetles. Instead, a quiet hush had fallen over the once bustling pathways of Arcadia.

Distant bird calls and the hissing sound of my robe running over ground were all I could hear. Somewhere, a Great Horned Owl hooted.

Iain's words from my previous dream resurfaced: *You are safe here, safe in Arcadia.*

I took the pathway to Guardian's Glade as I now knew it. They had names for everything here—the Boneyard, where they trained and discarded bones; Mender's Heath, where Asa healed any injuries or illnesses; the Yard, where most people congregated. And then there were the kitchens, the Tailor's quarters where they handled any fabric, the Hunter's Run where they store caches of previous hunts, and other places I hadn't heard of or visited.

The throne room felt soulless without people, without Silas. And I almost felt like I was trespassing.

You sort of are trespassing, I reminded myself.

Taking in a breath, I paused at Silas's bedroom door.

Would his people die for intruding like this? Am I allowed to do this?

Another image of Nyx flitting across my memory chilled my senses, making up my mind for me. As quiet as possible, I cracked open the door, peeking my head in.

It was bigger than my own, set up the same, only adding a few things. In the corner sat a desk with a massive, old book resting open. On both sides of the desk, shelves stretched tall holding books, trinkets, and scrolls as well as a large feather collection dangling from thread that decorated the branches near the edge of Silas's room. Across the space, a wardrobe stood with a mirror next to it. Beside the mirror was something like a makeshift coat hanger. Instead of coats, it held various woven crowns of branches and flowers.

And at the back of the room, Silas sprawled out on his bed, asleep. The sight of him shirtless and vulnerable made my heart flutter with anxiety.

This is a bad idea.

But I was already there. I stepped a pace away from the bed.

Do I sit down? Do I whisper his name?

I opened my mouth, but before I could speak, he interrupted. "Are you going to stand there or are you going to come over here?" Silas barely lifted his head from his pillow.

"You're awake."

What a stupid thing to say.

"Come here." There was a gentleness in his voice that beckoned me.

I sat on the edge of the bed facing him, the bed shifting beneath my weight. His eyes weren't even open.

Is he dreaming?

"Did you think I wouldn't hear you sneaking in?" he asked, voice

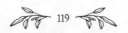

thick with sleep. His tone wasn't angry or upset but amused. "I'm a wolf, Eden. I can hear and smell you from farther than you know."

"Right." I refused to look at him, too conscious of how heavy my steps must be and how much I reeked of sweat and the woods.

Stupid. You're so stupid.

"What's troubling you?" He rolled himself over, head propped by an arm. His eyes opened, their shades of green black in the dark.

"I... I had a nightmare again."

I watched the muscles in his jaw tense. With a sharp inhale, he ran his hand through his tousled hair. "But you're all right?"

Nodding, I twisted my hands in my lap. "I think so. A little spooked."

A few moments passed in silence, the tension palpable. Silas moved forward and wrapped his arms around my torso, trapping my arms in my lap. He rested his chin on my shoulder, leaning his head against mine.

"I'll keep you safe. I promise." He grew quiet for a moment, and I relished the feeling of his body rising and falling with his breath. There was something calming about being held after having a nightmare, something protective about it.

And sleepy, protective Silas was intoxicating. Kingly duties didn't burden him. Grief didn't quite weigh him down.

This Silas was alluring.

He moved back. "We can talk more about it in the morning when I'm awake and clear-minded."

"I thought wolves were nocturnal." I turned my head towards him, heart lurching with how close his lips were to my own.

I wondered how it would feel to kiss his sun-tanned skin. Eventually, I assumed I'd *have* to kiss him—not that I would mind it—but it seemed strange to move from being hated to being cared for so fast.

"Oh, we are nocturnal. Generally. We also sleep a lot." He chuckled,

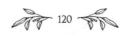

the sound reverberating in my ears. "And I have to be awake whenever I am needed, precisely why I sleep when I can, day or night."

I nodded, not knowing what to say or how to talk to him. There was so much I didn't know, so much I wanted to learn. I had always wanted to know more about the *virlukos*, ever since Iain pulled me from the river.

But now I *needed* to know.

So much had changed since that day. And if I accepted this crazy idea of being Silas's wife, their *queen*, I needed to know everything.

Absolutely everything.

I'd have to convince Caroline to teach me. Or I could borrow Silas's books and scrolls.

"Come here," Silas whispered, pulling me further onto the bed. He scooted to the side, making room for me.

Alarm bells rang in my brain, screaming in protest. What would his family say if they found me asleep in his bed? Did they have a protocol for Arcadian courtship?

He pulled me closer to him, laying a hand on my arm and tucking the other under his feather pillow. The blanket smelled like him, like the earth after it rains.

"Silas?"

"Mmm?" he mumbled.

"What happens if he–" I swallowed. A thought had occurred to me as the prospect of sleep grew closer and with it, the threat of another nightmare. "If he gets me?"

His hand cupped my cheek, his forefinger tightening under my jaw. "I'm not going to allow that to happen, Eden. I promise, I *will* keep you safe."

I nodded, afraid if I spoke that my words would turn into tears. I didn't want to worry Silas more than I had about such a strange connection to his enemy—*my* enemy.

My heart split into so many different directions while my brain followed countless thoughts. Thoughts of this wolf pack, how my research would help them, and learning to be a queen rolled around before being replaced by darker ones of the forest, the Spirits from the Festival of Kings, and Nyx.

What would happen if he reached me?

My only consolation was the warmth and presence of Silas next to me. It was comforting and in a way, natural. Like I'd been there before in his arms, like he'd known I'd fill this role when he'd brought me to Arcadia. Why did it feel so normal, so *right*?

Partners protected their own. So it only made sense that Silas would be bent on keeping me safe. Making me *feel* safe.

I closed my eyes.

That's what I am now, his partner. And he had promised me.

He promised.

It was a promise I would hold him to.

15

SILAS

MORNINGS WERE MY FAVORITE.

The precious moments before I had to act like an Alpha. Where I could be Silas. And I'd become addicted to the simplicity of the stillness. If I had the luxury of sleeping in, I often chose to lay silent and listen to the birds.

Mourning doves sang as the light filtered through the trees. The smell of moss drifted on the wind, the gray clouds causing everything to rest in a calming, peaceful quiet. In the distance, raindrops drummed on leaves.

I shifted towards Eden. She looked so beautiful at rest with her heartbeat slow and regular.

Our conversation from the night before drifted to my mind. She'd had another nightmare and sought me out.

At least she's not scared to talk to me.

So much had changed. I fought the urge to scoff. The past few days... All of it was inconvenient for the both of us.

I had been on routine scouting duty. She'd been studying plants on a hike.

I was struggling my way through my first year as king. She was being a human, doing her job.

I had been prepared for a match with a wolf. She hadn't planned on staying.

And now—now, I truly *saw* her for the first time. A mess of curls had sprung out of her braid and framed her face. Her eyes were closed, but the thought of her dreaming made me wonder about who she was under her skin.

I wanted to pick her brain and piece by piece pull out whatever it was that made her tick. I needed to know *everything* about her. The desire to know her darkest secrets and deepest fears overwhelmed me.

She had clung to that one encounter, meeting my family, for fifteen years. What resilience she must have to hold onto that, and the courage to go searching. Though she seemed timid, it seemed more like a timid curiosity.

I loved her occasional confidence the most, the logic she held behind it. When it decided to come out of her, it showed bravery, that she could stand up for herself if needed.

A wolf spirit.

I wondered if she would stay in Arcadia, if she would choose to stay with me. In all of our years in that forest, I couldn't remember a single instance of a wolf refusing a pairing. Not that they couldn't refuse, but why would they?

But what of a human?

She stirred beside me.

I brushed my hand over her bare arm where the sleeve of her robe had bunched at her shoulder, her skin soft and warm. She blinked a few times before opening her eyes. I watched as they fluttered around the room, like she'd forgotten where she'd been. She turned her head to me.

"Good morning." I smiled. "How did you sleep?"

She pushed her escaped strands of hair back away from her face. "I slept much better. I don't think I dreamed of anything."

"Good." I drew my hand across her cheek, tucking her hair behind her ear. She stilled under my touch.

I could still sense a tension between us, like she hadn't started falling as fast as I had.

But there was something there.

Something.

"So," I said, resting my hand on her shoulder. "You had another nightmare. Tell me about it."

Eden's face flashed with fear. I held her hand in mine, giving it a squeeze.

"He threatened me. He wants to take down Arcadia. He mentioned you and Caroline, and that it would be nice to have a reunion with Nash."

I stiffened. "Nash?"

"I don't know. It was just a dream."

Nyx probably knew that Nash wasn't the most reliable, flighty at the best of times. Would Nyx mention Nash to stir up discord?

Or was there something Nash hadn't told me about his time away?

"Pretty convenient that Nyx starts problems right when Nash comes home."

Eden shrugged. "I don't know. I was so scared. Nyx didn't explain, and none of it made sense. And he wants me to–"

She stopped short. Her hand gripped mine.

"You're safe here, Eden. Nothing," I whispered. "*Nothing* can hurt you here."

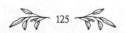

She nodded. "He wanted me to meet him."

"Meet him? Where?"

"My woods. My river. The Little River, where you and I first met."

"No way. Not happening."

"Silas." She sat up, shoulders slouching. "I don't want to be responsible for Arcadia's downfall. I don't want to sit by and let Nyx come and take whatever he wants."

I sat up, laying my hand gently on her knee. "I know. But there's no reason to rush into things without a plan."

"How could we plan for this?"

I shrugged. "It's simple. We plan an ambush. You'd be the bait, and we'd have Guardians waiting to attack."

"Won't he hear us coming? He'd know."

"Maybe. But maybe he's so confident that he won't care. You are human after all."

"Right." She picked at her nails. "Why would anyone want a human?"

"Eden, it's not like that. It's... complicated."

She shifted her weight. "Then explain it to me. What changed with you? Or is it some wolf thing I wouldn't understand?"

"No." My brow furrowed. "Well, maybe."

When she sighed, I took her hand in mine again.

"That's not what I meant. You just remind me of my father."

Her brow shot up in surprise. "I remind you of an old wolf man."

I squeezed my eyes shut. "No. Eden, I found something different in you. That day in the forest, you were curious and careful about nature rather than taking advantage of it. Even as a child, something about you was wild. I noticed it while watching you from the opposite bank before you fell into the river."

She sat up. Our knees brushed. "You saw me before I fell?"

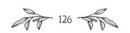

The memory pulled a smile to my lips. "I watched you standing stones in a circle. So odd. As a child, I figured it was your humanness, that *thing* that felt strange and alluring to me. But I think..." I shook my head and struggled for words to describe her.

"A wolf spirit," she muttered.

"Right. But when I brought you to Arcadia, I was conflicted. You knew so much about us, information that could put my people in danger. I worried about protecting my family. But I'm bound to take care of you, to rescue you, to rescue humans."

Her body flinched at the word *humans*.

"And you remind me of my father because of that day on the banks of the Little River. You remind me of lessons with my father, quality time with my family. It's bittersweet. And I had this—this complex that maybe keeping you close keeps the memories of my parents close. So I had a decision to make between my people, my duty, and my emotions." I ran a hand over my face. "I received no training for being a King. It happened so fast. I'm still trying to figure all this out."

The silence following my confession weighed on my skin like the words themselves buried me alive.

Eden squeezed my hand and laid her head on my shoulder. The movement eased the tension I'd brought on myself, the fear that I wouldn't be a good enough Alpha.

A fear that Nash had pointed out the night he'd come home, that maybe I wasn't making our father proud.

"From what little I've seen, you're a fantastic king, Silas. Those crowns look good on you."

I smirked, her words dispelling the negative thoughts I'd had. "So you think I look good?"

She lifted her head to face me. "I didn't say–"

"I think you did."

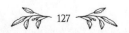

Her face flushed pink when she turned away, trying to hide a smile.

My heart lurched and my thoughts slipped back into darkness, thoughts of her leaving me behind. I'd sit alone with my grief having to explain to my kingdom that I wouldn't have a mate for another year.

I needed peace.

I swallowed my fear, offering her a soft smile. "Hey, I want to show you something."

I stood, pulling her up with me. Straightening the blankets and closing the Compendium that lay open from my studies the night before, I opened the door for Eden. Guardian's Glade was still in the early blue of the morning.

I closed the door behind us and slipped my hand into hers, searching her eyes for any sign of doubt or fear. Only curiosity lived in her gaze.

I led her South, through our forest where we were protected. I knew these trees. These trees knew me. Better than most of my people.

Somewhere, a murder of crows called into the early morning. Eden's gaze pulled towards them. The wind rustled around us. The call of the crows blended with the wind, a sound that brought a sense of comfort.

"When we were children," I glanced at Eden. "Nash and I used to race Caroline to our secret spot. A place where we were just a couple of wolf pups and not royalty. Siblings instead of heirs."

"It must've been difficult for you. Being royalty and not getting to be a kid."

I shrugged. "Some days, it could be frustrating. But it wasn't all bad. We got first pick for dinner, after our parents, of course. Then we were trained by our father, unusual for Kings. They typically leave it to the Betas of the group. But our father..." I smiled at the memory of him. "Our father wanted to be there for all of it."

TO LIVE AMONG WOLVES

"You must miss him."

"Every day."

"I wish I knew him more."

I met her eyes. So soft. So kind. I placed a kiss on her forehead. My heart fractured and healed all at once, my soul pulled in two separate directions. This was *right*.

How can I rule and raise heirs with a human? one half of me reasoned.

How can I imagine a life without her now? the other questioned.

My chest ached and I wished I could've talked longer with my father, asking him what I should do. He would've given me sound advice. No doubt he would've told me to follow my gut, to trust my intuition.

But what if my intuition was wrong?

16

EDEN

S ILAS LED ME THROUGH the woods on a small boarded pathway through the forest. I was getting used to the absence of shoes after leaving them in my room that first day. I could feel everything: the wet boards and the grass tickling my toes.

"Where are we going?" I whispered, something stirring inside of me—excitement and nervousness.

"Patience, young human." Silas chuckled. "We're almost there."

I flinched. I never dreamed that the word *human* would be an insult. But I found myself bristling every time Silas said it. It wasn't his fault. It wasn't even my fault. But to be human meant I'd always be less than the wolves of Arcadia.

The trees began thinning out, and gray light filtered around us. Craning my neck, I caught a glimpse of open sky past the trees, the sound of rain pattering on each individual leaf of each of the countless trees. My jaw slid open and my eyes wandered over the dancing branches.

Silas's deep laugh startled me.

"What?" I raised an eyebrow.

He laughed again, shaking his head. "You're so... human."

"Isn't that a bad thing?" I hated that I heard the doubt and fear of disapproval in my voice.

"I forget, sometimes, to appreciate the small things. But you remind me to pay attention a little more. That life itself is magical even in the small moments."

Silas pulled me forward down the boarded path, and soon the whole sky emerged like the mountains and trees had hidden it from view. A great big expanse fell open before me, light fracturing in so many shades, faded by the clouds. Mist blanketed the folds of the Great Mountains, trees punctuating where they met the horizon.

"What is this place?" I breathed, eyes taking in as much as they would allow.

"Welcome to *Rauha*, my secret place. *Rauha* means peace. *This* is my place of peace."

A light mist brushed past, sending a shiver down my spine. But the rush pulled a laugh out of my innermost being.

"Since we were interrupted before," Silas bowed his head, extending his hand to me, "may I have another dance with you, most esteemed guest of Arcadia?"

"A *human* dancing with the wolf king?" I mocked, sliding my hand into his. "How scandalous."

Silas grinned. "You forget he intends to marry her."

My stomach lurched at the words. It wasn't like marriage hadn't been part of the bound mates thing. It wasn't like I didn't realize the weight of what had happened in the previous twenty four hours. But something about Silas speaking the words aloud... It brought heat to my cheeks.

Marriage.

I would be his *wife* in three months' time.

He pulled me close, swaying in the drizzle. His eyes held secrets that I wished to unfold.

"Too bad we didn't know," he mumbled.

"What do you mean?" I gazed up at him, watching his eyes and lips.

"Back when we first met." Silas's voice reverberated in my chest. "We could've stopped ourselves from wasting so much time."

"We're here now," I whispered. "This must've been part of the plan. All of our history has led to this moment."

Silas grew quiet as something passed over his eyes like a cloud over the sun. "I wish my father could have known you better. He would've loved you."

As if dammed up by the sheer strangeness of the past few days, tears spilled down my cheeks like the waterfalls hidden in these mountains. I turned my face down, avoiding his gaze. We stopped dancing, and I tried to shake away the growing ache of profound loss. Silas bent his head down and met my eyes, a shadow of emotion casting over his features.

"Hey, it's okay." He said it in such a sweet whisper that a sob escaped my lips.

"I don't know why I'm so emotional over this." I sniffled. "I only met him that one time, but the knowledge that you all existed somewhere in the world confirmed that magic waited to be discovered. And knowing that he's gone is painful." I shook my head. "I'm sorry. It's unfair of me to be like this when he's your father. You must miss him so much."

"Eden." Silas hummed my name. "It's all right to cry. And I do miss him. And my mother. I miss having a complete family, and they were so in love."

I brushed away the tears with my thumbs. "What was she like?"

Silas held my hands in his, gazing out over the expansive view of rolling blue mountains. "Regal. Being a queen was in her bones."

I sniffed again, blinking to slow my tears. "I wish I could say the same about myself."

He grinned, rolling his eyes. "You're wild at heart. That counts for a lot." He sighed, dropping his head back so his eyes faced the foliage above us. "I thought losing my mother would be the hardest thing. I thought it would break me. I was fifteen."

"Silas, I'm so sorry."

He shook his head, pursing his lips. "My father turned into a shell for a while. The kingdom grieved for such a long time. And then, the sun peeked out again. Theirs was a passionate love, something that burned, a beacon for all of Arcadia. And when her light went out, we all lost our way for a bit.

"And I clung to my duties as an heir. They kept me afloat. Duty and discipline. I ate well, I hunted well, I patrolled and mingled and performed so well. But duty became my identity, and I lost myself in what I wanted to be instead. And then, after losing my father, I only had Caroline."

I held Silas's face in one hand, running my thumb against his light stubble. "A child should never bury their parents so young."

"But now I have you." He pulled me closer, arms wrapped over my shoulders as I buried my face into his shoulder.

I couldn't help but take deep breaths, like the smell of him brought me some sort of peace that I hadn't had since that day I slipped into the river. Or maybe it was this place—*Rauha*—that brought me to rest again.

"We should be heading back," he whispered into my hair. "They'll be needing me."

"Of course." I pulled back. "I'm sorry."

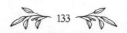

"Hey," he whispered, caressing my cheek like he'd done it a thousand times, like he didn't light my skin on fire with his touch. "You don't need to apologize to me. You come before duty, before ritual, before everything. You're going to be my wife. You're going to be my queen."

His words sent my thoughts in a spiral. The reality settled in again that I would have to lead a kingdom.

"Silas," I breathed. "I—"

"I can't wait until you see the ceremony things." He gushed as he brought me back down the path. "It'll all be perfect. The Tailors will make the most elegant dress for you to wear. And Caroline will help you with all the details."

The blood rushing through my ears drowned out his words.

Thump, thump.

Thump, thump.

Thump, thump.

Queen.

How will I ever be enough for this?

17

SILAS

I HADN'T TALKED TO Eden after our trip to Rauha. I'd gotten myself tangled in cleaning up after the Festival of Kings, preparing for the waterfall freezing over, protection plans with the Guardians for the border of Arcadia, and everything in between. I wondered what Eden would find to fill her time.

After planning another trip to re-supply and listing out what needed to be collected in the nearest towns, I was famished. I had sat down for lunch to study the Compendium when Nash burst into my room.

"I was thinking," he threw himself on my bed like it belonged to him. "Now that Eden is basically Queen, she needs protection when you're not around."

His words had the skin on the back of my neck tingling. Did he think that I hadn't already considered that?

"I mean," he went on, "she'd be fine on her own if she could shift. But since she's human, I wondered if I couldn't be of service somehow.

I could escort her, assist her with anything she needs, be a guard of sorts to keep her safe when you're busy with King stuff."

I raised an eyebrow. "You want to be her personal guardian?" The thought of him with her all the time didn't sit right, not after her dream. "You want her alone."

"What?" Nash scoffed. "No, I don't."

I tilted my head. "I saw the way you looked at her that first day."

A muscle in Nash's jaw tensed, but he said nothing.

"So you admit it then?"

"Yes. I mean, no!" Nash covered his face. "She's beautiful, of course, but I wouldn't... I couldn't–"

"Then why do it, Nash?"

He sat up, tucking one foot under his other leg. "I'm dispensable."

Dispensable. The word was harsh, but he was right in terms of hierarchy.

I pinched the bridge of my nose. "So you would take all of that responsibility on yourself? And if anything were to happen to her, you and you alone would answer for it."

"Yes."

I sighed, my chest tightening at the thought of harm coming to her. Nash was right. Eden needed someone when I wasn't around. "If you allow anything to happen to her–"

"I will lick the Glade floors clean for eternity. I know. I promise to keep her safe, Silas. I promise on my own life."

"One I'll hold you to."

Nash visibly relaxed. "Good. Now that it's settled, I need to ask you a question."

I dropped my head back. "What more do you want, Nash?"

"Why is Eden near Feru Falls?"

I stiffened. "She's where?"

It didn't take long for us to arrive at the Gateway, not with the fear coursing cold in my veins. I had no control over what happened to her outside of my domain, and I hated to think of what might happen if she wandered outside of it.

The borders of Arcadia were walled high. Our peaceful land rested in a valley between mountains, a place no mortal human had yet discovered. Other forest-dwelling animals came and went. They weren't difficult for us wolves to manage. But if Eden found her way *out*, what then?

Nash and I found her studying next to a stack of books with her back against a rock face. She sat mere steps away from the cleft in the stone wall surrounding the kingdom. Steps away from the door to the outside, to danger, to Nyx.

"Eden," I called out, coming to a halt. Nash nearly collided with me.

"Oh, hey." She smiled but arched an eyebrow, tucking a strand of her wild hair behind an ear. "Is something wrong?"

Curiosity bloomed in her like a flower caught in spring rain. Clearing my throat, I turned my eyes down. "No, I... It's just that... Well—"

"I asked him if I could be your guardian while he attended his duties as king," Nash interrupted. "We wanted to tell you in person."

"Guardian?" Her smile faltered.

"Not that you really need one," I started. "But considering last night..."

I could hear both Nash and Eden's heartbeats quicken for different reasons.

Nash stiffened. "What happened last night?"

I watched Eden, wondering what she would say. I wouldn't betray her trust, but Nash would find out. He would have to know.

After a moment, she swallowed. "I had another dream about Nyx."

"Another?"

"This time, he threatened to take down Arcadia," I explained. "In the little time alone I've had today, I've been trying to come up with a way we can deal with the situation with the least amount of death."

My mind flashed back to Nash being mentioned in Eden's dream. Something about it bothered me, but I couldn't put my paw on what.

I met Eden's gaze. She seemed so concerned, so worried. I hated seeing her stressed.

"You have to be careful, Si," Nash started. "This isn't us playing Alphas anymore."

"You don't think I know that, Nash?" I snapped. "I've been playing Alphas for the past year not knowing what the *silva* I'm doing."

Nash swallowed. "Sorry, I didn't–"

"Just stop." After a deep breath, I turned back to Nash. "Look, you've been gone. I've done my best here. You've made it quite clear you're disappointed in how I'm doing, but I'm the Alpha here. I will figure this out. And if I fail, I take the blame. Me, alone."

Nash nodded. I couldn't read his expressions as well as I used to. Too much time and too many things had passed between us.

Is he angry? Is he going to run again?

Eden cleared her throat. "You won't be alone in it. They'll blame me as well, considering it's my fault that..." She inhaled but didn't finish her sentence. She fiddled with the pages of the book in her lap.

"We'll figure it out." I knelt in front of her. "We're doing this together."

She still gazed down at the book.

I lifted her chin and smiled at her. "We're going to be fine."

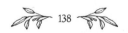

Though they were my own words, they were far away and cold like the winter threatening the world outside of Arcadia's walls.

Do I really believe what I said?

Will we figure it out?

"Eden," I murmured. "I have to go back. But—" I sucked in a breath. "Please don't go too far from Nash. He's sworn his life to protect you. I need you safe."

She nodded, though I could hear her fear, her heartbeat hammering and echoing even in my ears.

I walked away before I could change my mind.

18

EDEN

HAVING A GUARDIAN WASN'T like I expected. It didn't seem like an extended imprisonment, which comforted me.

Nash kept me company. He was so lighthearted that it kept my mind off of Silas and Nyx for most of the afternoon while we wandered around Arcadia, and I familiarized myself with its native things under the heavy gray clouds.

Occasionally, I'd glance over and look at Nash and see Iain instead. His gait, his smile, his hair, his laugh even. Except his eyes had a darkness to them. Yet, almost being in Iain's presence eased my anxiety, a reminder that I'd found what I'd been searching for.

But when dinner came and went, Nash returned to his room. The day faded into night, leaving me alone with my thoughts. Thoughts that lingered with the images I'd seen in my dreams.

I sat at the base of the throne in Guardian's Glade, feet tucked to the side. I felt almost grounded, sitting in the place where I had started only three days ago at the base of the throne. And here I sat, spiraling despite experiencing the truth of the dreams I'd had since childhood.

What has my life become?

"You seem like you could use some company."

I raised my head to see Caroline gliding towards me, almost floating. She dropped down to her knees and her silver robe pooled around her.

"Is it that obvious?" I groaned.

"You're in here alone. Without a lantern lit."

I noticed the depth of the dark for the first time since sitting down. I must've been sitting there for an hour or so. I could no longer make out the details of the double doors at the end of the aisle. I had lost track of time.

"I guess you're right." I sighed. "Did Silas send you?"

"Why would he send me?" She furrowed her brow.

"I had another dream last night. Nash volunteered to be my guardian when Silas couldn't be there, and Nash had other things to tend to after dinner. They think I need protection even inside of Arcadia. Does that mean I'm not safe here?"

Caroline grew somber. "Arcadia is a magical thing, but so is *he*. He's a Seer after all. Somehow, he's influenced your dreams. Who knows what other deep forms of magic he's capable of when he's desperate."

He seemed a lot more powerful than I first imagined him to be. All the nightmares, his uncanny ability to know things, those hollow, flaming eyes.

"Is Arcadia protected by magic? Or is there something we can do to ward him off? I feel restless, like I can't do anything to help."

"They banished him once, but history is a little foggy when it comes to the terms of his banishment. That's where you come in." Caroline gave my hand a quick squeeze. "We need you to research as much as you can alongside our other historians to read about encounters with

Nyx from the past. My hope, and Silas's, is that you can find the answer by reading our texts with fresh eyes."

"*Human* eyes," I retorted.

"I suppose so, yes. That's exactly why we need you. I've spent years reading the same texts. No doubt there's something in our books that could be an answered prayer, but only new eyes can find it."

I thought of the old books I'd begun to scour earlier, reading age-old words written by the ancient kings of the past.

Ancient *wolf* kings.

Kings like Silas.

The thought of him made my stomach twist.

Wolf. King. Husband.

Maybe everything would work out, maybe this would have happened all along. My doubts still swirled at the surface as I stood. I may have been human, but I'd help if I could.

"I want to be helpful."

Caroline beamed. "I knew there had to be a reason my father chose you. Come on. I'll find you some of our other histories."

I measured my breaths, thinking of how useless reading seemed to me at this moment. But if Caroline's words were true, somehow being human would be a benefit in the days to come. I only hoped I'd live up to the expectation.

19

SILAS

I COULDN'T THINK STRAIGHT all day. Nothing I did distracted me from the image of Eden sitting by the Gateway.

Then getting chomped in half by that *beast*.

Lycaon, I want to hold her and never let go.

I chided my childish desires, knowing that love wasn't grasping something and never releasing. That kind of love wasn't protective.

It couldn't be.

Love was freedom, the risk of the other one leaving you behind either in life or death.

Love was loss waiting to happen.

And I'd experienced so much loss.

I held my forehead in my hands, elbows propped up on my knees as I sat by the Great River's bank that lay inside of our borders. Its rumbling tone almost drowned out the thoughts that weighed my head and shoulders down.

The Great River flowed for miles, eventually branching into the

Little River where I had first met Eden fifteen years ago. Chance allowed us to meet once. Serendipity decided that we would come together again.

But the river reminded me of my father, and I missed him.

Losing him, becoming King . . . it overwhelmed me most days. But something about the sound of water drowned out my algae-like anxious thoughts: if I sat still for too long, the algae grew and infected the quiet waters of my mind, tainting it with green, floaty organisms. But movement, the rush of water over stones, separated me from my worries.

I almost decided to take a swim when a flash of burnished copper drew my attention as an *ugal* emerged from the undergrowth across the river. His scales stood in contrast against the green moss and woody trunks of trees.

I straightened myself and a feeling of anticipation passed over me. I gave the *ugal* a nod, hoping to prompt it to speak.

The *ugals* were one of the many magical races existing in the hidden parts of Appalachia, the Great Mountains, but they were mainly solitary creatures.

"*Han ar vene,*" the *ugal* said in the ancient tongue. "*Ar vaara innu feru. Han vole hon... Lo Kunin e Arcadia.*"

Nyx was causing problems, and he would come for my bride-to-be.

"*Kein?*" I asked.

"*Myt us Joulo.*"

Before the winter solstice.

My head swam. There was a reason humans called him the Smoke Wolf, and not because of his scent or dark fur. He evaded capture or attention with the thick fog that often accompanied him. And if he caused problems for the surrounding region, he'd wreak havoc in Arcadia soon enough if I didn't stop him first.

"*Bene, cara.*"

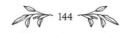

The *ugal* bowed and slipped into the Great River, sinking below its inky waters.

I picked my way back to the path while the darkness seeped around me. It was something I loved about my kingdom, something I had always loved, how the atmosphere ebbed and flowed like the riverbanks in spring. Movement and a flow like the river encompassed the kingdom, and the forest never stood still.

The mist, the light, the branches of the trees.

The river, the song, the hum of the birds.

It captivated me.

It soothed my spirit when the darkness came for me.

I arrived back at the Yard as the guards began to light the lanterns. In front of me, my path was illuminated, drawing me back to my throne, my room, my bed.

I wondered if I should go to Eden's room to check on her.

Is that what a human husband would do?

Jealousy crept up my bones, hot and heavy.

You gave that job to Nash already.

He had the freedom to be with Eden instead of taking care of the kingdom. He had the job I most wanted, all the fun with none of the responsibility.

I headed straight for my room, ready to collapse and tear off the professional mask of royalty I had to wear.

Is this what Father felt like? And why had I never asked questions when he walked with the living?

I remembered the personal training he had given me and my siblings. Not very traditional, but maybe it had been the only time he was allowed to be himself—Iain, not the King.

I remembered how wistful Eden had sounded when she first asked about him.

What happened to Iain, your father?

Her dreams had answered that question. I didn't know whether to be happy or angry. I shoved open the double doors to the throne room.

What I wouldn't give to ask my father why he'd revealed information to Eden and not his own children. I wanted to ask him what this all meant and what waited out there that Eden could help fight.

Or maybe she wasn't chosen to be a physical benefit. Yes, I'd already assigned her to research. I'd made an educated guess that she would be good at it, considering her meticulous attention to detail in her own research. She was intelligent.

Yes, maybe my father knew I'd need a fresh pair of eyes. A new perspective.

I opened the door to my bedroom surprised to find that not only had my lanterns been lit, but Eden hunched over some of Arcadia's old texts at my desk. She hadn't noticed me yet. I closed the door and leaned against its frame.

For several minutes I watched her while she worked. Dressed in her Historian robe, she looked like the night sky on a clear summer day.

It made me ache for memories long past of summers as a pup with Nash and Caroline, summers with our mother and father together. Summers where I was Silas rolling around in the grass on Midsummer's Eve gazing up at Lycaon's constellation in the night sky, nestled between the Scorpion and the Centaur.

I must've hummed a nostalgic sigh because Eden startled and whipped her head around. I shot her a smirk.

"I'm sorry," she mumbled and cleared her throat. "I didn't realize you had come in."

"Do you know you bite your bottom lip when you read?" I asked, stepping over to her. Her eyes flickered in the low lantern light. "It's cute."

"You think biting my lip is cute?" She chuckled.

I shrugged. "So what if I do?"

She shook her head and turned back to her books. "I did want to ask you something."

"Of course." I leaned back against the desk, folding my arms across my chest. "Anything at all."

"There's a section of this old book." She pulled the Compendium out, setting it on the desk with a thud. Dust danced in the lantern light. "I flipped through it, searching for anything that reminded me of *him*."

I noticed the way she tensed when she mentioned Nyx but said nothing.

"I found this." She pointed to a page illustrating a shadow with flaming eyes. "Can you translate it for me?"

My heart quickened in my chest at the sight. I moved to stand behind Eden, arms propped on the desk on either side of her body. She shifted and I leaned my head over her shoulder. "Which part?"

"Um," She cleared her throat. "It's here, I think."

I squinted at the scrawled font on the brittle, yellowing pages. The illustration of the Smoke Wolf glared at me as I stumbled over the curling letters. "*Innu lo veime...* In the distant past." I traced the line with my finger, squinting to read the words in the faint light. "*Lo municci rikas innu rauha sur lo feru...* The city lived in peace with the wild."

"Is this a legend?" Eden asked, voice reverberating against my ribs. "Or history?"

I smiled to myself. "You forget that we are *both*. But if I'm being honest, I'm not even sure. I would have to imagine that it's history, but so many of our stories merge with local folklore. It's hard to say."

She tilted her head up. "Keep going. Please."

Taking a deep breath, I pulled my attention away from her soft,

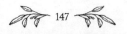

brown eyes and back to the text. "*Autem vaara art vene e l'orizun...* But danger grew on the horizon." I swallowed and adjusted my left hand as I retraced the line of curling letters. "*Lycaon art kunan e lo myt, au han avi vele nemicci...* Lycaon—he's the god and first king of Arcadia—was king at the time and had many enemies."

"Lycaon," Eden whispered, pronouncing each of the syllables. "He's your ancestor?"

I nodded.

"So you're a demigod then?"

"Demigod?" I raised an eyebrow at her.

"So you don't have any super cool powers?"

I smirked. "You mean besides my rugged looks and the fact that I can phase into a wolf?"

She chuckled, brushing her hair out of her eyes. "Yes, besides that."

"Then no." I moved to lean against the desk so I could face her. "I hope you're okay with what you're stuck with."

She smiled. "More than happy."

"I hope you mean what you say." The words spilled out before I could stop them, but my chest felt like a dam had been opened.

Eden wasn't only brains or a pretty face. I felt a little bit more like my old self with her, the Silas I knew before so much death and loss. The Silas who hadn't grieved his parents. She brought him back out, and I liked who I was with her.

I didn't have to wear a mask.

I could be myself.

Her smile faded. "I always mean what I say. Always."

I cleared my throat, returning back to the text. I tilted my head so I could read sideways. "Lycaon was king at the time and had many enemies... *surin e alla art: lo Nyx...* The chief of them all: Nyx, or the Smoke Wolf as humans call him."

I picked the book up and read silently, afraid to voice the next part out loud.

He arrived without warning or sound, devastating the town. He brought with him a mist so dense that many were lost in a few days. Making a decision for the greater good of the kingdom, Lycaon met Nyx on the banks of the Great River, offering his own life in the stead of many.

For a brief moment, the wild quaked and stilled from a binding contract between kings of separate kingdoms. It's said that in the wake of the earth shaking, the sound of stone and metal rang through the trees. And when the sun drove the fog away, Arcadia was left with a second king and no enemy in sight.

"Silas, what does it say?"

"Um... It's about their battle, or what little is known about it. A fog came over the kingdom and an earthquake. Then sunshine and a second king taking Lycaon's place."

"Lycaon was killed?"

I shook my head, eyebrows furrowed. "The text is unclear. He offered himself in the place of his kingdom and the surrounding villages and towns. The fog rolled over, obscuring everything. The next thing written is that Arcadia had a new king."

Eden bit her lip. I wondered how long she'd been in my room, pouring over these old books alone.

"Eden." I wet my lips. "You need to rest."

She inhaled as if to protest but surprised me with a nod. After stacking her books in a neat pile on my desk, she started towards the door. I caught her wrist in my hand, pulling her back.

"Where do you think you're going?"

"My room. Or am I being assigned a new prison cell?" She raised her eyebrows in a challenge, a grin on her lips.

"Would you consider the king's room a cell?" I pushed myself away from the desk until she and I breathed the same air.

She pursed her lips. "Maybe it doesn't *look* like a cell, but I would have a cellmate."

That pulled a chuckle out of my throat. "Is that all that I am now?"

"Among... other things." She turned her eyes down at her bare feet on the soft, mossy floor.

"Be careful with your words, human," I whispered in her ear. "You'll give the king a big head."

She tucked herself under my chin, wrapping her arms around my waist in a hug. "You didn't need my help for that. You already have one of those."

I rolled my eyes, holding her, arms folding around her slim shoulders. My breath caught in my throat, the weight of the story settling on top of my lungs. The Seers and Historians always said that history was bound to repeat itself.

Silas.

Of the forest.

I'd been told to never fear the depth or be fazed by the darkness of the trees. A blessing over me at my birth, now a curse.

Was it my destiny to take the place of my people, standing in their stead and stopping Nyx for once and for all?

If Lycaon could do it, I could, too. His blood coursed through my veins.

"Come on," I mumbled. "Rest."

I backed away, stepping over to the bed where I slipped under the blankets. Eden hesitated but followed after blowing out the lanterns. I lay on my back and gazed at the foliage above us as she nestled her head on my chest.

She hummed in contentedness and I stroked her wild hair.

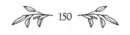

"Goodnight, Eden," I whispered.

"Goodnight, silly little king."

Eden soon fell asleep. I yawned, trying to imagine what it would be like to stand off against Nyx, two kings pitted against each other from the beginning. I tried to imagine dying at the hands of my enemy, or at least bow to him in submission.

I stood next to a wolf I had only seen sketches of.

Lycaon sniffed the air. He hunted something. I hadn't figured out what yet.

He trotted away from the Yard to the heart of Arcadia. I had been to the sacred ruins countless times with my mother when she tended her gardens there. But it was unrecognizable when we approached. Not a ruin but a beautiful centerpiece to a sprawling forest, and in place of my mother's garden were stone markers.

Lycaon slowed his pace as he walked up to the entrance of the stone gazebo. He waited for something. Or maybe someone.

I turned my head and realized that a fog approached.

Lycaon stepped onto the stone floor of the gazebo, tail swishing in his wake. I followed, too anxious to speak.

There were carvings in the stone, much clearer than anything I could read the times I visited the stone ruins in the past—or future, considering this place seemed brand new. The dream's time felt off. The markings resembled the ceremonial paint the Seers painted at Sarva.

Angular lines cut into the stone, speaking a language I had tried my best to learn. I memorized as much as I could, memorizing line after line and curve after curve, wondering if my father decided to reveal information from the Other Realm.

Lycaon drew my attention now, bowing his head in the center of the gazebo.

I heard his prayer in his head but couldn't make sense of it. Surely he wasn't praying to himself?

But if not to himself, then who?

The fog grew more dense. I heard three heartbeats: my own, Lycaon's, and–

Lycaon emitted a low growl, rumbling like thunder. "You dare come to my father's resting place, disturbing the peace?"

"He was my father, too, you know," a snarky voice snapped from the fog, echoing in every direction.

"You left. You wanted your own rules," Lycaon said. "You chose your destiny, and I chose mine. I can't help that you chose wrong."

"Please, brother. I only want to talk." A dark figure emerged from the mist, a heap of matted fur. He loomed large, but I could tell he had been through a difficult season.

"Talk? You had your chance to talk at your Council meeting. I am the Alpha and you're the Omega now. What's done is done, Nyx. I can't change that. I can't reverse the banishment."

My heart lurched in my chest. Brother?

Nyx growled. "You're the King of Arcadia. You can change anything."

"I am a servant of the Wild. The Wild changes me, not the other way around."

Nyx snapped at the air with a bark. "Know this, Ly: I will seek retribution. And you will pay for choosing the wrong side of this war. I will reclaim what's mine even if it takes a millennia. I am nothing if not patient."

With that, the wolf melted into the mist. Lycaon howled, low and mournful. As his call echoed in the trees, an easterly wind blew the fog away revealing a normal forest behind its tendrilled curtains.

I turned to Lycaon when a flash of light blinded me. I shut my eyes, refusing to see the god-like king in physical form.

I jolted awake, taking a few seconds to readjust my eyes, trying to make sense of what I had witnessed. Eden lay asleep next to me, hair splayed around her head like a crown.

A flicker of lantern light caught my eye around the edges of my door.

20

SILAS

C AREFUL NOT TO DISTURB Eden, I slid out from under the blankets. Praying that it wouldn't make much noise, I slipped through the doorway and into Guardian's Glade. One of the double doors across the room shut with a soft click.

My bare feet made no sound as I jogged over, wrenching it open, hoping to catch the lurker. To my disappointment, no one waited outside, but the light of a lantern bent around the right corridor of trees.

I followed, unsure of what to do when I caught up to whomever I followed. I wanted answers, though. Answers I couldn't find by going back to sleep.

The light bent further, following the path I had walked in my dreams.

The ruins.

My mother's garden.

With a quick pace, I followed the light, my prey rustling ten steps ahead of me.

Who would be outside my door at this hour? And why are they headed to the ruins? Could they see my dreams? Has my father reached out after all?

While my footsteps fell to the rhythm of my heartbeat, I thought of my dream.

It can't possibly be true.

But then again, how could I have imagined those runes with markings that I'd never recalled?

I pressed onward, noticing how close we were to the heart of Arcadia. I strained my ears, searching for the other person's heartbeat. But the pounding of my own drowned it out.

I rounded the corner, thinking of the gazebo from my dream, but was met with the sight of the ruins as I had always known them, my mother's flowers circling the old stones. A tall, violet-clad figure stood at the center of the platform of the dilapidated gazebo. The figure held a lantern low in front of its body, casting shadows on his face.

"What is this?" I asked.

"Poetic justice," the oily Seer voice spoke.

Ransom.

"What exactly is being justified?"

"Arcadia." The Seer lifted his lantern, casting its light over the faded runes. "What do you make of it, my king?"

"You know I never did well with runes, Ransom." I stepped closer, wary of this strange man. "Why have you led me here?"

"Something must be done about our Enemy." He didn't turn to me, but I could tell that he paid close attention to my words, heart rate, and body language.

It was currency to him.

"You *knew*... about Lycaon and Nyx, that they were brothers. This

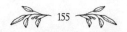

155

whole time, you knew?" My eyebrows pinched together.

"Knowing," Ransom mused, running his free hand over the eroded stone. "Such a funny little word. I am a *Seer*, my king. Not a knower."

"Semantics."

The Seer continued without acknowledging my comment. "I can see what has passed, what is passing even now, and what might come to pass if one's intentions succeed to fruition."

"Speak to me plainly, Ransom. I am your king, but I am first and foremost a peer, one who grew alongside you as a pup."

He met my eyes now. They were a piercing shade of gray, like a hawk. He stayed silent for a long moment before stepping down the cracked steps of the gazebo, an arm's length away from me.

"There." He pointed at the pocket in my robe. "That is your answer."

Sticking my hand in my pocket, I pulled out the piece of cedar that he gave me at the Festival of Kings. "I still don't understand. What does this answer?"

"When burned, cedar purifies, leaving protection and positivity in its wake." He repeated the same words he had spoken during the Festival of Kings. "It would mean pain, but it would also mean immortality, my king."

That same sense of foreboding doom settled over me. "You mean, I'm supposed to–I have to..."

I couldn't say the words out loud. It would feel like it was set in stone, like the faded runes on this memorial stone. And maybe I, too, would fade from the world, only a broken ruin in a forest of memories.

I would repeat history. I would face Nyx alone. And I would burn.

"There have been rumors." Ransom licked his lips, like this whole business enticed him. "History is often bound to repeat itself."

My lips parted to form another question.

But I already knew the answer.

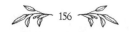

I'd already seen the parallel between me and Lycaon. And this could be a hint that Nash could be more than he appeared to be. Maybe Nyx and Nash had more in common than I thought. And maybe somewhere lurked a hidden history.

But he was my brother. My blood.

Could he really be capable of treason?

Even if Nash was innocent, I knew I would have to face Nyx. I was King, after all. Death was my duty.

"Silas." Ransom's eyes softened and he offered a tight smile. The use of my name pulled at the edges of my heart. "Our life is for Arcadia. And this is your destiny."

My head swam, shadows clouding my vision. "What if I fail?"

The Seer took a long, deep breath. "Then we'll pick up the pieces and continue living. Though, if it encourages you, I will tell you this: You will always succeed when you follow the path laid out before you. Obedience is the first step."

"And if I succeed?"

Ransom chuckled. "Then Arcadia moves on, honoring the second coming king who stepped down to bring the rest of us life. There will be monuments and songs and feasts in your honor."

"And Eden?" My voice cracked.

Ransom went to speak, but no words fell out of his mouth. He stood there, mouth open like he had been frozen. He bowed his head. "I cannot say, my king. The future is... uncertain."

"Will she live?"

I had to know.

That same tongue-tied expression took over his face. "I cannot say."

I ran my hand through my hair, gripping my roots in a tight fist. My chest ached.

"*Je kunan, ja doleo.*" His words in the ancient tongue pulled my gaze back to his.

My king, I'm sorry.

"Why now?"

He only smiled. "I have to get back. I hope you will come to understand, my king. But I know you will do what is right for Arcadia, for your people."

He bowed and left, violet robes swishing against the Solomon's Seal and the lantern light dancing between the trees until it disappeared.

I was alone. Alone with my thoughts, darker than the night sky.

21

EDEN

T HE SWEET AROMA OF tree sap pulled me from the heaviness of sleep that gripped my limbs. Adjusting my eyes to the gray light, I tried to remember if I'd had any dreams. I couldn't recall anything specific and took that as a good sign.

Having no dreams felt better than having bad ones.

I shifted from my spot in Silas's bed. The blankets were warm and the morning held a comfortable chill. Autumn had edged her way past summer even within the magical borders of Arcadia.

I slid my arms under the pillow, burying my face in the silky fabric.

"Good morning." A familiar, tenor voice broke the silence.

I rolled to my side, squinting my eyes at Silas who sat at the small table with breakfast and two steaming cups in front of him.

"Good morning," I mumbled.

I swear I could feel his chuckle from across the room. His voice had this timber to it that rattled between my ribs.

"Tea?"

"At what point in Arcadian history will y'all learn to make coffee?" I pulled myself to a sitting position.

"Tea is better for you."

I tried to gauge his expression and raised an eyebrow. "You've never had coffee, have you?"

"Never." He smiled. "You'll have to make some for me sometime."

I slid out of the bed and sat across the table from him, noticing an open book resting on his knee. "What's that?"

Silas shrugged. "Books of glyphs and runes, the older written language of Arcadia before the Ancient Tongue."

"Ancient Tongue being the language that the Compendium is written in?"

He nodded.

I picked up an apple from the spread of fruits, cheeses, and bread. "Will you teach me?"

His face crinkled with his pensive expression. "You want to learn the Ancient Tongue?"

It was my turn to shrug, swallowing a bite of apple. "If I'm to be the Queen of Arcadia, it only makes sense to learn as much as I can. And besides, how am I supposed to research if I have to keep pestering the king to translate?"

His frown melted when he inhaled. "I suppose you're right. It's only fair, after all. I'll have Caroline bring you some books."

He sipped his tea, and I took the opportunity to study him. His eyes were bloodshot and his hair lay flat against his head. That bright, vivid green in his eyes had dimmed a little.

"How did you sleep?" I cupped the steaming mug of tea, averting my eyes from his, hoping he'd take my bait.

"Fine until…" He swallowed like it hurt to say it out loud. "One of the Seers had a vision of sorts."

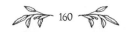

"Seers? Like Aubrey and Ransom?"

"Ransom, yes."

I glanced up at him. The muscles tightened in Silas's jaw as he sat his mug back on the table and tore into a piece of bread.

"What did he have to say?" My heart stuttered. Whatever Ransom had seen must've unnerved Silas if he acted like this. Or maybe Silas didn't like Ransom. Or maybe waking up in the middle of the night two nights in a row left him sleep deprived.

Silas jerked his head as if dismissing it but cleared his throat. "Warnings about Nyx." He licked his lips. "I need to sit down with Caroline and Nash. Figure out our tactics."

"Can I help at all? It's driving me crazy being useless."

He met my gaze, eyebrows raised. "All I need for you is to read as much as you can. I want your perspective on everything. There may be something I'm missing."

"But I thought if I joined your meeting that maybe I could–"

"Eden." He held his hand up, silencing me with a glance. "I need you to be researching, not talking in circles with us." He exhaled and turned his eyes on me again, green even duller now. "I need you, Eden. You're the key to ending this."

"But I'm only human."

"Exactly. You're human."

I took another sip of tea, letting the woody taste and warmth slip through me. "If this is what will help you."

He stood. "See you at lunch?"

I nodded.

He sighed something sounding like relief, stepping over and kissed the top of my head. With a small smile, he ducked out of his room into Guardian's Glade.

Yesterday, I might have hoped he'd kiss me, but today I wanted

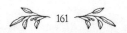

things to be different. I wanted to be a part of this, regardless of the consequences.

And I wanted him to trust me like he did his siblings despite their differences.

I want to feel like I belong.

My stomach twisted at the realization, and all of the sudden, the room spun in front of my eyes. I blinked a few times, pushing away the tea and breakfast. I thought back to my childhood, all the years spent like an outsider, never invited to parties or movies, never included in group projects or conversations, alone at the cafeteria.

Alone.

Is it that I'd wanted—more friends? More control? To fit in?

No.

I wanted to belong without changing a single piece of me. I wanted to belong by being myself and not pretending to be something I wasn't.

"That's what this is," I whispered, squeezing my eyes shut. "This is all pretend."

My body burned hot and ached as tears slid down my cheeks. My hands shook. My body felt altogether weak and sick.

This is all pretend.

This is all pretend.

This is all pretend.

Maybe I doubted too much.

Or maybe I had believed so hard that werewolves existed that I convinced myself of this complete delusion. Maybe my body lay strewn across the leafy floor of the forest in the State Park. Maybe Arcadia and Silas and betrothal were my brain's way of hallucinating through hypothermia.

Maybe this was dying.

Because none of this could be real. No way I could be a queen. No way I could be a wife. No way I could be friends with wolves. No way I could *belong* to this place.

I snapped my eyes open.

A rustling at the door caught my attention a moment before it opened.

"Good morning," a golden voice sang. Caroline stepped to Silas's desk, dropping four thin booklets and a larger tome with a thud.

She turned and frowned. "Eden, what's wrong?"

I shook my head, willing myself to stop shaking. I failed. Instead, my chin shook and the floodgates opened.

In a moment, Caroline led me to sit on Silas's bed, pulling me into a warm embrace. I released everything, sobbing against her shoulder, the tang of lemon and dirt fresh on her robes. I squeezed my arms around her shoulders, not wanting to be alone like this.

It felt good to have a sister, a friend.

Eventually, my breaths evened out, and my tears stopped coming. Caroline moved away to take a good look at me.

"What happened?"

I shook my head, not knowing where to start. "I can't do this."

"Can't do what?"

I shrugged, my robe sleeves slipping over my skin. "Any of this. Be a queen, marry Silas, stop a war, fight Nyx."

"Where is this coming from?"

"I'm not good enough for Arcadia. I'm not good enough for Silas. I'm not strong like you. I'm not even that special. I guarantee that you could pick any girl in Tennessee, and she'd be the same as—if not better—than me."

Caroline smiled, shaking her head. "But then she wouldn't be Eden."

I threw a hand in the air. "Exactly."

Caroline tilted her head to the side. "Arcadia would miss Eden very much if we picked a random girl."

I shook my head but said nothing.

Caroline stood and walked to the desk, taking one of the smaller booklets. "Silas told me to bring these to you. He said you wanted to learn the Ancient Tongue. I am impressed by you and your attitude in all of this. You are brave, you know."

"How am I brave? I'm crying about my inadequacy, and I'm scared of my own dreams."

Caroline raised an eyebrow. "Dreams aren't something to be taken lightly. My, uh—Markus—the one you met the other day, is a Seer. He's always told me that dreams can reveal a lot about a person."

"I still don't see how I'm brave."

"In time, you will." She placed the book in my hands. "Start with this. Come find me if you need any help, okay? I'll be in the Yard."

And with the air of a bird in flight, she glided from the room.

I opened the booklet, curious about what lay between the pages. The first part had been inked in English, tight boxy letters introducing the concept of the Ancient Tongue and why it should be kept. Apparently, the animals in the Appalachian Mountain range spoke the Ancient Tongue, but as far as I knew, whitetail deer hadn't made any noises similar to the words Silas had spoken the night before.

But maybe it was like the mental conversations with Iain. Maybe there weren't physical words involved, but mental communication in the old language.

With a mix of excitement and anxiousness, I dove into my studies, knowing that I couldn't surface until I'd mastered at least something.

I'd prove myself worthy of Arcadia even if it killed me.

22

SILAS

"I STILL DON'T UNDERSTAND." Nash paced along the edge of the Great River where I had met with the *ugal* days previous. His feet curled around the stones piled along the edges.

"I don't understand either."

I had recounted my vision from the previous night, editing out the parts that made it seem like Nash and I were to repeat the feud between Lycaon and Nyx. While Eden's dream and my own vision both leaned towards the belief that Nash would be dangerous, I wanted to believe the best about him.

"It sounds like you have to die to save Arcadia from ruin." His voice shook. He swallowed. "Is that what you got from it?"

I shrugged. "Maybe, but I'm not sure if that future is definite or only one possible future."

Nash sighed, turning away. I watched the hem of his robe grow more damp as the river water climbed up the fabric. I didn't want to die. I wanted the opposite. But who was I to doubt a Seer? Who was I to fight fate? Who was I to step away from the heroic history of Lycaon?

I glanced up as Nash's shoulders tensed. He straightened as his eyes met mine. He stood in shadow, eyes dark and sinister. "Nightshade."

"Nash, I don't think–"

"Hear me out, Si," he interrupted, stepping closer. "You take a small dose, and we can have Ransom and Markus there to help if things go south. Seers do it all the time."

"Nash," I fixed my eyes on a wren rummaging through the underbrush of the forest. "We don't know if it will help."

"It can't hurt."

"We know that it can! Seers have died from taking too much."

Nash shook his head. "I think it's the only way."

"*Sen sun ferulukos.*"

"Maybe I *am* crazy." Nash shrugged. "But it could mean the difference between us knowing you're going to die and hoping to change that outcome."

I hated that he made at least a little sense.

It might be my only way to know for sure.

I may be able to see Lycaon again.

"Okay."

"Okay?"

I nodded. "Let's do it. Now."

Nash stayed close behind me as we returned to the maintained trails of Arcadia. I moved through the mix of wolves and people when we arrived at Mender's Heath. Asa, robed in faded evergreen with a group of pups, slathered a salve of waybread over one of their chests. Another kid must have bitten the victim while wrestling.

They noticed Nash and I and bowed.

"Stand up straight," I corrected my own posture.

The children clambered to stand straighter than the child on the right or left. Asa patted the shoulder of the injured boy who leapt off the narrow bed. Together, the group scampered back to the Yard, chattering about the injury when they left.

"My King." Asa bowed his head to me. "And Prince Nash. To what do I owe the pleasure?"

He smiled and turned back to tidy up the waybread salve.

"I need a small dose of nightshade." I tried to speak evenly, hoping that the Healer couldn't detect my own nervousness.

He fumbled with the lid for the salve. "Nightshade?" He hesitated as he replaced the jar on a shelf with a dozen other unlabeled bottles. "Whole or crushed?"

I glanced at Nash. He shrugged.

I swallowed. "I need enough to produce a state of Sight, enough to envision."

"I see." Asa nodded once. "I take it Ransom has your feathers ruffled again?"

Nash raised his eyebrows at me.

Frowning, I shook my head. "Do you have what I need?"

Asa sighed while he rummaged through a basket of smaller bottles and jars. "I do. Of course I do. And I will not question you but warn you. This is playing with fire. Fire can warm and feed and protect, but it can also burn and destroy and kill." He pointed a stare at me. "I will be here until midnight should you need my assistance. Send word."

He handed me a dusty bottle with a cairn drawn on the front.

"Take a three-fingered pinch with your tea. The effects are difficult to predict; even the Seers wouldn't know how your body would react until you take it. Be on guard, and do be careful, Silas."

The elderly Healer smiled at me. He'd been the one to bandage my wounds after Nash and I had fought. He'd healed every sickness, disease, poison ivy rash, and everything else for my entire life.

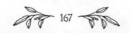

My resolve faltered. "Thank you, Asa. I will. I promise."

I turned, ducking through the doorway as I went. Nash followed, and I led us down into the tighter, darker portion of the maintained trails towards the Sage Brush where Ransom and Markus would be.

It always struck me strange that the rest of the forest could be so light and breezy, but it grew darker and colder the closer one got to the Sage Brush. The ghost beetles buzzed around the ferns and underbrush, drifting away when we passed.

"Si." Nash's whispered voice broke our silence.

I stopped, turning to face him.

He worked his jaw side to side for a moment before shaking his head. "Do you trust them?"

"You're the one who had this idea in the first place." I glanced to the side, drawn to movement beyond the shadows. "We're being watched."

I turned back, pushing forward with as much confidence as I could muster.

It's not that I don't trust them. But do they trust me?

I kept my eyes down until the faint, golden light of lanterns illuminated the soft, dirt path in front of my bare feet. Upon first observation, the darkness enveloped the forest like midnight. However, sunshine leaked through cracks here and there. The effect unsettled me as I stepped through the woven archway where two lanterns had been hung and lit.

The rest of the pathway had lanterns hung at intervals, leaving some spaces in shadows. The light played tricks on my eyes, shadows bending and swaying while I made my way to the ceremonial grounds.

We crossed paths with the first violet-robed Seer a few minutes into the walk. She lowered her hood when we passed, and she bowed.

"Still weird," I muttered under my breath.

"Do you know where you're going?" Nash hissed behind me. Panic lurked at the edges of his voice.

"Yes. I've been here a few times since..." I couldn't bring myself to say it out loud in this place.

"Yeah." Nash walked up next to me. "But you know what you're looking for, or where they'll be?"

"I have a feeling he already knows we're coming." I swallowed, my mouth dry.

When we turned the last corner, the blue-tinged flames of the ceremonial grounds stopped me in my tracks. This place didn't comfort or ease pain. The Sage Brush was a place of confirming worst fears.

Taking a deep breath, I crossed the threshold. The flames from the pit in the center of the clearing leapt high, imitating my wolf form in eerie blue flame, and another thinner and darker wolf followed behind, imitating Nash.

A group of Seers were working on a variety of things: writing in books, examining leaves from native Arcadian plants, and charting stars. One hooded Seer held fire in his bare hands, illuminating his chin and lips.

"Ransom," I muttered.

"*Onni, je kunan.*"

"I'm sure you know our reason for seeking you out."

Ransom folded his hands, extinguishing the fire. Gray ash-stained skeletal fingers on his palms. "I do, indeed. I must say, I hadn't expected such action from you considering..."

With a flick of his hand, the fire in the pit leapt again, and a figure swirled into focus, all wild hair twisted among honeysuckle vines.

I licked my dry lips. "She knows what she needs to know."

Nash turned his head towards me.

Had he assumed I told her about the vision?

Why should I worry a human who can't do anything about it?

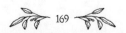

Why should I worry anyone who wouldn't understand?

"Of course. And I take it, you wish for Markus to join us?"

Another Seer approached the fire, lowering his hood to reveal a broad-shouldered, blond-haired man with a heavy-set jaw. He bowed and met my eyes.

I had seen him often with my sister. They'd grown closer since the death of our father. And he spoke honestly with me, which I appreciated.

"It would be wise to have double the knowledge," I said.

"I couldn't agree more, my king." Ransom held an ash-stained hand out towards a dark path. "If you will follow me, we can begin."

I was glad to be following Ransom as the path in front was unlit and pitch black. I knew you had to have the Sight to reach the deepest parts of the Sage Brush without becoming hopelessly lost.

Ransom stopped abruptly, and I collided with his back. I paused, focusing all my attention on what lay ahead. It smelled of sage and burnt wood and summer rain. Ransom blew on his hand and the eerie blue lanterns ignited.

The small room had a narrow bed like at Mender's Heath. A basket lay next to it, along with a low table containing various things like herbs and water.

"My king, if you'll take your place." Ransom motioned towards the bed, and I obeyed.

I met Nash's unreadable gaze as I settled down, my legs draped over the end. He stood on the opposite side of the bed facing Ransom and Markus who busied themselves at the low table.

"May I?" Markus asked, holding his hand out towards me.

I passed him the bottle of nightshade. "Asa said, a–"

"Three-fingered pinch with your tea," Markus finished. "Forgive me, my king, but this is not our first experience with nightshade."

"Right." I swallowed. "What should I expect?"

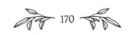

"There are..." Markus searched for the right word. "Many potential symptoms."

Ransom blew on his hand again, igniting a sprig of something and placing a mug over it.

"Many have experienced nausea, others have trouble breathing or feverish symptoms. The key is to keep your mind clear of dark thoughts."

"Like that's possible in a place like this," Nash grumbled.

Markus continued like he hadn't heard my brother. "If you keep your mind clear and focus on the question you want answered most, with mine and Ransom's assistance, you'll be able to find the answers you seek."

"Is it as simple as that?" I asked, my voice betraying my doubt.

Ransom lifted his head now, holding something crushed in his hands. "It is as simple and as difficult as you allow it to be."

Nash disguised a scoff as clearing his throat. He folded his arms over his chest.

Ransom moved from lantern to lantern, garnishing them each with a dash of something that caused the flames to turn white, casting the world in shades of gray.

Ransom flipped over the mug, tendrils of smoke dissipating in the air. He passed it to Markus. When Markus put tea in the mug and covered it in hot water, the smell of licorice and conifers filled the already sage-scented air.

My breaths slipped in rapid succession, the anticipation wearing on my nerves. I closed my eyes, forcing myself to exhale with each breath.

It's just tea.

I'm just going to drink a cup of tea.

I looked back up in time to see Markus put a three-fingered pinch of crushed nightshade into the hot tea, muddying the usually clear liquid.

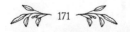

"Whenever you're ready." Markus passed me the mug.

It smelled extra earthy, like someone had put greens into the drink. But it reminded me of the swirling dark waters of the Great River after a storm.

Like it waited for this moment, all my fears of leaving the physical world rushed to me. I thought of my mother, my father, all the kings before me. I wondered about my people, about Caroline and Nash, who I'd leave behind if I passed over Realms. I thought about Eden, who would be left untethered once more.

What have I gotten her into?

Without thinking about it, my cup moved to my lips and I drank. For a moment, nothing happened. I gulped it down despite its scalding heat and watched the two Seers and my brother. They observed me closely.

I shook my head, opening my mouth in an attempt to speak. My body burned. My heart thrashed in my ears, feet, hands, and head.

Relentless pounding.

My vision darkened.

"What's happening?"

I'd heard Nash's voice, but I couldn't see him no matter where I turned. The darkness covered everything.

Had Ransom doused all the lanterns as swiftly as he'd lit them?

"My king," Ransom said, but again I couldn't find him. "You need to clear your mind. Allow the nightshade to assume control."

"Here," Markus placed something woven in my hands. "It's a basket if you need to–"

My body responded before I could. I expelled the contents of my stomach into the basket. I brushed my hand over my lips. My tongue tasted bitter.

"Silas." Ransom's voice was sterner this time. "Clear your mind.

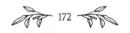

What question is it to which you seek answers?"

I growled though no words escaped my lips.

Am I human?

Am I wolf?

No, that's not it.

My thoughts rambled incoherently.

"Do something!" Nash's voice strangled with panic.

A muffled voice muttered beside me across from Nash. The words were in the Ancient Tongue but flowed like rushing water through my ears, a calming presence.

The fog that had occupied my mind since finishing the tea cleared as if from a western wind.

I wish to speak to Lycaon. I want to know what really happened the day he disappeared and the next king assumed the throne. I want to know what I must do to protect my kingdom, my people, my family, my future wife.

The chanting grew faint, and I wondered if the nightshade hadn't worked. I began to see light again and realized that Ransom must be relighting the lanterns.

But I found myself seated on a familiar outcrop of rock overlooking the valley. I was at *Rauha*, miles away from the Sage Brush. But the valley seemed different.

Is this the past?

Footsteps sounded behind me. I turned around. A massive white *virlukos* stepped through the branches. I had seen him the night before in my dreams.

"*King Lycaon.*" I bowed, realizing that I stood on all fours, my wolf paws beneath me.

"*Rise, young king.*" His voice rumbled in my chest, rattling my bones.

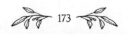

I stood, trying to make myself look tall. I wanted to have it all together, to make him proud after all he did for Arcadia, after all he did for me.

"You wished to speak to me." He huffed out a laugh. Whatever I had expected, this wasn't it. My request wasn't meant to be amusing. *"Speak, young king."*

I found myself speechless in front of him. Here I was, this puny child trying to protect the kingdom for which Lycaon had sacrificed everything.

What did I have to say that would mean anything to him?

He exhaled, and the hot breath rustled my hair. My tongue-tied mouth had been freed.

"My King." I inclined my head. *"I... I saw..."* I swallowed, unsure how to continue.

"You saw the day my brother, Nyx, betrayed our destiny." Lycaon raised his head high, gazing out over the valley, the place under his care. *"And you would like to know what really happened that day."*

"Well... yes." I frowned. If he could read my thoughts, why did he want me to speak at all? *"Did he kill you?"*

"Take a good look at me. Do I seem dead?" He turned to me, a mischievous glint in his eyes.

I poured over every inch of his body visible from where I sat. His body was completely intact, not injured in any way.

"Not that I can see."

"Then no. I would say he has not killed me."

"But then what happened? Where did you go? Why did you make them mourn when you could return to them?" Frustration laced my words. If I drank nightshade to not find answers, I would be furious.

"I chose to leave my Spirit behind, like all the other kings and queens of Arcadia."

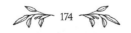

"*But my father—*"

"*Iain is very lucky to have a son like you, a daughter like Caroline, and a son like Nash.*"

"*But—*"

"*Silas.*" My name from Lycaon's lips sent a shudder through my body. "*Wherever you go, I am with you. To the end of the age. Am I not alive?*"

"*Well, you are, but—*"

"*Am I not with you even now?*"

"*Yes, but—*"

"*Silas.*" Lycaon spoke gently, but it stopped me mid-sentence again. "*You already have what you need to bring light to the darkness.*"

My eyebrows furrowed. "*But what is it? What will I see?*"

"*My son, you shall see wonders.*"

My face grew hot. "*I'm not worthy.*"

"*What you do does not make you worthy.*" His fur brushed against mine when he sat beside me. "*It's what's inside of you that makes you worthy.*"

I turned my head to the side, gazing over the valley under my care now. "*And if I fail?*"

"*Then you learn. And we try again.*"

My vision blurred and I bit back tears. After a moment of expectant silence, I took a shuddered breath. "*And if I die?*"

"*What an adventure that will be.*"

A whimper escaped my lips. "*I don't want to die. I can't. I can't leave them. Not now.*"

Lycaon's breath rustled my fur, but he said nothing.

"*I can't do it,*" I choked.

"*When the time is right, and you'll know when it is, peace will follow you across the realms. And you'll once again be reunited with your mother, your father, and the ancients before you.*"

"*But my family... I can't leave them.*" I rubbed my muzzle against my shoulder.

"*It's up to you to take the next step on the path. You aren't called to jump ahead of your destiny. Don't worry about the future; doing so will only cause you to lose your way.*"

"*But how will I know which path to take?*" I looked up at him, unashamed of my tears.

"*You will. Know this: you will make me proud.*" He met my gaze with a gleam in his eyes. "*I am sure of it.*"

I tried to speak, but my breath caught in my lungs.

Lycaon stood, bowing low, and disappeared into the forest.

I turned my gaze over the valley while time sped up, the sun rapidly falling behind the hills, darkness surrounding me.

Vene vaara elo dumahn.

Danger is in my future.

He was coming, and I would die fighting.

23

EDEN

CAROLINE BURST INTO SILAS'S room, startling me from my studies. "Up, now."

"What's going on?" I closed the book I had been studying, learning the equivalent of vowel sounds of the Ancient Tongue. "Is it *him*?"

She grabbed my wrist and dragged me through the doorway, Guardian's Glade, and down path after path. The silence ate at my insides.

"Caroline." I tried to pull my wrist loose, but she had an iron grip. "What is going on? Let go."

Caroline adjusted her hand and pulled me down a dark pathway. "Silas has done something utterly idiotic."

My stomach lurched. Images of Silas lying broken, bruised, and bloody filled my mind. Images of Nyx covered in blood.

Is he dead?

"What's happened to him?" I tried to keep from stumbling, but between being dragged from the room and fears about Silas's well-being, my legs hadn't had the chance to loosen.

The forest grew even darker, the light disappearing, difficult to imagine that it wasn't midnight.

Caroline sucked in a breath. "Eden, I don't know what state he will be in. It's best to prepare for anything at this point."

"What do you mean? What happened? I thought you had meetings. What has he done?" I pulled and yanked on my arm, but her grip grew tighter.

We passed through a lantern-lit archway into an ethereal place. The blue lightning bugs from *Sarva* drifted like stars in an endless midnight sky. The lanterns cast elongated shadows over the pathway as we passed several terrifying people in violet robes.

It dawned on me that we must be where the Seers worked, though the dark seemed ironic since I could barely see a thing. I wondered about Ransom and Aubrey and if they were here somewhere.

The dark consumed everything until it didn't. A bright, azure fire blazed in the center of a room with similar fire in all of the lanterns. The flames in the pit leapt, and a bright wolf with piercing eyes jogged through, followed by a swirling image of myself, wrapped in robes and honeysuckle.

"Caroline," a woman's voice called from across the fire. Aubrey stepped over to us. "Markus said—"

"Take us," Caroline commanded with an authority I hadn't yet seen her wear. It fit her like a glove. "Now."

Aubrey bowed her head and turned on her heel. She led the way down a pitch-black pathway, Caroline still gripping my arm. Up ahead, a faint silver glow seeped through the dense trees.

"Thank you, Aubrey," Caroline breathed and we stopped.

Sidling up next to her, I could see the faint reflection of silver in her eyes. Tears had pooled at the base of her eyelids.

Aubrey left us, and Caroline pushed forward into a room that smelled of licorice and bile.

"Oh, Lycaon," Caroline muttered, releasing my arm to cover her mouth and nose.

Despite the awful stench, the sight scared me more. Silas sat like a statue at the edge of a narrow bed, if it could be called that. He choked, and something dark had dried to his chin.

"What did you do to him?" I breathed, finding my voice. I made myself turn away from Silas and at the other people in the room.

Nash stood in the dim light of a lantern, both hands clutching the back of his head, eyes wide and wild. He shook his head but said nothing. Ransom sat across the room, eyes focused on Silas. He must not have heard me.

"Caroline," Markus spoke and stepped closer to Caroline.

She took a half step back. "What did you do?"

Markus shook his head, speechless, and he turned his eyes back to Silas.

I moved to Silas's side and cupped his face in my hand. He barely turned at my touch, but it was a response.

"Silas?" I muttered.

The green of his eyes had flooded pitch black like the forest around us, and with the lighting it felt like we were in some horror film like *Nosferatu* or *Hour of the Wolf*.

"What's wrong with him?" I asked the room at large, hoping someone could explain if this was a weird wolf disease or a strange ritual. But based on everyone's grave expressions, this couldn't be normal.

"He wanted to See, so he asked us to facilitate." Ransom stood. "He's taken a small dose of nightshade."

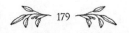

"Nightshade?" Caroline bellowed.

I turned, startled by her outburst. Her eyes burned with rage as she rounded on Markus.

"It was his choice," Markus started. "He is our king. We did what he asked us to do."

Caroline snarled, pushing him aside and she shoved Nash in the chest. "And this was your brilliant idea, huh? Make *him* take the poison. Make *him* do the stupid thing. It'll be fun. Right? Just like old times."

Nash shook his head. "I didn't—"

"Am I wrong?" She snapped.

"He—"

"Am I wrong?" Caroline repeated, all hints of kindness gone.

Nash couldn't look her in the eyes.

"Nash, we aren't pups anymore. Silas is supposed to be leading the kingdom, not playing your stupid games."

"Caroline, what do I do?" I asked, turning back to Silas who still couldn't breathe.

"He needs water. And talk to him." Caroline moved to the table next to me.

"Si?" I asked, watching his black eyes. They unnerved me. "Can you hear me?"

I heard someone, no doubt Caroline, pouring something. None of the men had offered to help, and Nash paced.

"Silas." I inhaled. My hands trembled. "It's Eden. I need you to talk to me."

His breath shuddered in gasps, but he no longer choked.

What had he swallowed?

I moved my hand to his neck. His skin burned. I moved my hands to his forehead, his shoulder, his arms. Fever inflamed his entire body.

"Caroline, he's feverish. Burning hot."

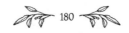

"He will be fine if you give him water," Ransom spoke in an indifferent tone. "This is normal."

"Normal people don't ingest poison," I grumbled, pushing Silas's hair out of his eyes.

"Here." Caroline passed me a mug of water.

Gently, I tilted it to his lips, hoping he could at least swallow. At first, he sputtered, dripping some of it down his chin, but he drank the rest with ease. His breaths steadied after a few silent moments.

"Silas, can you speak?" I whispered.

"Eden." His hoarse voice cut through the crackle of the lanterns.

"Oh, thank God." I leaned my forehead against his shoulder, the heat still burning through his skin.

"I can't see," he mumbled. "Are the lanterns out?"

I whipped my head around to Ransom, where he stood behind Caroline.

"Your sight will come back, my king," he reassured.

Turning back to Silas, I brushed my thumb over his cheek. He leaned into my touch, such a small movement, but filled with so many unspoken words. I wiped away what smelled like vomit from his chin.

"What were you thinking?" I whispered.

"I needed answers."

"Were they worth it?"

He sat silent for a moment, his eyes unseeing. "Yes."

I leaned once more into him, and this time, he wrapped his arms around my shoulders.

"At least warn me next time. You scared me. I thought you were about to die." I sat up again, brushing his sweaty hair out of his face again. He clenched his jaw tight, his skin pale.

He blinked once, then twice, and smiled. "Glad to know you're worried about me. For a while there, I thought you didn't care what happened to me."

I bowed my head, my face burning with embarrassment. "Not really worried. Only a little worried. Normal amount of worry."

"Mhmm, sure." Silas smirked, closing his eyes when I brushed my thumb over his forehead.

"How are you feeling now?"

"Better, now that you're here." His smile caught my attention.

Despite the experience he'd had, he was smiling... About me.

"Silas." Caroline slid her hand on my shoulder. "Can you see yet?"

His eyes fluttered open, finding my own. "Things are starting to come into focus."

"My king." Ransom stepped forward. "I recommend lots of water in the next few hours and plenty of rest tonight. Don't be concerned if you have..." He pursed his lips, searching for the right word. "Unsettling dreams."

Silas nodded. "Thank you."

Ransom bowed, turning to Markus. "I'll let you see our guests back."

Markus bowed to Ransom, avoiding Caroline's cold demeanor. "If you'll follow me."

He started down the dark path, pausing at the door to wait for us. Nash and Caroline walked at the front closest to Markus.

"Come on." I slipped my arm under Silas's and helped him off the narrow bed.

"I can handle it," Silas muttered.

He swayed on his feet, his hands shaky at his sides.

"Si." I reached for him, and he pulled me into a tight hug.

His breath ruffled my hair. "I need to appear strong in front of my people until we reach Guardian's Glade. Help me?"

A question, not a command. I backed up, giving him a slight smile.

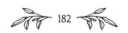

"After you, love," he murmured.

I stepped in line behind Nash, and together we melted into darkness. My last glimpse of the ominous silver flames showed Ransom dousing one of the lanterns, casting his face into partial shadow.

Behind his polite smile, I could've sworn he bared his teeth.

24

SILAS

WALKING BACK TO GUARDIAN'S Glade sent excruciating pain throughout my body. It took everything in me to keep walking forward, a steady expression plastered on my face, though I'm sure it was more of a grimace.

When Caroline shut the doors behind us, I collapsed onto the throne. All of the nervous energy sapped the strength from my bones. Everything ached. And my head pounded, resisting the brightness of the afternoon.

"Nash," I croaked. "Tell me everything."

He stopped his pacing, exhaling before glancing at me. "You'll have to fill in what you saw. But you guzzled the tea and then vomited it into the basket. And then Ransom started chanting in Ancient, and then you sort of..."

"What?" I prompted.

Nash shook his head. "You sort of went rigid. And your eyes grew all black. You were convulsing, and I didn't know what to do."

He ran a hand over his eyes. Eden slid her hand into mine.

"I'm sorry, Si," he whispered.

I shook my head, holding a hand up in the air. "Don't apologize. It was worth it."

"It better have been worth it," Caroline snapped.

"What happened?" Eden asked, eyes searching mine. "What did you *see* when you were..." She swallowed but didn't finish her thought.

I closed my eyes and leaned against the throne that shouldn't belong to me, the throne my father should still be sitting in. "I saw Lycaon."

"What?" Caroline and Nash said simultaneously.

"The wolf from the legend?" Eden asked.

I nodded. "He talked to me about... about what I have to do."

Nash grumbled in frustration. "Well, what do you have to do?"

"Whatever it is, you have us behind you," Caroline offered.

I pushed myself up to a seated position. "He told me that I have what I need to bring light to the darkness. That he's with me."

"Silas," Caroline breathed. "You have Lycaon's *blessing*."

My heart sank, and I couldn't look at her anymore. I turned to Eden, who studied me.

"Whatever he's asked you to do, we're with you." A hint of a smile tugged at her lips.

"Thank you." I turned to Nash and Caroline, both having expressions of elation and disbelief. "Will you two take care of things today? I'm not sure I can."

Caroline beamed. "Of course. I am so proud of you."

If only she knew.

When she and Nash closed the doors behind them, I sank lower into the throne with a sigh, the branches lifting my weight.

"What is it?" Eden knelt in front of me.

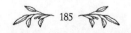

"I'm exhausted."

"You drank poison. You're lucky you aren't worse off."

I couldn't help but smirk at this human who'd already become such a big part of my life here in Arcadia. She slipped into the natural rhythm with only a hiccup.

I hoped she stayed.

"Let's get you to bed, yeah?"

"It's only midday." Despite my protests, I allowed her to lead me to my room. The lamps were still lit, burning golden in the afternoon light. Eden's books were scattered over the desk, a few pages marked with leaves.

I slipped into bed, pulling the blankets over my body.

"If you need me," Eden said, "I'll be working on my Ancient."

I watched her for a while, paying attention to all of her little quirks. How she furrowed her brow when she couldn't make sense of a word, how she muttered under her breath when she struggled to pronounce something, and how she picked at the edges of her nails.

"Eden," I said, voice hoarse.

She perked up, raising an eyebrow in question.

"Come here." I patted the bed.

Marking her place with a dried oak leaf, Eden closed the book and plopped on the bed, sitting cross-legged in front of me.

"What's up?" She pursed her lips, studying me.

For a flash of a second, I considered what I was about to do, the confession I would give. Somehow, I knew and *had* known for a while. But it solidified into a formal emotion. No longer resting beneath the waves of my subconscious but living and breathing in my active thoughts.

I didn't have to be a king around her. I could be me. She sparked a curiosity in me that had been dormant for so long. And though I didn't know her well, I wanted to know her.

"*Ja rakassen,* Eden."

I love you.

It felt easier to say in Ancient, like a secret, despite finally being said out loud.

"I... something..." Eden shook her head. "What's that middle word?"

I smiled, brushing her hair out of her eyes. She had two pieces tied back so that it still hung loose, but the bulk of it out of her eyes.

Those entrancing eyes.

"You'll have to translate for me." I closed my eyes, leaning back, sinking in comfort.

The bed shifted when she moved back to the desk, rifling through the pages.

"Book three," I indicated.

I heard her set the first book down and pick up another. Pages flipped for several seconds. Then silence.

I strained to hear any slight movement. The songbirds whistled above us and a light breeze rustled the leaves and needles.

"*Rakas?*" she repeated.

"*Rakas.*" I opened one eye, heart pounding in my ears.

She stared at the page, shoulders slack and eyebrows furrowed. She closed the book, gazing up at the lantern over the desk but not really seeing it.

"*Ja rakassen,* Eden," I repeated, watching her.

She turned to me now, something like disbelief resting in her eyes.

I wondered for a moment if she didn't feel the same. It sent a wave of ache through my entire body. Had I mistaken her touch, her concern, her care for something more?

"It's okay," I started in an effort to hide my embarrassment. "You

don't have to say anything. I wanted you to know."

"Can I..." Eden spoke like I was something fragile in her hands. "Can I get you anything? Tea, lunch, a rock?"

My face twisted. "A rock?"

"I don't know, I figured you'd read all the books. And it's not like you have many things to keep you entertained in here."

I propped myself up on my elbows, glancing around the room. "I guess I've never thought about it. I've never really been sick or injured where I couldn't leave. And not that I can't leave our—my room now," I amended, rushing to cover the mistake. "I don't want my people to be worried about me. They don't know what kind of threat we're facing, and I need to handle it in the most diplomatic way possible. I don't want them asking questions and committing mutiny because their king can't stand straight without swaying like a reed."

Eden laughed under her breath. "You don't have to explain yourself to me, Silas."

My chest warmed at her words. It wasn't *I love you,* but as good as. And if this arranged marriage wasn't for love, it could at least be for friendship.

But Lycaon, please let it be for love.

"Thank you." I nodded. "Lunch would be great, if that's not taking you away from your studies."

"I need a break anyway." She stretched and then headed to the door.

I sat up. "Oh, and if you find a nice rock..."

A bemused expression crossed her face as she rolled her eyes and she shut the door. I flopped back on the bed, a sigh escaping.

This balance of whatever *this* was... it was tiring. But not how I had expected.

I thought it would have been more difficult to slip into this position of lover, of friend, of constant companion. But it felt like buttoning my robe. Second nature.

But it tired me in other ways. Her fragility frightened me, knowing she couldn't defend with teeth and claws like *virlukos*. It infuriated me to no end that I didn't know how she felt. And I struggled to keep my thoughts positive knowing she might one day choose to leave me and Arcadia behind.

Am I going to be the first King whose pairing selection failed?

I shook the thought from my mind.

I had to stay positive.

I closed my eyes and slipped between memories, thinking of my mother, my father, our faded happy past that eluded me. I thought of the peaceful moments under the trees in the heart of Arcadia, my mother tending her flowers and her children playing behind her. So close to me, yet so far away.

What will she say when you see her again?

I wanted a love like my mother and father's, one filled with laughter and playful moments. I wanted a love both fierce and tender, loyal to a fault.

I heard the door open before Eden spoke. "It's not much."

I leaned forward, eyeing the steaming bowls on a wooden tray. I inhaled the scent of roasted meat and sage. "Venison stew?"

"Mmm." She hummed, setting the platter on the desk and bringing me a bowl. "I hope it tastes okay. When I asked for some, the cooks said it wasn't quite ready. But I thought a bit of protein might be better than carbs on an empty stomach."

"This is perfect, Eden. Thank you."

She climbed into the bed next to me, setting a stone between us.

I picked up a round, smooth basalt rock.

"You asked for a rock, so I did you one better and found one that reminded me of you."

A smile slipped onto my lips. "So I'm round and dark?"

Her eyebrows furrowed, lips parting. "No, more your personality."

"Stony?"

She rolled her eyes, shoving my knee. "No! Smooth and stoic. And well-rounded."

"Uh-huh. Sure. I'll believe you."

She sighed in frustration.

"I'm only teasing, Eden. Thank you." I ran my thumb over the surface of the rock as I scooped a spoonful of potatoes and venison into my mouth.

As I swallowed, my stomach turned. I covered my mouth with my hand and waited to see if it would twist further. I'd assumed I might be sick after the nightshade, but I hoped against it.

They did warn me.

"Silas?" Eden's spoon hovered halfway to her mouth.

"Fine." I nodded.

I forced myself to take another bite, worried I would give it right back up. After swallowing, my mouth grew wet with saliva and my throat burned.

"Silas." Eden set her soup to the side and pulled mine away. "What's going on?"

I stood, licking my lips. I pulled tree branches aside to reveal the small side door I rarely used and slipped out before expelling my stomach onto the forest floor.

And again.

And again.

I glanced around, ensuring no one was nearby. The *micca* peered around the trees and from under the ferns with their golden eyes. Birds flitted in the branches, mocking me.

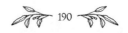

I half-waved toward the *micca* before throwing up again.

"Here." Eden ducked through the side door and passed me a mug of water.

I glanced back up at the *micca*, but they'd disappeared. Or at least they'd gone into concealment like the little hide-and-seek masters they were.

"Thank you." I tipped the edge of the mug to my lips, taking in water.

She shrugged, and I wiped my lips with the back of my arm. "It's not quite holding your hair back, but it's something."

I raised an eyebrow.

She shook her head. "Never mind."

The sound of leaves rustling for a moment snagged my attention.

"What was that?" Eden asked, stepping back behind me.

Despite my eyesight and lifetime in the forest, I couldn't find the source of the rustling. But I knew better than to believe it was nothing.

"*Onni, micca. Rauha ussen,*" I croaked out.

"Hello... something... Peace with you?" Eden stated more as a question than a translation.

I flashed her a smile. "Peace *to* you."

"Who's here?" she asked, eyes scanning the trees.

"I don't know who, but it's the *micca*."

"*Micca?*" Eden's brows furrowed.

I turned my gaze back to the forest in front of us. For a moment, all stayed still. Then, like they were welcomed by my words, a group of *micca* appeared spaced out in a semicircle around us.

"What are they?" Eden slid a hand on my shoulder, the warmth of her touch sending electricity down my spine.

"*Micca.*" I smiled at the closest one.

He was no taller than a large dog, his braided beard dusted the

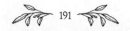

mossy forest floor. He blinked large eyes at me, golden like an autumn sunset. His clothes were mottled browns and greens, mimicking the colors of the undergrowth of the forest, and his slightly pointed ears stuck out beneath his long hat.

"*Onni, je kunan.*" He bowed his head to me and then turned to Eden. "*Je kunin.*"

"What did he say?" Eden whispered, hand tightening on my shoulder.

"He says, hello, my king." I turned my head, her fingers mere inches from my lips. The desire to kiss them nearly overcame me. The idea of her saying she loved me back invaded my thoughts. But then the remembrance of her lack of words only moments ago doused the fire. "My queen."

"Queen." Her voice trembled.

"*Rakas ar lo surin rauha innu feru,*" the *micc* said.

"Love and peace and wild." Eden muttered.

"To Love is the greatest peace in the wild," I translated.

Against my better instinct, I place a light kiss on her knuckles. I stepped forward, letting her hand slip off my shoulder.

Kneeling in front of the *micc*, I met his gaze. "*Kanin sun nahn?*"

"*Rusna.*" The *micc* beamed at me, golden eyes glimmering in the afternoon sun that filtered through the foliage.

"*Rauha*, Rusna." I held my right hand over my heart, bowing to him.

He bowed low, beard rustling over the moss and ferns at his bare feet.

I stood, turning to Eden. "He says his name is Rusna."

"What do they..." Her question hung, unsaid.

"They kind of do their own thing. They're still pretty secretive and isolated even with us, but the *micca* are the forest caretakers."

"Like park rangers and game wardens?"

A chuckle escaped me. "Not quite. If *virlukos* protect humans and lead them back to safety, *micca* care for the forest and ensure things work how they should."

"Like gardeners?"

I shrugged. "Something like that."

With gracefulness I hadn't expected, Eden knelt in front of Rusna, who stepped back. His face tilted upward, showing off his larger nose and odd eyes, his skin tanned by the sun. Eden held out her hands. Slowly, Rusna slid his small, wrinkled hands into hers, his golden eyes watching hers.

"*Rauha us sen.*" She stumbled over the Ancient words.

"*Ussen,*" I corrected.

Rusna beamed and then bowed low again, his beard brushing against his feet. "*Rauha ussen, cara e micca.*"

Eden turned to me, eyebrows pinched together.

With a chuckle, I licked my lips. "Peace to you, friend of the *micca.*"

Something about seeing Eden smiling at Rusna, bridging the gap between humans and the magic of *Shaconage,* brought so much hope and courage to my spirit.

I only hoped it would last.

25

EDEN

LONG AFTER RUSNA AND his friends had left, I stared into the forest where they had disappeared.

To think, after nineteen years of living in the foothills of the Appalachian Mountains. After centuries—millennia—of people living in these hills, these creatures, the micca, stayed hidden.

"Eden," Silas hummed in a sing-song voice. "You can't stand here forever."

I turned towards him. He'd worried me. He'd been so sick before, so weak. When he'd come out here, I worried I'd have to call Asa to do something.

Instead, I'd met an entirely new species.

"How many other creatures have I missed?"

His eyebrows drew together. "What do you mean?"

"How many other species have I been unaware of? How many are there out in the world?" Curiosity danced on my tongue.

"In the world?" He ran a hand through his hair and down his neck.

"I can't say. I haven't been farther west than the Mississippi River."

"But to there? How many live between here and there that I've never dreamed of existing?"

His face softened into a smile. "Countless."

My breath escaped me.

Countless.

And I had been content with my ferns and coyote tracks when magic, *micca,* and *virlukos* existed.

How had I never known?

But in a way, I *had* known. I believed in werewolves with steadfast faith when everyone else believed it to be a myth. All of those folklore stories I had clung to, the renaissance festivals where people dressed like humanoid fauns and five-foot tall fairies... Were they based in truth?

"There's a pack," Silas started, shifting his weight. "Another kingdom of *virlukos* that live in Kentucky. They're migratory, so they don't have a specific place. Father brought us—Caroline, Nash, and me—after our mother had passed. Elder Macon had assumed the role of leader in our father's absence. And we met our distant cousins."

"What are they like?" I asked.

He shrugged, his robe fluttering with the motion. "Much like us. But they're proficient at hiding their kingdom in plain sight. And they eat feasts every day. They also interact more with humans than Arcadia. But their mountains are tinted orange and stunningly beautiful."

"Will you take me someday?"

He smiled. "Someday, *pilukos.*"

"What did you say?"

He stepped to me, sliding his hands around my waist, tugging me closer. I was swept up in a sea of evergreen, mischief glinting behind a carefully crafted mask. His breath tickled my ear.

His words from earlier drifted across my mind, making me feel chosen rather than assigned to be someone's wife, but the fear of not being enough dimmed the fire that burned in my ribcage. I wondered if his love would be enough to make me worthy of a crown.

"Someday, little wolf."

There was much to discuss over dinner. Silas and I hosted Caroline and Nash in Guardian's Glade so he could talk about Nyx and his plans for the winter. Most of it, I didn't understand since their ways of life weren't known to me yet.

"I plan to keep an eye over the waterfall during the cold snaps to make sure the gate stays open for us. As for *Joulo*, it's on the twenty-first of the month. We could choose to celebrate early or wait until after."

"Why not the day of?" Nash asked after taking a sip of his tea.

Silas shook his head. "If Nyx hasn't moved before then, he'll plan for the solstice. I feel like he'd want to make a show of it. And I'd rather be on top of it that day than distracted by feast preparations."

"And if what the *ugal* said was a ruse?" Caroline set her bowl down. "What then?"

"Since when do you not trust the creatures we serve? The ones that serve us in return?"

I stuffed my mouth full of stew, wanting to avoid confrontation as much as possible.

"We can't be too careful, Silas," Caroline murmured while staring down at her bowl.

"I'm not a pup anymore, Caroline. I understand that better than anyone. But life must continue despite our desires to freeze time."

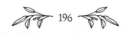

The table grew quiet. The birdsong sounded unsettling with the brewing tension between the siblings.

"Si," Nash started. "It's not that you aren't being careful or trying to delay the inevitable, but *ugal* are cunning. What if he delivered false information in exchange for something?"

Silas scoffed, swirling his potatoes around in his bowl. "Inevitable. What do you know about the inevitable? What do you know about life and death to make you an expert?"

"Silas–" Caroline began.

"What do you know of destiny and worthiness?" He snapped like a broken bone. "What do you know of immortality?"

Nash shook his head. "Brother, you aren't making sense."

"The story," I muttered.

"What?" Caroline pointed a gaze at me. "What story?"

Silas sighed, leaning back and dropping his head back so he could gaze at the foliage above the Glade drawing his siblings' attention. "*Lo Sain e lo Feru.*"

"What about the legend?" Caroline turned back to me.

"I studied the books like you told me," I pointed out, hoping not to draw her frustration onto me. "And there was a story in Ancient with a smoky illustration. Silas translated it and–"

"And you think Lycaon received immortality for his sacrifice?" Nash asked.

I couldn't tell what they were thinking from their expressions. They were all so difficult for me to read.

"Lycaon told me so himself," Silas said. "Ransom confirmed it last night."

"Last night?" Caroline shook her head. "But you talked to Lycaon this morning. How could–"

Silas interrupted. "You know how the Seers work. Don't tell me

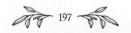

Markus has you fooled."

"Don't bring Markus into this," Caroline hissed.

"Why shouldn't I?" Silas pointed a hand at her. "If the lineage is in jeopardy, do you really want a Seer's blood mixed in?"

Caroline slammed a hand on the table. Our cups rattled. "You're one to talk! You're marrying a human, for Lycaon's sake. And you want to risk it with *her* blood?"

"Don't you think I've already thought of that?" Silas shouted.

The table grew silent, and I was painfully aware of Nash's eyes averting from mine. My face flushed from embarrassment.

When Iain had bowed at my feet and that night passed by in a blur, I hadn't been thinking of lineage, only the fact that I had been chosen to live in a fairytale. But with marriage, I realized I risked the royal line by being human.

Here I was, enamored by the world, and Silas had to think about heirs.

"I can't help that Father chose this for me. You know that I have no choice." Silas sighed, defeated.

I recalled his words from earlier in the afternoon, words confessing his deepest emotions. I hadn't responded then because I wasn't sure what to say. Attraction maybe, but love? It was an emotion I wasn't super familiar with.

So how could I respond to that? Promising in words that might not prove true?

But was all of that a lie for my comfort?

My heart hung heavy in my chest.

Maybe this wasn't love, but maybe it could be. Someday.

But this—realizing that he didn't choose this, didn't *want* me—why did it feel so painful?

I cleared my throat, willing my voice to not betray my hurt. "I'll

leave you all alone... to talk. Humans aren't really good at managing frozen waterfalls."

"Eden." Silas sighed. He grasped my hand, but I pulled away and slipped my fingers through his. I slid through his bedroom door with ease. I noticed the lit lanterns and the Compendium underneath a pile of Common to Ancient translation books. I picked up my leather journal, fingering the familiar pages.

I had dozens of drawings in the pages, things of the natural world. But the *micca*, now *that* was something I wanted to add to my journal. I wondered if Rusna would be willing to sit for his portrait.

With a deep breath, I slipped out the side door into the darkening forest. The blue-colored lightning bugs drifted around the fronds. The half-moon glittered through the leaves of the trees high above me. And somewhere, the sound of running water pulled my attention.

Stepping through the trees, ducking under branches and around underbrush, I found my way to the banks of a wide river. It gurgled along, the inky surface reflecting the moon. I pushed aside my fear and the thoughts of the day I'd been swept away by the Little River. Things had changed, and this was a different river.

I watched the blue beetles glide around as if dancing to the melody of the water. And I realized they were too big to be beetles.

Careful not to disturb the creatures, I sat on a boulder that jutted out in the river, wary not to scoot too close to the edge as I didn't want a repeat of my childhood.

I pulled out my journal and the pen clipped to it. As my eyes adjusted to the lighting, I could see more than light around the glowing creatures. Body parts, legs, arms, wings.

I must be dreaming.

Across the river, movement caught my eye. A figure, no bigger than a chicken, had rolled out from under the undergrowth. Its large iridescent eyes blinked once, like a lizard's eyes, as it climbed up another boulder in the shallow water. There, it sat cross-legged and straight-backed as it watched me.

A voice croaked from the creature, and it took a few moments before it dawned on me that the creature spoke Ancient.

"*Ja doleo?*" I asked, hoping the creature would repeat itself in its frog-like tone.

"*Onni, kunin e virlukos.*" The creature tilted its smooth head sideways.

"*Onni. Rauha ussen,*" I whispered.

"*Ar lo surin slava usavi e lo feru.*"

"Slau wah?" I repeated.

"Honor," a male voice spoke in English behind me.

I nearly dropped my journal in panic when I faced Markus.

"I'm sorry, my queen." He bowed his head. "I didn't mean to startle you."

I fumbled for words, glancing back at the creature, but his eyes remained on me. I turned back to the Seer. "It's Eden."

He motioned to the rock next to me.

"Please. Sit." I regained my composure.

Markus gazed at the moon and the stars shining around it. "The Princess is bright this evening."

"The Princess?" I followed his gaze, squinting up at the stars.

"There are sixteen stars depicting the Princess who'd been tied to the rock to be eaten by a river monster. The bottom star and the far right stars are her chains." He indicated the stars above us. "But instead of greeting death, a hero saves her. And she reigns, beautiful and beloved." He turned to me. "The *ugal* said it is the greatest honor to have you in the wild."

I turned to the amphibious creature whose lips stretched wide,

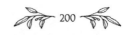

eyes blinking sideways. *"Bene, pila cara."*

The creature bowed low, and with one leap, he plunged into the dark waters, a ripple the only sign he had been present.

"Amazing," I breathed.

"I forget how little humans know."

"More like how little we're worth," I mumbled.

He hummed in response.

For a moment, the croaking of the frogs swelled, the crickets chirped, and the flutter and buzzing of little glowing wings rustled over the babble in the river. And I wondered what the people of Arcadia thought of the intrusive human barging in on their peaceful kingdom, bringing war to their front doors.

"You are worth much more than you believe," Markus spoke.

The frogs quieted.

"How can I be? I am nothing in comparison to you or your people."

He smiled at the Princess constellation again. "People see much more in you. They see past the veil. They see what you cannot." He turned his gaze to me again. "And when the time comes for you to be bound to the rock, you will emerge and reign, both beautiful and beloved."

26

SILAS

I WATCHED EDEN CLOSE the door to our room—my room—then melted to the table with a groan.

"Way to go." Nash patted my shoulder. "I think that sold the whole marriage and giving up the human life thing."

"No, it's my fault," Caroline mumbled. "I shouldn't have pushed, it's..." She growled in frustration. "It's unfair to you, all this pressure. Eden is a nice person, but she's *human*. Why would Father choose her? When he knows that you can't go against his word, why would he choose her over any woman in Arcadia?"

"I asked him," I said. "He said to trust him, so that's what I'm doing."

"I know." She laid her hand on my folded arms. "I know. And I'm sorry, Si. I'm confused by all of this. And then when you brought up Markus–"

"He's cute, by the way," Nash commented, talking with his mouth full.

Caroline rolled her eyes. "At least act like a prince on occasion."

"Caroline." I sat up, placing my free hand on top of hers. "I want you to be happy. And if Markus makes you happy, then I look forward to having him for dinner." I took a deep breath, the words falling out before I could stop them. "I'm jealous of your freedom, your ability to pick whomever you choose. I didn't have anyone particular in mind before, but having an option–"

"I know, and I'm sorry." She smiled at me. "If it helps, I don't think Markus is interested."

"*Please*," Nash scoffed, setting down his empty bowl. "Like this morning was any indicator."

"What do you mean?" Caroline seemed bewildered.

I scratched my forehead. "Come on. You didn't notice it? He acted like an injured pup when we were leaving. And you *sounded* pretty angry. I bet you *looked* even worse."

Her jaw dropped, and she smacked my arm. "You would think I'd receive civility from the crowned King and Prince, but no. I am insulted."

Nash smirked at me, and I finished my stew.

"You should go talk to her." Caroline set her bowl down. "Eden will understand, but you have to be gentle about it. She didn't choose this either."

I exhaled between my teeth. "I know... It's... I told her I loved her today."

Nash choked on tea.

"You what?" Caroline's eyes widened.

"I wanted to be honest! After this morning, things kind of fell into perspective for me. And I don't know, it sort of slipped out in Ancient, and then she translated and brought me lunch."

"What did she say?" Caroline asked.

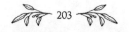

"Nothing. I told her that she didn't have to say anything, no pressure. And she brought me lunch along with basalt."

"She brought you a rock?" Nash laughed.

"A *basalt* rock," I corrected. "She said it reminded her of me."

"Hard?" Nash laughed. "Stony?"

"Silas." Caroline sighed. "You need to work on your tact."

"If she stays, then I don't need tact with women, right?"

"That's *if* she stays." Nash frowned. "She did compare you to a rock."

"*Talk* to her." Caroline motioned to my bedroom door behind the throne.

I stood. "Talk. That's all it is, talking."

I took one last look at my siblings before slipping through the door. The dim room had been lit with lanterns in the deepening dark of the evening. I turned to the bed first, wondering if Eden had turned in early, but it was still made. She wasn't at the desk either, and her journal had gone missing from the stack of books.

There wasn't another heartbeat in the room besides my own.

I turned in a circle, eyes finding the side door.

My heart quickened its pace as I stepped into the night.

Lycaon, please don't let me lose her.

Please don't let her run away.

Ghost beetles had settled for the evening, lounging on their beds in flowers and ferns. A barred owl hooted, shrilling in the autumn air. Somewhere, a *micc* played a flute serenade for the trees while the crickets and frogs sang along.

My eyes drifted from side to side, wondering where she'd gone.

Water.

The faint sound of a splash reached my ears.

I recalled summer evenings when the weather stayed humid late

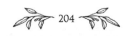

into the night. I would take Nash and Caroline to the Great River, where it ran deep and wide enough to swim.

The thought of Eden in the water startled me. Both the image of her swimming without a robe *and* nearly drowning in the Little River as a child assaulted my mind.

When I inched closer to the bank, I heard voices.

Who is with her?

What is with her?

My heart pounded.

I ducked around a tree and spotted Markus sitting on a rock a few feet away from Eden. She had her journal in hand, and her eyes were fixed on the stars. I glanced to see the Princess shining bright above the river.

As my panic subsided, I took a deep breath. He had to hear my heartbeat, knowing I worried for her. But Markus gazed at her unflinchingly.

"And when the time comes for you to be bound to the rock," he said, "you will emerge and reign, both beautiful and beloved."

I stepped into the open between them on the bank. "Good evening, Markus." I bowed my head in his direction. "May I?" I motioned to Eden.

"Of course," he said while he stood. "And if I may ask, my king. Caroline...?"

I couldn't stop the smile from edging out of my stoic professionalism. "She's forgiven you already. She should still be in Guardian's Glade if you want to speak with her yourself. I'm sure she would be delighted to see you."

Markus stared at me, open-mouthed.

A chuckle rumbled in my chest. "Go. You might miss her."

With a bow, he sped off, nearly jogging through the trees. I watched his figure disappear into the dark before turning to Eden and assuming Markus's seat.

"Before you say anything," she shifted her body to me, "I know you have a duty to your people. And I know I'm not your first choice. Why would I be? I'm only human. So you don't have to apologize. I understand."

What a strange creature she is.

Here I sat trying to apologize for my hurtful words despite the situation, and she consoled me. But I needed to apologize, to make things right, to make her understand why and *how* I felt.

"Eden, I truly am sorry. My words were unkind and harsh, considering you haven't had much of a choice either."

"I could've left."

"Would you have left?" I feared that I wouldn't like her answer. Even worse, she stayed silent for eons while I listened to the steady beat of her heart.

She shook her head. "I don't think I could ever leave this behind. Not now."

"But what about your home, the life you left behind? Are you willing to give that up to stay here? Because this..." I opened my arms, palms facing the sky. "It's forever or not at all—no one can know about Arcadia for the safety of the kingdom and my people."

"*Our* people," she said, and her words made my heart stutter. "At the beginning, I might have thought differently. And I still might miss my human family and the luxury of technology. Also coffee. But I have a family here, or at least I'm starting to have one. And I couldn't leave, not when there's still so much to learn, so much to explore. I mean, I spoke to a lizard in an Ancient forest language."

I raised an eyebrow. "What did the *ugal* say?"

"It called me a friend of the wild and then said that it's the greatest honor to have me here. *Me*, an honor."

"It is a great honor to have a human amongst us." I smiled at her, wondering how good her night vision was. I could see her as clear as day.

Her hands gripped the edges of her journal even when her shoulders relaxed, rising and falling with her breath. And her eyes, moving from the river to the Princess constellation above us and to me.

"What good is a human?"

I stood, stepping to the rock where she had perched. "Oh, humans do much good for us forest creatures. And they're so powerful."

She scoffed. "More powerful than a shapeshifter?"

"Equal in power and strength. I haven't had much experience with humans, given my status. But you are by far one of the bravest I've met. The river, the forest, even the wind is in awe of you, *pilukos*."

She shook her head but said nothing.

"Hey," I whispered.

She didn't move.

"*Onni*," I tried again.

Still, she didn't move.

Gently, I brushed her face with my hand, lifting her chin. Her eyes watered in the light of the moon. "You are worth so much more than you believe."

Without a second thought, I pressed my lips against hers, knowing full well that I could be rejected.

Everything in me exploded, the sky erupting in sparks and dazzling light, like the stars themselves were all burning out at once. My heart the wind and my brain the river, my body the forest rooted in place.

And I realized why: she was kissing me back.

My fingers slipped through her wild hair, my thumb finding its place below her ear. Her hand found my arm, holding me tight.

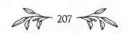

I pulled back, heart shuddering in my chest.

She laughed.

"What?" My voice came out rougher than usual.

She shook her head with a small smile. "Don't tell me I'm dreaming. I never want to wake up from this. Lizards and a kiss from the wolf king?"

Laughter bubbling up from deep inside of me, and I pulled her close. She tucked her head against my neck and shoulder, burrowing into my arms. I held her tight, kissing the top of her head like I had done it a thousand times before.

"You make me feel like Silas again," I mumbled into her hair.

She hummed against my neck, her breath warm against my skin.

This was something new. All of it. This weightlessness... I hadn't felt like that since I was a child.

Since before my father died.

Since before my mother died.

When everything was still whole.

Is this what love is?

If love bound up the broken things, I never wanted to be without it. If love stitched up the loose threads of my soul, I would never let it run out of string. If love filled the cracks of dry soil, I wanted rainy days forever.

Eden didn't want to wake up from this dream, and neither did I.

27

EDEN

I STARED AT THE tree branches swaying overhead.

I could still feel Silas's lips on mine.

We had walked back to his room hand in hand, and I almost fell too many times from the dizziness of the whole experience. It's not that I hadn't kissed anyone before, but never with such intent. Never with such tension.

Silas had said goodnight and fallen asleep. But my mind raced at the thought of him, so I lay very much awake. And though it meant no nightmares, a girl can only stare at dark branches of trees for so long.

I wonder if Asa is still at Mender's Heath.

The thought of Arcadia at dark had scared me my first few nights. But I recognized the safety here, the structure, the sense of community.

I edged out of the bed trying not to wake Silas. He had exhausted himself with the nightshade incident.

I slipped out the door into Guardian's Glade. It, too, slumbered in silence, not hosting any courts or meetings or feasts. Its lanterns had been doused hours before, and only the light of the moon and stars illuminated the path before me.

I gazed upwards, noting that the Princess constellation had moved quite a bit in the sky. I thought about Markus's words, shivering at the thought of being tied to a rock.

Did he mean it figuratively? Or am I literally going to be tied to a rock?

I frowned at the thought, wondering if I'd missed a strange wolf ritual in my brief time researching. I had barely read through the first quarter of the Compendium with its hundreds of dusty pages.

I opened one of the double doors at the front of Guardian's Glade, closing it behind me. The temperature had dropped a bit, and I could smell the rain headed our way. The crickets chirped along with the back-and-forth call of the owls, a midnight symphony only for me.

The pathways ahead glimmered with soft yellow light. I caught a whiff of something sweet in the air. Crouching to get a better view, I noticed small bell-shaped petals underneath the deep green alternating leaves.

Solomon's Seal.

For wisdom, peace, and healing.

Straightening, I realized that plants lined the entire path. But here, in the magic that Arcadia protected, they glowed in the dark.

"I will never *not* be amazed by this," I whispered to the forest.

I picked my way through the trees, coming to the quiet room of Mender's Heath. Two bodies lay sleeping on beds, both in wolf form. I slipped through the door, not wanting to wake them.

My eyes traveled over the room's contents. A shelf filled with things stood straight across from the door, flanked by two beds. A basin of water, a pile of flickering embers, a simple desk, a mortar and pestle, and a thick book decorated the room. But I didn't see the head healer.

Maybe he went home for the night. Maybe there's a night shift.

"*Ruaha*, Eden."

I bit back a startled shout as I turned to face Asa. He stood in the doorway, lantern in hand.

"*Ja doleo.* I didn't mean to frighten you."

I shook my head, trying to settle my brain for long enough to find words.

"Are you having trouble sleeping again?" He swept past me, evergreen robes brushing my ankles.

"Again?" I repeated.

"Your husband mentioned you had trouble sleeping. Something about nightmares."

The word husband had me frozen in place. "We aren't married yet."

"Are you thinking of leaving?"

"Well, no."

"Then he will be your husband eventually, no?" Asa turned away from me, rifling through his herbs that rested in bowls, bottles, sachets, and anything else that could carry a plant. A set of dishes sat nestled in the corner of one shelf across from a kettle.

"I suppose so."

"You sound disconsolate. Would you like some tea?" He lifted the kettle from its place with a grunt, settling the thing on the coals. He poured the water and turned back to his desk of herbs.

"It's not that I'm upset. I–" I stopped short, not knowing how to put it into words. "I've been dreaming of finding this place for nearly fifteen years. This... this *life* is something I've dreamed of for as long as I can remember."

In a way, it was true. I couldn't remember much before that fateful day in the Little River. And this had been my only real dream.

"But you're still discontent." It wasn't a question.

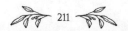

"I don't understand it. I don't think I expected... I *know* I didn't expect to come here and marry a king. Silas is wonderful, but I–"

The words lodged in my throat.

I can't do this.

"My dear." Asa turned, giving me his full attention. "No one is ready for marriage. Even if a person thinks she is ready, she never knows what to expect. She only knows who she is at that moment, and if one has enough resolve and knows that marriage means choosing their partner despite everything life deals... Then she is as ready as she will ever be."

I set my gaze on the corner of the closest bed. "But what if she isn't good enough?"

"*Autem.*" Asa chuckled along with the word. "Are any of us ever good enough? Who are you not good enough for? Our late King Iain— may his spirit find peace among trees—considered you good enough. Our Silas considers you good enough. Are you standing in the way of yourself?"

I squeezed my eyes shut. He'd been so gentle that first afternoon in Arcadia, tending my bruises with salves and putting another poultice on my head where I'd fallen in the forest. He'd talked like he knew how difficult this transition would be for me, knowing that whatever happened wouldn't be simple. But I couldn't look at him now.

Because he was right. Me and my reservations held me hostage. Only me and my doubts held me back.

"I am old, *je kunin*. Old enough that I've married, had my own children, and my children have given me grandchildren. I am old enough to know when reluctance is really the mask for self-doubt and fear."

He turned, pulling the kettle off of the embers. Setting it on the desk, he pulled out a cup and spooned in some tea. He hesitated, then pulled a small jar down from the top shelf and tossed in a pinch. After capping and replacing the jar, he poured a small amount of steaming water over the tea. He gave the cup a quick swirl, and poured the rest of the water, filling the mug to the brim.

Asa lifted the kettle again, returning it to its home. "My dear, your hesitation is not uncalled for, nor is it uncommon. But you have the spirit of a wolf inside of you." He turned back to me. "You may not feel it like the rest of us, but we can hear your heart beating in time to ours. You are one of us, even when you don't feel it. You are."

A hot tear slid down my cheek. I swiped it away as Asa passed me the cup.

"I put a bit of valerian root in your tea. That should help you fall asleep."

I inhaled the steam, the smell of woods after a rain filling my senses. I took an experimental sip.

I swallowed the soothing liquid. "I wish things were simple."

"Nothing beautiful is ever simple. Life is artfully complex even when things seem plain on the outside."

He whistled a strange melody, and a bird I'd only seen in photos perched on his finger.

"Is that an Eastern Whip-poor-will?" I tilted my head sideways, observing it.

Asa bowed his head. "Such a small thing, simple buff coloring, and yet..." Asa stroked the bird's back, and it began to sing its haunting song. "Its call is seen as an omen of death. A simple thing turned massively complex, haunting *and* beautiful."

The bird flew away, flourishing its wings as it disappeared into the dark of the night. Asa turned his eyes on me again. His eyes, once warm and kind, now had a strange shade to them. My stomach churned.

Trying to maintain my calm appearance, I downed the rest of my tea, chewing on the leaves I'd sipped. I passed him the cup with a nod. "Thank you for the tea, Asa."

"Of course, my dear. You know where to find me if you need anything else."

Taking that as my cue to leave, I hurried off, knowing that the increase of my heart rate betrayed my anxiety.

How am I to hide my emotions in this place?

My heart was practically on my robe sleeve while I rushed back to Silas's room. I relaxed my shoulders when the door shut behind me. Silas's steady breathing and soft snoring filled the air. I slipped back under the covers and lay on my side.

Sleep, sleep, sleep.

I tried closing my eyes, though sleep stayed far from me. A bird rustled in the branches over the bed, causing me to jerk my eyes open. The same darkness met me, shadows of branches shifting.

The branches dissolved into a clearing with a stone building in the center. Strange carvings adorned the structure.

Picking up the hem of my navy robes, I moved to stand in the center of the gazebo-like place. I lifted my gaze to the ceiling, words written in a language I didn't understand. Between the words, images of wolves and men shifted like they were alive.

The air moved around me, and I was aware of another presence. Turning, I caught sight of a tail swishing around the outer wall. The figure of a white wolf slipped into view, his massive paws making a sound as he met me in the center of the building.

"My daughter." His voice rumbled in my chest, reverberating off of the walls and ceiling around us. "Do not be afraid."

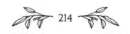

I knew he could hear my heartbeat. I knew he could read my thoughts in an instant. But his words softened the edges of my fear. He smelled of juniper and mint, something so familiar.

"Eden," he hummed.

"Lycaon," I breathed, the word escaping my lips before I even thought it.

He smiled at me. "Dear one, rauha e Arcadia. Be at peace."

I stepped forward, holding my hand out. With such gentleness, Lycaon pushed his large head against my palm, his fur sliding between my fingers. The similarities to my meeting Iain were not lost on me.

"Welcome home, daughter of Arcadia, spirit of the wild."

I couldn't take my eyes off of him. I was interacting with a god, the one who shifted virlukos history, dividing it into two pieces. And he comforted me, a human.

"You desire to belong." His words were soft and strong all at once.

"Yes."

"It is before you already; in this forest. In this kingdom lies your answer."

"But how will I know?"

"You will find your way. One way or another, you will find your place, little queen."

My heart jumped at the mention. "Will I be married to Silas?"

"Only you and Silas can say."

Lycaon lifted his head, looking out at the clearing. Figures began to emerge from the undergrowth, micca and ugal and kuslar and other creatures I hadn't seen or imagined.

"It's almost time for my departure," he rumbled. "I have plans for you, daughter. For hope and for your future. Call on me, and I will answer you. Maybe not in voice, but I will listen and answer."

He shook his coat and phased into a man made of sunshine

through the rain clouds, refracting every color imaginable. The smell of mint and juniper lingered. He smiled, and the tears ran freely down my cheeks.

"Daughter, vener e rauha."

28

SILAS

I.
Silas.
Wake up.

Disoriented from the nightmares about my father with details I couldn't remember, I blinked back the sleep in my eyes. The sky behind the trees faded to a shade of dried cornflower, misty in the early morning. The rusty scent in the air reassured me that autumn colors were coming soon, winter cold on its heels.

I shifted on my elbows, forcing my face away from my pillow. Eden's knees angled to the side, her posture stiff and wary.

"What is it?" I rotated my body and pulled myself to sit up.

I noticed the tears that streaked down her face.

Another nightmare with Nyx.

"What happened? What did he say?"

She shook her head, biting the inside of her lip. She turned her gaze away, unfocused.

When she said nothing, I rubbed her knee. "You're safe here, Eden. I promised on my life that no harm would come to you."

Maybe a poor choice of words considering what I would have to do soon to ensure the protection of Arcadia, but I meant it. I meant every word. I would give my life away before I saw Eden in pain.

"Si," she breathed. "I saw Lycaon."

My hand stilled, goose flesh climbing up my arms and snaking down my legs and spine.

"You... You *saw* him?"

It wasn't that I thought she lied—why would she?—but the thought of Lycaon visiting a human unsettled me.

She nodded. "He met me in a stone structure and told me that I'd find where I belonged." She pointed her gaze at her hands twisted in her lap. "And he phased in front of me. I-I can't explain it."

"You saw his human form." The realization took longer to process. My eyes widened. "What did he look like as a man?"

"Bright. Radiant. Iridescent."

I could almost picture it. But in the end, Lycaon's human form looked too much like my own father, and a tide of grief welled in me again.

I cleared my throat. "So he said you would find where you belong? In Arcadia?"

Eden shrugged. "I think so, maybe. I guess I have to find out."

She grew silent for a while. I thought about hidden meanings in Lycaon's words. He spoke in riddles, and I wasn't certain he meant tangible answers.

"Eden." I ran my hand along her knee and thigh. "Are you sure he wasn't confirming *Sarva*? That you would find peace here and call this place home?"

She met my gaze. "I think I already call Arcadia home."

I opened my mouth to speak, but no words formed. Had she changed her mind so quickly? Was it the kiss from last night? Or was it something Markus had said to her?

I focused all my attention to my ears, the rustle of the blankets, the swaying of the tree branches above us, the first birds waking, the rippling of the creek, Eden's heart beating in time with my own.

Eden's heart is beating in time with my own.

Such a simple thing had such a heavy impact on my body, mind, and spirit.

"Silas, can I tell you something?"

"I'm listening," I mumbled.

"Last night, I went to Asa, and he gave me valerian to fall asleep."

I straightened but forced myself to stay quiet.

"He sensed my distress, and I realized something." She licked her chapped lips. "I'm scared. I am so afraid of messing up, of not being enough for you or Arcadia, of failing to be the Queen and wife you need. I went searching for answers. I arrived here and detested you. You acted arrogant and biased against humans. And worst of all, blamed me for exposing Arcadia before allowing me the chance to speak."

I started to speak, but she continued, clawed hands pushing her hair back.

"And I was starting to tolerate you when Iain bowed in front of me. I didn't know what was going on, but it happened. And then you were arguing with him, your siblings, and everyone else about me being human and about your heirs. And if that wasn't enough to stress a person, there's still the threat of imminent danger from Nyx, thinking that *I* might have brought him in. Not to mention, I met creatures that shouldn't exist and discovered there are other *virlukos* in Kentucky, making my world expand in a thousand different directions. And then there are prophecies and hallucinations and visions and nightmares and Seers, and all of it is so..."

She inhaled and held her breath for a moment. "Overwhelming! I am so overwhelmed. By you, by myself. I don't know. But I'm so scared that I'm going to fail. And I'm scared because I think I might come to love you, and I don't know what that will do to me." She wilted, covering her face with her hands. "I don't think I can do this, Silas. I can't do this to you or your family. I won't allow you to end your lineage or–"

I leaned over, wrapping my arms around her slender shoulders, her hair tickling my neck. I had heard every inflection of her voice, every tremor, every sped-up heartbeat, and all the meaning behind her words.

"Eden," I rasped. "You are more than worthy."

I pulled back enough to run my thumb across her cheek, wiping away her tears and inhaling the scent of tea that lingered around her. "This has been messy and stressful, but that doesn't mean it's not worth trying." I searched her eyes for any hint of her emotions. Her eyes welled up in the blue light of dawn. "I want you, Eden. I want you forever."

"Forever is a long time," she gasped through tears.

I grinned. "I want to love you for a long, *long* time."

She buried her face in my shoulder, so I held her tight, rocking her. It's what my mother used to do when I was a pup and got scared or hurt. She'd scoop me into her arms, whispering comforting words in Ancient and rock me until I fell asleep.

I missed those days.

I missed her.

I wondered for a moment how heavy the grief had been for my father after her passing.

Lycaon, is it ever easier?

I brushed back Eden's hair as a breeze wrapped around us in a

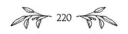

swirl. A voice whispered on the wind in Ancient.

Us rakas ar rikas, lo surin rauha autem vaara.

To love is to live, the greatest peace and danger.

The wind had answered my thoughts.

"Did you hear that?" I sat up.

"Hear what?" Eden croaked.

I paused for a moment, straining my ears for anything out of the ordinary. When nothing suspicious made noise, I shook my head. "Nothing. It must've been the wind."

Eden burrowed back down into the covers and pulled me with her. Despite having spent the past several nights in the same bed, I hadn't been so conscious of her body this close to mine. I always had other things clouding my thoughts, but now the sky had cleared and I *only* noticed her body close to me.

Her legs brushed against my knees, and I pulled back so I wouldn't touch her. My skin burned hot under the blanket. Her hand found my own, fingers tangling with mine.

Her eyes closed. She took one long, deep breath and exhaled, her shoulders relaxing. I brushed her hair behind her ear, and Eden's face softened like my touch alone comforted her. It made lying next to her more unbearable. I only had so much self-control.

"You know," I started, the tension rising in my limbs, "you're kind of cute when you ramble."

Her eyes shot open, and she raised an eyebrow. "You think my incessant rambling is endearing? You must be nuts."

I sat up, trying to push away the tension in my gut. "Speaking of nuts, are you hungry?"

She chuckled. "I could eat, I guess. Are *you* hungry?"

"Please. I'm part wolf. I'm always ravenous."

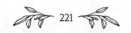

29

EDEN

WATCHING SILAS IN THE kitchen was like watching a nine-year-old make breakfast. He didn't know where anything should be stored, and when he did find the right bowl or pot, he'd make so much noise that I swore it would wake the whole forest.

"Silas!" I laughed, whispering his name. "You have to be quiet."

He gasped. "Do you... Do you think there are wolves in these parts?"

I rolled my eyes. Something new had control over his body, like all the stress had dissipated for a morning, and I didn't want to spoil it. This version of him was special, and maybe only a handful of people had seen this Silas.

"Silly little king." I pushed myself up onto the tabletop, my feet dangling inches from the floor.

He hummed, a smile on the edge of his lips as he made his way to me. He fit his knees between mine and leaned his arms against the table on either side of me.

"You pretty little queen." He smirked, kissing me with such gentleness. My stomach turned, loving how relaxed he seemed.

It shouldn't have surprised me again and again, but the image of the Silas I'd met my first day in Arcadia and the goofy guy standing in front of me were almost two separate people. He moved back, smiling at me.

"So what are we having for breakfast this morning?" I asked breathlessly.

He raised his eyebrow at me.

"Ah." I nodded. "My apologies. What are we having for breakfast this morning, *your majesty*?"

He rolled his eyes, nudging me. "Har har. Nothing a king can't handle."

He pushed back from the table. After pulling the kettle from its hook, he filled it with water and placed it over the remains of a fire. I watched while he systematically built and lit a fire, causing small flames to climb around the wood.

Leaving the kettle and fire, he tugged a large jar off the shelf, his muscles tightening from the weight of it. Silas pried the lid away, revealing pounds of oats. He grabbed one of the bowls he'd found earlier and spooned several scoops into the bowl.

"So tell me what life is like for a human." He glanced at me and returned the jar, grabbing an apple and a small knife.

I shook my head, raking a hand through my unruly hair. "Nothing special."

He stopped, eyes finding mine. "I'd have to disagree."

I swayed my feet under the table. "It's just life. It's not magical like this."

He dropped his hand with the knife to the table. "Life is magical in and of itself. You are teaching me that every day. It doesn't need shapeshifters to be special or important."

I focused on the fire, wood starting to crackle. "Fine then. It's life. It's education in concrete buildings in straight rows of desks. It's having the pressure to plan your entire life before you're even considered an adult. It's–"

My words stopped when I remembered my life before all of this. "It's music playing so loud your heart matches pace. It's witnessing sunrises, sunsets, and stars so beautiful you *know* that your problems don't matter in comparison, that there's something greater beyond your minuscule life. It's eating good food and drinking iced coffee in the summer and apple cider chai in the autumn. It's screaming in the car on a road trip alone when you're free. It's simple and complex and ugly and beautiful all at once."

"Do you miss it yet?"

I met his gaze. His eyes were shadowed in the dark of dawn.

I nodded.

"Maybe–" Silas started, cutting himself off. "Well, Someday."

His attention was off of me and onto the apple, slicing through its skin with such precision. He cut the pieces into chunks, gathering them together in a pile. He tossed the core through the trees to our right.

It hit me anew that the kitchens were one of the places that didn't have walls. Caroline had first explained to me that everyone ate together in the kitchen. Sometimes the royal family ate with their people, and other days, they ate their meals in private.

But the way the kitchen had been built aligned with communal living. There were no walls, only trees and grass marking the transition from forest to room. The center, where the table, shelving, and furniture rested, had a thin layer of small rocks and clamshells that clinked and crunched whenever Silas moved around.

"So we're having oatmeal for breakfast?" I peered around him at the fire where the kettle steamed.

"Mother's recipe."

I thought I heard pain in his voice, maybe nostalgia.

His body froze aside from his chest rising and falling. "She always made the best breakfast. Oatmeal, cornbread, deer meat over the fire. It was always a special meal, even for a normal day. She was just like that."

"She sounds wonderful."

"She was," he said, then shook his head. "*Is*... I guess. I don't know."

He wrapped the edge of his robe sleeve around his hand and turned to reach for the kettle. He poured the boiling water over the oats, then replaced the kettle to its hook. He pulled four small jars from the shelves.

I watched him while he added what looked like salt from one, what smelled like cinnamon and nutmeg from two others, and a greenish-gray colored herb. Scooping them up in his hands, he added the apple chunks. He then grabbed a spoon from a drawer in the shelving and stirred the contents of the bowl until they were mixed.

"Lycaon," Silas spoke, holding a hand at the base of his sternum. "*Veime kunan, surin lukos. Rauha ussen. Bene.*"

He passed me a spoon and dug in.

I took a bite, the flavors melding in my mouth. Silas had added thyme, the mystery herb. I never would have thought about adding it to oatmeal, but it balanced the tartness of the apple.

"Tell me about your wolf life," I said between mouthfuls.

He shrugged, swallowing. "You know a lot of it. I grew up as a prince who might one day rule Arcadia. Nash and I fought constantly, and Caroline always thought she was better than us. And our mother passed to the Other Realm when we were fifteen, only five years ago, though it's like I've spent a lifetime without her."

"And Iain?" I urged.

Silas shook his head. "He was always a father to us, not a king. Just Iain. And he taught us well growing up. Only when Nash started disappearing for long lengths of time did things start to slip away from us."

"Disappear? What do you mean?"

I knew he'd missed Iain's passing. That much was evident from his lack of knowledge when he'd barged into my council hearing. But now that I tried to understand the timeline, how long had Nash been gone?

Silas shifted where he stood, shoulders tensing.

"The first time Nash disappeared, he'd been gone for two days— about a week or so after burying my mother. When he returned, our father was grateful he'd come back. And alive, at that. We hadn't been allowed out alone. No *virlukos* is until they reach sixteen. So Nash wasn't trained and could've gotten into serious trouble."

"But he kept disappearing?"

Silas clenched his jaw. "He started disappearing for longer periods of time. He'd been gone for about a month when—" He swallowed, clearing his throat. "When Nyx murdered our father."

"I'm so sorry, Si," I whispered. .

He shook his head. "It's not your fault that he wasn't there. My father had been searching for Nash when he... And Nash stayed missing for eight more months. He stayed missing for almost an entire year. I mean, who does that?" His voice snapped. "I've never demanded answers from him. Not once."

"Silas, I'm sure—"

He threw his spoon back into the bowl. "You know, come to think of it. Why did he decide to return now of all times? Now, when you're here and Nyx is causing problems again. A bit of a coincidence, really."

"Silas—"

He wasn't listening to me.

"I'm going to find him."

"Silas."

I reached for him too late.

He dropped his robe and phased, disappearing into the forest.

30

SILAS

THE DIRT FELT COLD on my flushed skin.

I hadn't ended up going after Nash. Halfway to his room, my temper had subsided, and I knew better than to start a fight with him like this. We needed to talk, but arguing out of hurt and anger would accomplish nothing.

Instead, I found myself kneeling in the Aisle of Kings again.

Alone.

Under the cover of heavy gray clouds, the row of standing stones seemed ancient, like nothing had moved in centuries. Like the Spirits hadn't howled a few nights ago.

I grabbed fistfuls of the soft, rich dirt around my parents' resting place. The immediate chill of the dirt subsided and my body heat overpowered it. I felt feverish again.

Eden and I were having a simple conversation that turned sour like rotten fruit. It's not that I hadn't been mad when Nash began disappearing. Caroline and I tried so many times to convince him to stay, to talk, to open up. He never listened.

My father was a great king, but there were days when he was too kind to us.

Nash had needed someone to sit him down with a firm hand and make him talk for a moment to realize that he wasn't alone. He needed better coping mechanisms than running. But that's what made me the Alpha and him the Omega.

Presence.

Reliability.

Maturity.

And he had been gone.

No one had discussed with my siblings who would take the throne until a week or two before our father passed. I wish I had seen it then. The Seers had grown restless, but I assumed it had been because of the solstice. The days were short and bitter cold, and the nights were longer and even colder. The waterfall had frozen two weeks earlier than expected, causing a panic about the gateway.

Could I have been that unobservant? Did I not see the signs?

My father had summoned Caroline and me into Guardian's Glade. He'd stepped out of what was his room and *would* be mine. He wore his silver robe, and the long hair framing his face had been braided, the rest curling wildly around his shoulders and neck. He'd held the Compendium under one arm and a cup of *Joulo* tea in the other.

He'd sat on his throne of branches and beckoned us closer.

I still remembered the expression on Caroline's face, so determined and tuned in. I was careless, flippant even.

Father had assigned us our positions, where we would be stationed from day to day, and who we were to learn under. Caroline would train under the Historians.

I could almost see his eyes boring holes into mine. He had promised

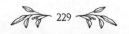

to train me in everything I would need to know to be King of Arcadia. He had promised to guide me, walk by my side while I stumbled through the systems.

But he didn't live long enough. I had abused the little time I had with him.

The last time I saw him whole and in one piece, I had been short with him. We had been discussing what to do about Nash with the feast approaching and how long he had been gone. I had condemned my brother to whatever fate he had chosen since he'd chosen everything *but* his kingdom, his people, his duty.

His *family*.

Father had defended him.

And I'd had enough. The fighting exhausted me, but I carried so much bitterness. So I'd shaken my head, shoving past my father, muttering about me being the king and not him.

I hadn't meant it.

I hadn't meant it at all.

And I would give anything to take those words back.

The dirt, damp from sweat, stuck to my palms. I wiped my hands on my shoulders and tried to stop or at least limit their shaking.

Ransom had mentioned side effects—nightmares, fever, fatigue, nausea. The ache and my chest grew so painful, I wondered for a moment if Ransom hadn't tricked me, if the nightshade had more powerful, lasting effects than momentary blindness and vomiting.

Nightshade.

The ache pulsed when I thought of the vision, so real. I had spoken to Lycaon, felt his fur, heard the rumble of his laugh.

I could take nightshade to see my father and ask him for forgiveness. I can sit with him and ask for advice.

I stood, swaying with tingling legs. The ground rumbled as distant thunder moved towards the valley Arcadia slept in.

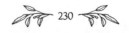

Phasing with a single bound, I trotted with a purpose down the fern-covered path into the Yard. More people milled about now, bowing their heads when I passed. I headed straight for the Sage Brush, knowing my intentions would be frowned upon by Asa, Caroline, and Eden.

Eden.

She would be furious when she found out.

Another rumble, closer and wilder, rattled my bones when I ducked into the darkening forest. The light leaked out through the foliage. I approached the first lantern when a rustling to my left froze me in my tracks.

The forest stood still around me. This calm before the storm unsettled me. The undergrowth shuffled as golden eyes and fur slipped above the plant line. I shook my head, phasing and ducking low. "What are you doing here?"

My sister phased beside me, her skin contrasting against the deep greens. "I could ask you the same thing."

"I asked first. And I'm in charge."

Caroline rolled her eyes. "Look, I'm–" She swallowed. "I'm spying on Markus."

My eyebrows shot up. "*Spying*? Do you think he's up to something?"

She shook her head. "Not that I'm aware of, but with the nightshade incident yesterday–"

"And he talked to Eden last night by the Great River." I gestured behind us where the water gurgled miles away.

"He was with Eden?" She furrowed her brow.

I shrugged. "I guess he went to check on her after she ran out of dinner."

"How did he know where to find her? He should've been eating dinner–"

" –in the kitchens. With everyone else. Why was he behind my

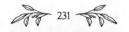

room in the first place?" I turned my eyes to the entrance to the Sage Brush like talking about Markus would summon him.

"Si," Caroline muttered so low that I thought I had imagined it.

I turned to her. Her eyes were pinned to the path leading through the doorway.

"And you're sure he doesn't know?" Markus hurried next to our brother.

"Trust me, he's too busy with Eden." Nash shook his head.

"I hope you understand what this means for me if someone finds out." Markus ran a hand through his dusty-colored hair. "Especially your sister. I... I wouldn't want to hurt her."

Caroline's body went rigid, eyes blazing with cold fury. Lightning flashed, illuminating the two men in the path, followed by a low rumble of thunder echoing in my chest.

Nash put a hand on Markus's shoulder, stopping him before the first lanterns in the archway. "Listen, I know it's been difficult. I know I haven't been around for awhile, but I'm trying to make amends. If there's anything else I can do for you, please let me know."

Markus bowed his head to Nash and melted into the darkness of the Sage Brush. Nash watched for a moment until Markus' heartbeat passed out of earshot, then he turned and headed up the path, shifting as he went.

When I could no longer hear his footfalls or his heartbeat beating in time with our own, I stood, intending to follow Nash. But Caroline grabbed my arm.

"Silas, you can't follow him. He'll know we overheard, and I don't know what he would do. We don't..." She shifted her eyes up and down the path. "We don't know him anymore, right? He's been gone for so long. What if he's the reason that Nyx is back?"

I started to deny it. But doubt whispered in my ears with the force of a tornado. It had lived there since Nash had arrived. He'd been so quick to defend Eden...

What if he'd defended Eden because *he* was guilty?

Rain began to patter against the leaves. I blinked the water away, turning my head down the path.

What if Caroline was right?

What if he's not really our brother anymore?

31

EDEN

I F THE BELONGING IS somewhere in this kingdom, I better start searching.

Walking through the trees towards Guardian's Glade, I thought of my conversation with Silas. It's not that I regretted asking him about his life, I only wished it hadn't resurfaced so much hurt. Nash had only returned, and I caused Silas more pain.

And I'd spoiled such a nice morning with him. I hadn't had many of those since arriving, and I'd gone and ruined this one.

I slipped through the double doors of Guardian's Glade. Edging around the throne, I ran my hand over its twisted branches.

Will I have a throne like this one? Will I sit and preside over court like Silas does?

I lingered for a moment before slipping into Silas's room and shutting the door behind me. My books still towered on the desk, but I heaved the Compendium into my arms.

My eyes caught on something red resting on the table. Doing a double-take, I spotted a pair of apples along with some fresh water, bread, and pecans.

"I could get used to room service." I sighed.

Resting the Compendium on my hip, I slipped an apple into the pocket of my robe and stuffed a piece of bread in my mouth. I headed out the side door towards the river I had sat at only last night, where I gazed at the stars and interacted with strange creatures.

I should have been learning language and culture and etiquette, but I really wanted to know about the expansive world that continued to grow around me. These *creatures* I encountered, the amount of magic that had to exist, the mere thought of multiple shapeshifter packs. It tingled at the tips of my fingers. My entire body pulsated with the energy from daydreaming.

I plopped down on the same boulder from last night, the Compendium in hand. The river ran faster than I had thought the night before. The sight of those waters quickened my heart; I slid back an inch or two on the boulder. With the book secure in my lap, I chewed my first bite of the spruce bread.

When I pulled open the book, the pleasant crackle of page against page met my ears. Accompanied with the babbling river past me, it felt otherworldly.

How is this my life?

Will this ever feel real, or will I always anticipate waking up from a dream?

I combed through pages of stories in slanted writing with a mix of runes and the Ancient Tongue. Images depicting death for natural reasons, death by in-fighting, death by attack, or death by hunting littered the pages. Illustrations of plants lined some entries, an awful lot like my own journal.

My hands stilled over an image.

A wolf.

Eyes that recognized me from the page.

Impossible.

A breeze rippled through my hair, and I closed my eyes as I turned my head up towards the sky.

How can he recognize you on a page? How can he know you at all? It was a dream. He's a hero of history. Nothing more.

My eyes opened, finding that image again.

Lycaon, glowing in the afternoon sun, standing tall amongst the trees in Guardian's Glade. It felt strange to think of that place as ancient. But as far as I knew, Arcadia could have existed as long as the world had.

I shook my head. My brain couldn't process the weight of that thought. I turned the page to find the illustration of Nyx I'd found earlier. Somehow, seeing his face after Lycaon's... it made the dark wolf less scary.

Another breeze gusted around me, pushing the pages faster than I would have thought possible. Immediately, the wind died, and my chest tightened.

About two-thirds through the Compendium, a drawing had been made of a wolf print filled with something red. I prayed it wasn't blood, because the words written under it turned my stomach.

A Vision regarding the newborn pups of King Iain and Queen Ellie. Silas, Caroline, and Nash. May they find peace among trees.

Shaking my head, I glanced over the words in the entry.

Thank Lycaon they're written in English.

"Under the light of a full moon on the last day of the seventh month during the second year under the rule of King Iain, Queen Ellie delivered three new rulers to Arcadia." I stopped reading to think.

July 31st.

"The firstborn. He will be called Silas for the forest that keeps Arcadia safe. A blessing spoken over him that he would never fear the depth or be fazed by the darkness of the forest. Next, the princess. She will be called Caroline for her strong and free-willed spirit. A blessing spoken over her that she would never back away from the truth, always taking it in stride despite the hurt. And last, the immortal. He will be called Nash after the ash tree. A blessing spoken over him that he would protect until death, a solid foundation leaving an immortal legacy behind.

"Elder Macon, the one who pens these words, performed the royal birth ritual, peering into the potential that the three pups had in store. A dark cloud passed over the moon, blotting out its light when the ritual began. The fire sparked with life, images swirling in its smoke and flames. There weren't only three, but four in the flames. A dark shape split the fire in two, revealing a human on Arcadia's sacred ground."

I swallowed, realizing that my mouth had gone dry. "What is this?"

The wind rushed past me again, blocking my vision with my hair. Struggling to push it aside, I turned and froze. Amidst the gale, Elder Macon made his way toward me, staff in hand, unbothered by the wind.

"My queen." He bowed his head and stopped a pace away from me. "May I escort you back into the forest? It is about to rain, and I would hate for centuries of history to be ruined by the unforgiving elements."

The wind stopped.

I squinted at the sky, the dark clouds bringing images up in my head of what that night must have been like with the vision.

"Elder." I closed the book. "Tell me about July 31st."

His face remained impassive, but a slight smile tugged at the corners of his lips. "Let's walk, *je kunin.*"

I obliged, pulling myself to my feet and adjusting my robe, the Compendium held against my waist. The stones crunched under Elder

Macon's feet as he led me back into the forest.

"What you are doing," he turned so I could see his right eye, "is admirable but will be fruitless."

My brow furrowed, and I inhaled, ready to defend myself. But he kept going.

"For years, I have waited for your arrival, debated your identity with Iain again and again." He turned on me, robes swishing in the ferns. "Would you be the one to destroy Arcadia? Were you a lone *virlukos* seeking to take over a pack? Or were you in league with some darker enemy? Or were you a human threatening to bring the weight of the modern world on our shoulders, revealing our secrets to the masses?"

"I would never–"

"Ah, but how would we know?" He smiled, but it resembled a cleared field amongst a thriving forest—worn. "I advised Silas to keep you *contained* until we knew more."

"So you're the reason they all hated me?" My anger boiled underneath the surface.

He shook his head, picking up his pace. "They do not hate you. And I don't think Silas knows about the vision. The past year, he has been so distracted by picking up the shattered pieces of our kingdom that he hasn't had the chance to go through the Compendium cover to cover. He's been on guard physically and emotionally, protecting his people, not resting until his body gives in to sleep. Back then, he wouldn't eat for days. He wouldn't sleep. He would pace. Silas nearly became one of the Spirits in the trees, a ghost, a shell. But I fear for him now."

"What's coming that we don't already know? What more is there besides Nyx?" I quickened my pace in return.

"You cannot stop it, Eden. I've already seen it. And the Princess shines bright." Elder Macon froze in a dense patch of trees, glancing from side to side.

We stopped in what resembled any other part of the forest. And by this point, I was far more lost than I expected to be. Elder Macon craned his neck, tilting his head to the side like he listened for something.

And with a sudden gust of wind again, the trees bent and bowed, forming a path where there hadn't been one. The old man stepped through the opening of the tunnel of trees.

"Follow."

I did as commanded, mystified by the round path through the trees.

"How did you–"

"A gift." The Elder gave me a smile over his shoulder. "From Lycaon himself."

"Lycaon?" I stumbled over my feet.

"A gift all *virlukos* are granted *if* they only ask for it." He held a branch aside as we stepped into a furnished space like a library. Instead of the walls being made out of the thorny plants, they were trunk and wood, still alive. Books lined the shelves that grew from the walls, and books continued to fill up other spaces like the two tables and cot.

"What is this place?"

"Eden, welcome to the house of the Elder." He leaned his staff against a bookshelf. "Please make yourself comfortable. I'll be needing to borrow your book while we speak."

I gazed down at the Compendium, aware that I'd been trapped in a room of bookshelves with a man who had been talking crazy and made the trees move.

"It will never leave your sight, and you can take it with you when we're done." He held his hands out. "It's my duty."

I lifted the heavy book with effort after carrying it for so long, and I worried that Elder Macon would struggle. But he accepted it with the ease of someone who had held that thing a hundred times.

And he likely had.

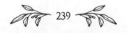

I sat on the edge of the cot. Settling down at one of the tables, he opened the book near the page with the bloody paw print illustration and Silas's birthday prophecy. Elder Macon began writing, the scratch of the tip against the page filled the small space. The rest of the world seemed muted.

"Why am I here?" I whispered.

"Why are any of us here?" He shook his head while he wrote in the book. "To live, to love, to learn."

"But why me? I'm just—"

"That's right." He cut off my words with his own. "You are *just*. *Just* human. *Just* right. *Just* Eden. And who are you to say that *just* Eden isn't what Arcadia needs?"

I sighed. "None of it makes any sense!" I dropped my face into my hands.

"*Rauha ussen*, Eden." I heard him shift, and my eyes found him pondering, left hand tapping at the edge of the Compendium. "It doesn't need to make sense. It simply needs to exist."

"You said he doesn't know." I pushed myself off the cot.

"No. He doesn't know about the vision. And even I can't predict what will happen. I have to trust the powers that be."

"Powers being?"

He raised his eyebrows. "You, Silas, Nash, Caroline, Nyx... and others."

"Me? But—"

Elder Macon raised a hand to quiet me. "Eden, I don't know the details. I only know that there will be a moment of decision and we'll have an opening to take down Nyx once and for all."

"If this *vision* involves Nyx, will you tell Silas then?"

Elder Macon paused, eyes flicking around the room. With a sigh, he turned to me. "I will wait until he has to know. This isn't the kind of

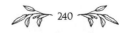

weight he needs to bear."

I crossed my arms over my chest. "But he's the king. Silas is strong. He can handle it."

"Perhaps."

"Tell me about July 31st." I stepped around the table, flipping the page back to the bloody paw print. "Tell me everything about your vision."

Elder Macon passed a hand over his eyes. "I am not proud."

"Please," I whispered.

"It's a common practice to take a glance into the royal family's future through the potential in its pups. So common that such jarring imagery threw me. Visions like this were more historical, not modern. I thought that it could never be true, but twice I did this ritual."

"Twice?" I turned to the page, studying the lines of the paw print. It resembled the track I'd sketched of Silas's the day this all began.

"Once at birth on July 31st. And once after our queen passed across to the Other Realm. May her spirit find peace among trees."

"Why did you decide to look again?" I bent before the old man and placed my hand on his. "Please. You might be the only one who knows anything."

"Lycaon, I hope so." He shuddered. "I saw how hard grief hit them, Nash especially. He hid it in jokes and acting out. And, of course, he disappeared for days, weeks, and months on end. Silas hardened his resolve, lost hope for humans being any good, and blamed them for his mother's death. Caroline guarded her heart after that, afraid to lose any more of her family and afraid to open up to any men who wished to pursue her.

"So I sought their potential again, hoping such a shift wouldn't tarnish their futures, only this time it burned vividly. More details had been added within the decade or so of life that had been lived."

He dragged his fingers across the drawing of the print. "Silas's print. But whose blood has filled it? Is it filling in the gaps of his soul, putting him at ease? Or will this empty his soul even more? Did it predict how Silas would have to fill in his father's prints after Iain passed?" He shifted in his chair before continuing. "I saw the meeting."

"Meeting?" I furrowed my eyebrows.

"I saw you, so young, almost lose your life. That thunderous rumble in the distance warned of what would come when you matured, a storm awaiting you. I saw Iain dive into the river to rescue you. I saw the pups leave their mother to go find their father. I could hear her thoughts like she spoke to me from the Other Realm."

His eyes drifted closed. "She is wrapped in energy and power. She is wise, though she does not know it. She will laugh, at ease with her fate. And she will treat our people with kindness."

His eyes opened, meeting my gaze.

"You're trying to tell me this is destiny?" I willed my breaths to slow and started pacing. "Or fate? Or... I don't know, something stupid?"

"Eden." Elder Macon closed the book, watching me. "It's not fate. Ellie *chose* you. She saw great potential in you even at such a young age, even while she watched from the trees rather than speak to you in person. She *saw* something in you. Who are you to doubt her? Who am I to doubt her?"

Shaking my head, I said nothing.

No way. No way can this be happening. A vision? My life planned out without me even knowing?

My eyebrows furrowed, and the question formed before I could think. "Did you send him? That day in the park, did you send him to meet me?"

Elder Macon smiled and stood. "That? No, that wasn't me. Only Serendipity doing her job."

32

SILAS

I LET MY FEET guide me as I wandered among Arcadia. Paranoia hung over me like the storm clouds. And my stomach felt like Ransom had tied it in knots while I spoke with Lycaon. And something in me felt a twang of jealousy that Eden had received a vision without any assistance or pain.

Maybe she has the Sight and that's why Father chose her to be the queen.

Or maybe Asa had given her nightshade in her tea.

Or maybe that's how Lycaon works.

I groaned in frustration, sending a cluster of ghost beetles in different directions. Then the rain started.

Once again, I'd wandered to the Aisle of Kings.

"Cursed place," I mumbled under my breath and turned around.

Instead, I walked with purpose to the ruins and my mother's garden. I didn't care that it rained. I didn't care that thunder rumbled over my kingdom. I didn't care that I had left my sister behind at the

Sage Brush. I didn't care that I had left Eden in the kitchen. I didn't care that I hadn't been a very good king the past week.

They were all better off without me, a king who didn't know how to be a king.

What good am I in place of someone like my father? How can I lead a country when Lycaon's words don't make sense, and I can't even lead my own family?

"How can I do this without you, Father?" I licked the rain off of my lips. "How can I do this at all? Lycaon, what am I supposed to do?"

I arrived at the ruins, the flowers dancing under the force of the rain, and noticed how bland and normal it seemed in the gray of day. It had loomed ominous in both my vision and after when I'd followed Ransom in the dark.

Rubble, ruins of a past life. It meant nothing.

With a groan, I flopped onto the mossy ground around the base of the old gazebo, closing my eyes and letting the rain pelt my skin.

Wash me clean. Help me start over. Let this horrid year start over.

We grew closer to the anniversary of my father's death every day, closer to the first full year of my reign.

What do I have to show for it?

What will the Compendium say about me when I'm long gone?

Am I the weeping king who accomplishes nothing, or will I be remembered as a hero, dying for the betterment of my kingdom?

I still hadn't told anyone about the details of my conversation with Lycaon. It burned my insides, a secret like a festering wound. It would kill me if I wasn't careful. It might still kill me even if I *was* careful.

Elder Macon would know. He would know what to do. He'd lived a long time; surely he had some wisdom he could give his king.

"Thought I might find you here."

I sat up, opening my eyes and blinking away the rain until I saw the

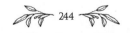

person who stood before me.

Nash.

"A few *micca* saw you come this way. Did you decide that a swim would help clear your head?" He smirked, dropping to sit next to me.

I eyed him.

"Did Nyx steal your voice or something? Or is that a reverse effect of the nightshade? I can get Ransom, and we can fix it. I just hope for your sake and for Eden's that you don't have to chop your tongue off or worse–"

"Nash."

He stopped his rambling with a single eyebrow raised. "So you can speak! Fantastic."

"What are you and Markus hiding from me?"

Nash's face fell, the color draining to match the sky above us. All humor had been sucked away. Lightning flashed, and fear reflected in my brother's eyes. A few seconds later, the thunder cracked so loud it shook the ground we sat on.

"I'm your king, Nash. You have to answer me. I'll wait through this storm until you say whatever you need to."

"Si, I didn't–" He swallowed. "I didn't want Eden to know. I didn't want you to tell her. And I didn't want to involve Caroline if it meant she'd break it off with Markus."

"Break *what* off? And how does this concern Eden?"

Nash shook his head. "I didn't mean to find out, I swear. But Elder Macon and the Feast... you know I can't help snooping. And in my defense, I was unattended, so–"

"Spit it out, Nash!" I growled, standing. "What did you find?"

He scrambled to his feet, pausing with his mouth open. At that moment, he seemed so young despite his scruffy facial hair and long, loose curls like our father's. He looked the part of king much more than

I did with my smooth face and slimmer shoulders.

But I hadn't seen that expression of pain in him in a while.

"Silas, I saw the vision. Both of them."

"Both?" I raised my eyebrows.

He nodded. "Markus had taken the Compendium during the feast. He needed it for documentation to catch up on everything that had happened and Father's choice for your mate. The Elder would've done it, but Elder Macon has been training Markus on ceremonial things and tradition. But Markus found something while bringing it to Elder Macon's study in the forest."

"Markus stole the Compendium?"

"For Elder Macon!" Nash raised his hands in defense. "Only to document history. But he saw the prediction made at our birth, our name meanings and all of that."

"But we knew that. It's not a secret."

"But he told me about the rest."

My heart quickened. "The rest?"

"I'm sorry, Silas. It's all my fault." Nash ran a hand through his dark curls, eyes blinking fast. "When they named us at birth, they sought our potential. And I'm supposed to be the one who protects our kingdom, who dies for it. Not you. I've gone and messed things up again. I mess *everything* up."

"Nash, what are you talking about?" I grabbed his shoulders, but he flinched under my touch. I realized that tears had mixed with rain on his cheeks.

"I'm sorry, Silas. I'm sorry."

He shook where he stood, repeating those two words in an airy voice.

"Nash, I need you to talk to me."

He shook his head. "It's unforgivable. It's treason. I can't."

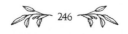

My conversation with Ransom flickered in my mind when I moved my head to look my brother in the eyes. I needed him to feel safe with me again like we had been as pups. "Nash, whatever you do, you're still my brother."

His shoulders shook under my hands. Thunder cracked again, shaking the ground below our feet. "I think I did it. I think I brought Nyx to Arcadia."

I stepped back, dropping my hands to my sides. "You... you led him here?"

History folded in on itself.

Nash sobbed. "I swear it was an accident. I had left. I went to Lukosan in *Kahtentah*. I needed to leave Arcadia—leave *Shaconage*—and the in *Washita*... I've lost a good chunk of my memory from traveling."

He trembled, fisting his hair between his fingers. His chest rose and fell, his heartbeat quickening.

"Nash, you have to breathe. Look at me."

He shook his head. "I remember leaving Arcadia and the Great Mountain and then *Shaconage*. I remember arriving in *Kahtentah* and finding Lukosan. And I remember Andra and Archer, but then my memory goes dark after that. Dark and lonely and wild. And I think Nyx did it. I can't prove it, and I don't understand. But my memory goes dark until the day I came home. And my name..." He ran his hands over his face. "It should've been me protecting the kingdom through my death. You were supposed to care for our people after. I should've been the immortal one. You are the king, the one who keeps Arcadia safe. But I turned it around, and now–"

He cut himself off with a choked cry.

The confession hurt, and I had so many questions about his time away from these mountains, but he wasn't in the mental space to answer questions. As for Nyx, I had started to resign myself to my fate. I had to do the right thing, even if it meant my death.

"Nash, I don't care what happened anymore. I promised Father that I would find you and bring you home, but you came back on your own. And I promised him that I would protect Arcadia. If that means that I have to die in your place, so be it. As long as I've made our father proud and done what's right for our people. That will be enough."

The truth of my words surprised even me.

Yes, he betrayed Arcadia.

Yes, he lied.

Yes, he could be blamed for a lot of things.

But he was my brother, and he would *always* be my brother.

"Nash, I need you to promise me that you won't tell Eden yet."

He rubbed a hand under his eyes, pushing the rain and tears away. "Well, yeah. I don't have nettle for brains."

I rolled my eyes. "No. I need you to not tell her that I have to stand for Arcadia. The vision from the nightshade... Lycaon's words were cryptic, but I think he meant for me to die in place of the kingdom. I have his blessing to stand before Nyx and right the wrongs of our history."

Thunder boomed again. Nash's eyebrows pinched together. "You knew you were going to die."

I shook my head. "Vaguely. I thought of talking to Elder Macon about the details before you arrived now."

Nash straightened. "I think we should. Maybe we can figure out a way for me to take the fall instead of you. That is, if you still want me with you."

I pulled Nash into a hug. "Of course I want you here. There's no one else I'd rather have standing with me now to walk this journey with."

He patted my back twice, backing up. "Where's Caroline?"

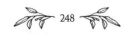

"Busy trying to figure Markus out."

"And Eden?"

I sighed, thinking of the morning. I had been so furious with Nash, that I'd never once questioned him about disappearing. But it seemed clear to me now that he had enough of his own guilt to last a lifetime.

"I left her in the kitchen this morning. She's probably studying in our room."

Despite the somber mood, Nash raised his eyebrow.

I shoved him aside with a shake of my head. "Yeah, yeah. I know."

33

EDEN

"SO WHAT DO I do?" I tried to keep pace with Elder Macon in the pathway he'd bent in the trees. I tripped over a root that had slithered back into place, catching myself before I fell. I jogged to catch back up with him and his blue-lit staff, a beacon in the rain. But it was much harder lugging the Compendium in my arms and attempting to keep it dry under my small frame.

"You keep quiet, for now. It's all potential and not fact. There may yet be things that change. I think it would be best if you didn't discuss the what-ifs with him. Think of how you'd react if I told you that *you* had a mark of death in your future."

I swallowed, feeling like the mark hung over me and not Silas. "It's all so cryptic."

The Elder chuckled. "Such is the way of Seers. Wonderful amounts of knowledge and magic, little foundation to base any truth or fact upon."

I groaned. "So he *could* succeed in banishing Nyx but die facing him or he *could* succeed in banishing him and live. Or he *could* fail. Or he *could* be fine and someone else dies? None of it makes any sense."

The Elder stopped, turning to face me. "Yes. There are countless possibilities. Which is why I don't want to worry him. I promise, I will tell him. If he comes seeking answers, I will give them. But until then, we must keep our hope up."

We walked the rest of the path.

"But what if he knows there's something wrong?" I sighed. "Or asks me what I've done today?"

"You must figure out a way to bend the truth to protect him for a little while longer. If he finds out the entire truth of the matter all at once, we may lose him."

We reached the end of the passageway of trees, and Elder Macon cut a hard left.

"This isn't the way to the river." I glanced back over my shoulder.

"I'm taking you through the heart of Arcadia. That way you can come around a way that's natural, like you were walking in the woods enjoying a stroll."

I noticed the ferns around us rustling. "Elder Macon?"

He turned his head, and the rustling stopped. A brawny *micc* slipped out of the underbrush, whispering in Ancient. Elder Macon stiffened. The light from his staff flickered like his tension affected its glow.

"What is it?" I turned to the *micc* who had already disappeared into the ferns again.

In response, the Elder gripped my elbow and turned us in the opposite direction, pulling me along while he swept through the forest.

"What's going on?" I hissed.

He let go but continued in a fast stride. "Silas. And Nash. They're heading this way."

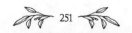

"Do the *micca* follow your orders?"

He stopped, piercing me with his gaze. "I have eyes and ears all over Arcadia and beyond. I am not in control of them, but we are in harmony. As the Elder, it is my job to see and hear everything."

He began walking again, but before I could ask any more questions, Silas and Nash stepped out of the thick trees and onto the path ahead, both bare and soaked to the bone.

Elder Macon froze, and I collided with his shoulder. I saw Nash and Silas both spot the Compendium in my hands.

"Eden." Silas cleared his throat. "Elder Macon. How are you?"

"Wonderful, thank you, *je kunan*. I told Eden about all of the creatures she might find that seek refuge in Arcadia. She had met an *ugal* but hadn't met any of the *kuslar*. But it began to rain, so I'm taking her back on the fastest route."

Nash glanced at Silas, who frowned. "Right. Well, Nash and I were wanting to talk to you about..." His voice trailed off.

"Eden," Elder Macon turned to me, "I presume you can find your way back?"

I nodded with a tight smile, then turned and hurried away.

Please don't ask any questions, Silas. Please don't make me lie.

"Eden?" Silas called.

I froze, then turned to face him. His head tilted sideways, watching me like a hawk. "Yes?"

"Can I have the Compendium, please?"

My body shivered from the autumn rain, but my cheeks flushed. With a quick glance at Elder Macon, I passed the heavy book to Silas, who accepted it without breaking my gaze.

Something shifted in his eyes. But he pulled me in for a short hug, kissing my temple. "Shout if you need help, okay? Someone will come for you."

I swallowed hard, and left them. In a feeble attempt to slow my breathing, I pushed air out of my lips. I glanced back to find Elder Macon opening the tree path again, watching me as if he feared the outcome of the vision even now.

An hour or so passed, and I decided to work on my Ancient in the Yard where others congregated. It gave me an excuse to ask people to quiz me, and it protected me from the rain. Some sort of magic covered the gathering areas, shielding them from the weather.

Some of the pups even napped around my ankles, and it warmed me to be accepted among the people.

They didn't have to take me in, but they chose to do so.

And I grew more comfortable day by day with bare skin. I wasn't quite there myself, but it didn't shock me as much. It seemed ancient, primal in its own way.

Maybe one day I'll get there.

I grinned down at the pups rolling at my feet.

One of them phased to a small boy. "Watch this!" Scrambling to his feet, he launched off of a nearby boulder and phased midair, twisting his body and landing with an unstable plop onto the grass. The other two pups roared with wolfish laughter and bounded after their playmate.

I stacked my booklets and gazed up at the clouds above, biting my lower lip. As much as I enjoyed studying the ancient language of my future kingdom, I worried about Silas and whether the Elder would tell him what had been made known to me.

I sighed, noting my stomach aching with hunger. On my way to the kitchens, I noticed more people milling about. I smiled at anyone I made eye contact with, hoping to come off friendly. One older woman

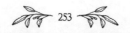

beamed at me, her skin not deeply wrinkled yet.

"Have you been told about the Revel?" Her eyes twinkled.

"Revel?" My eyebrows pinched together.

The woman chuckled. "You're in for a treat, my queen."

She filed in with the rest of the crowd surrounding me. And I realized that it indeed was a crowd—almost the entire kingdom—all filing towards the kitchens like me.

In the kitchens, we filed into the area, spreading out wide. One of the heads of the kitchens met my eyes and beckoned me forward. I glanced around, but everyone chatted amongst themselves. I walked to the woman, clothed in a rusty robe.

"*Je kunin.*" She bowed her head. "Welcome to the Revel."

"Thank you very much, but I—"

"Eden."

I whirled around to face Silas. Nash stood beside me, stiff as a tree trunk. They were both still damp from being out in the rain, but at least they had donned their robes before coming to the kitchens.

"Hi," I breathed. "Will someone please explain to me what's going on?"

Like my confusion eased his tension, Nash's shoulders relaxed, and his lips quirked into a grin. "The little human is about to get an education."

"Education?" I turned the woman beside me, but she counted the people under her breath.

Silas slid closer to me, so close I could smell the rain on his skin. "Arcadia has designated Hunters."

I blinked a few times, trying to reign my thoughts in, distracted from our close proximity. My brain flooded with both memories of our first kiss and the playful breakfast, his anger at Nash and the vision from only five years previous. It all stirred in my head like some hodgepodge soup.

"Hunters."

Silas nodded. "They go out and hunt for game once a week or so, and we store caches around the edges of Arcadia for slimmer months. The Revel is when we all feast on the meals our Hunters have brought home."

"Raw meat?" My brow wrinkled.

He smiled. Whatever storm had been hanging over him, clouding his eyes, it had been blown away by my humanness. "Yes, raw meat, *pilukos*."

"Enough flirting." Nash rolled his eyes. "I'm starving over here."

A dark expression flashed over Silas's eyes, but it disappeared. He turned to the group at large when Caroline emerged. I watched her walk toward us, head high, while the Seer, Markus, lingered behind with the crowd.

"Arcadians," Silas began in a commanding voice, "it is time for the Revel."

Murmurs and hums rippled through the crowd.

Silas grinned at me. "And this is our future queen's first Revel, a pleasure I don't think any one of us has ever witnessed. This is a day of making history!"

The crowd erupted in applause and howls.

I shook my head at Silas, who kept watching me with that stupid grin.

"Eden and I will share the first bite, then you all will fall in line in rank, Caroline following after Eden, and so on. You all know how this goes. Hunters?"

A mix of men and women approached, large pieces of wood held between a pair carrying large quantities and arranged cuts of meat.

"Close your mouth. You look like a cave." Silas whispered with a chuckle.

I turned to him, frowning.

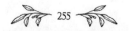

"You didn't think we ripped apart flesh and bone and fur, did you?" He smirked.

"I guess…" I sputtered for an explanation.

I *did* think that it would be a full deer carcass or something. I hadn't expected a meat board on a platter.

"We are wild, Eden. But we're an ancient race of people, far separated from the wolves you've studied. There is dignity and honor here, and a family with a chain of command." He held my hand in his, surprised to find his skin warm to the touch despite the chill in the air. "We are unique. And you are a part of that now."

The pairs of hunters spread out amongst the people, the crowd readjusting based on rank and superiority. The last pair stopped in front of us, lowering the platter to table height.

While grateful that it wasn't a carcass, it still hadn't been cooked. I'd had sushi a few times, but nothing like this. It was like a ribeye stared up at me, still breathing.

"It's only venison." His smile softened.

Still holding my hand, he used his right hand to pick up a small piece of meat. He motioned his head to the board, and I picked out a piece about the same size.

"Ready?" He lifted his piece like it was a toast.

You're being ridiculous, Eden. It's meat.

I nodded. "Ready."

"*Rikas e lo Feru!*" Silas called out.

To Life in the Wild.

34

SILAS

NEVER, IN ALL OF our people's history had a human stepped foot on Arcadian soil, much less participated in a Revel. No one knew what to expect from this human standing beside me.

Eden chewed the tender piece of meat like she feared she'd be sick. The people around us cheered and hollered, all filing in line to receive their own meal.

Caroline stepped up to our platter with a smile. She picked a couple pieces, meeting my gaze. She arched an eyebrow.

I glanced at Markus, who watched us from the sea of purple in which he stood. Turning back to Caroline, I nodded.

She moved towards Markus, and the crowd hushed.

Two historic things in one day.

"What's going on?" Eden muttered. She stepped behind me now, trying to find a better view of Caroline.

"It's a sort of betrothal between herself and Markus."

"*She's* proposing?" I could hear the surprise in Eden's voice, and a smile crept to my face.

"He does have the chance to decline later, but in good custom, he'll take the offer now. And we'll have a family gathering tonight."

With grace like our mother, she held out a piece of meat to Markus. His ears flushed pink when he accepted, but he beamed. She whispered something to him, and he rolled his eyes.

The people around us erupted again in cheers, followed by howling and hollering. I joined in, glancing down at Eden. Her eyes sparkled.

Everyone quieted after a moment and returned to the Revel. Caroline stayed standing close to Markus.

I leaned down, my lips close to Eden's ear. "Just you wait. Our ceremony will be much more wild than this."

Her cheeks flushed pink when her eyes cut to mine.

"And we're making a substantial amount of *Kulas*." Nash leaned his head between us.

I put my palm over his face, pushing him back with an eye roll.

"*Kulas*?" Eden asked. "Isn't that gold? You can make gold?"

Chuckling, I shook my head. "It's a drink. It only seems golden. But good job with the translation. Keep it up, and you'll speak Ancient better than Nash."

"Oh, whatever. I always communicated better than you." Nash bumped my shoulder when I took another piece of meat.

To my delight, Eden picked another piece up.

"Admit it," I mumbled through my mouthful of food. "You like living with wolves."

She smiled, swallowing. "I never said otherwise. I'd rather live with wolves than run from them."

We settled into a peaceful quiet while the crowd mingled and ate. The heads of the kitchen ate near us, discussing plans for the *Joulo* feast in three months' time.

I had expected fear to overcome me at the thought of the feast—one I might miss if I didn't make it through the coming darkness. Instead, indifference greeted me. What a gift to not feel anything at their words, no stab of pain at the thought of missing my father. Call it peace or acceptance or sheer stupidity, but I felt grateful that anxiety and fear hadn't conquered my body.

"Nash, are you not hungry?"

I snapped my head to Eden who had noticed Nash not eating.

Status was the current of our culture. We had to have some sort of order, otherwise we'd accomplish nothing and people would lose their way in the undertow of confusion. But Eden didn't feel its constant ebb and flow, the fluidity behind it. Sure, Nash had been born a prince, but he'd chosen to be the outcast when he left. He wasn't present, and he dealt with the consequences.

Nash cleared his throat, but he didn't act embarrassed. "I have to eat last now."

"Last?" Eden turned to me, and then her eyes roved over the crowd.

Pups were scarfing down what food they could eat, youngest first. They needed to bulk up before the winter. Then the elders, including Elder Macon and the Branches—the heads of each guild. Then mothers and fathers, along with all of the Guardians. And so on.

And then Nash.

Before my coronation, I thought it would be fun to gloat when he returned, shoving it in his face that I'd been better. That I could best him. The Branches had told my father they thought I would make the best leader out of my siblings.

Whether they were right or not, I wasn't sure.

But Nash returned and was accepted without discussion or even thought.

The new Omega.

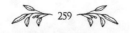

While people collected all that they wanted, Caroline and I included, Nash stepped to our platter and picked up two pieces, glancing at me.

I nodded, and he picked up two more.

"And you're okay with this?" Eden muttered.

I took a breath to answer her, but Nash started first. "Eden, it's all right. I did this to myself. I left, I made poor choices, and I have to live with that. That's life here."

She seemed broken, the sparkle of intrigue gone now.

Nash bumped her shoulder with his elbow. "But hey, it means I get the short stick to make the *Kulas* for *Joulo,* so I'll be sure it's extra strong for you."

With a wink, he sauntered off and plopped down against a tree away from the rest of the people.

Eden watched him for a moment before shaking her head. "This isn't right."

I put an arm around her shoulders. "He decided to leave. But he can earn his place again. It takes time."

She leaned her head against my shoulder. "I still have so much to learn."

I smiled as she sighed against me. "So much, *pilukos*. So much more to learn."

35

EDEN

I SPENT THE RAINY afternoon at the Tailors' quarters trying on a few different robes. Silas had promised that I would be invited to the family dinner but that I needed more than one robe since mine grew filthier by the day.

I had, up to then, been borrowing robes. Even the navy Historian robe didn't hang right on my frame, though I thought all robes were "one-size fits all." Apparently, I was wrong.

The group of sewists flitted back and forth around the organized room, the very first room in all of Arcadia that had a real roof. It consisted of branches stripped of their leaves, layered together, darkening the room. Lanterns hung on the posts, the entire place seeming like a seamstress took residence in someone's backyard pergola or gazebo.

There were posts on all four corners with branches acting like hangers for different colors of fabric. And there were lots of colors.

I listed the colors in my head, along with the Branch it represented.

Navy for Historians.

Light green for the young and learning.

Silver for royalty.

Violet for Seers.

Light blue for Guardians and Hunters.

Evergreen for Healers.

Rusty copper for the Cooks.

Mustard for the Tailors.

Beige for the ones without a Branch.

Then there were colors I had seen but didn't know their function. There were other shades of green and brown, as well as reds and pale purple and black, even a small bit of oranges and pinks.

The Tailors that worked with me now had picked three different colors: navy, white, and silver.

"Turn." The Tailor at my feet twirled her finger. The man next to her held out a handful of needles and pins.

"Please don't take this the wrong way," I started, shuffling around to face the opposite direction. "If you all don't really mingle with humans, how do you come across some of the stuff you have? Like paper and needles."

The woman scoffed. "Just because we don't mingle doesn't mean we don't ever go around humans. We try not to. Obviously, we stand out a bit. But..."

The man spoke up. "We send a group into town from time to time for a resupply. It's different now that we have certain commodities. Before, in ancient times, we acted more like wolves and less like humans."

"So I know the navy is for the Historians." I motioned down at the blue fabric hung over a branch. "And the silver is for members of the royal family. But what is the white for?" I gazed down at the robe they were fitting me for.

The two Tailors exchanged a bemused glance before busting out in laughter.

"What is it? What's so funny?"

The woman giggled. "It's for your ceremony. White is for special occasions."

Ceremony.

Wedding.

How stupid am I?

"Right. I almost forgot."

"How could you forget about your own marriage ceremony?" The man chuckled. "My wife went on about ours the entire time leading up to it. She couldn't plan it enough."

"What all is there to plan?" I asked.

"Oh, *you* don't need to worry." The woman pinned another part of the robe. "As long as you show up and speak, everything else will be done for you. Part of the perks of being betrothed to a royal."

"What are your ceremonies like? Is there dancing?"

The man nodded his head, eyes wide. "A lot of dancing."

The woman turned to the man, craning her neck. "Can you bring me the knife? I want to try something."

With an expert hand, she sawed off a piece of the fabric.

"What if we did a straight neckline instead of a V-neck?" She motioned at her chest where her mustard robe dipped in a V-shape. "And then we could pull the sleeves in at your wrists instead of having a wide opening." She held one sleeve tight in her hand. "And then we could make a band or something to hold it together and give it definition." She tied the cut piece of fabric around my wrist, turning the knot towards me so she could see what the flat and sewed version might look like.

"I love it." The man folded one arm against his chest and the other under his chin. "It's very flattering on you."

I tilted my head. "It's difficult for me to imagine, but I trust you two more than I trust myself with this."

She beamed. "Perfect. I should have the other's done within a week or so. I'll have to wait on this one for a bit, but we'll finish it in no time so you can try it on. And you can make changes if you'd like before *Joulo*."

I smiled. "Thank you."

While she unpinned the partial robe dress, reality sank deep in my bones... again.

I'm marrying a king. I'm getting married and I'm not even twenty years old.

I blinked a couple of times, looking down at the seamstress who watched me, like she'd asked a question and waited for an answer.

"I'm sorry." I shook my head. "Lost in thought. Did you say something?"

The woman laughed. "I only asked how you're settling in here. It's not often that we have human visitors."

"You mean never," the man called from across the room where he worked on the Historian robe.

The woman rolled her eyes. "Well, yes. Never. Most of us have had some interactions with humans. Comes with the territory, I guess. But what's it like?"

"You're scaring the poor girl." The man threw his arm out.

"Is it impolite to ask?" The woman bit her lip. "You *are* our queen, but you're human, and it's not so strange. Like you were one of us before."

One of us—the words I had been dying to hear my entire life. The status I had been seeking since forever. Though I never found it among

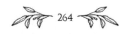

humans, I had found it among wolves.

"It's definitely an adjustment." I slipped my borrowed Historian robe back on.

"What's been the strangest thing to you? The phasing? The ceremonies? Being betrothed to the king?"

The Tailor rolled his eyes. "You're so dramatic."

"What?" The woman gave him an exaggerated shrug, drawing out the word. "Every girl dreams of being an alpha!"

Even wolves want to be somebody—anybody—other than themselves.

"I think the clothing has been the strangest," I said. "That, and the fact that there are magical races of creatures that I didn't know existed until now."

"It's always funny to me how humans make up all these stories and then don't believe them." The woman started replacing her tailoring things.

The other Tailor motioned with his knife. "And then there's the humans who don't believe in wendigos or raven mockers, but they'll believe in sasquatches."

"So not all cryptids exist but some do?"

They answered me with guffaws of laughter.

"You have a lot to learn, *je kunin.*"

"So I have been told," I grumbled.

"All right, shoo." The woman flapped her hands at me. "If you don't leave now, you'll be late for dinner. And I'm sure you won't want to miss tonight."

With a final wag of her eyebrows at me, she turned back to her work.

I found my way down the path quicker than times before, curious about this dinner with Markus. He wasn't likely to reject Caroline, that

much I knew. All of it fascinated me. The child who became Alpha had a mate picked for him or her, but the siblings had the freedom to choose whomever they truly loved.

It seemed unfair. And yet, Iain had chosen me.

Why?

A flash of violet in the bushes caught my eye.

"Markus?" I called out, wondering if he was heading to Guardian's Glade for dinner.

But a face I didn't recognize peeked out of the shadows. The man bowed, his ghostly pale face contrasting his jet-black hair. His milky eyes stared into mine.

"My queen." He bowed. "I do not recommend you go any farther."

"And why is that?"

"It is gruesome."

My heart cinched. "What's gruesome? What's happened?"

The Seer shook his head with a sigh. "Come and see."

He pushed through some branches into the forest with no path, yet he walked with direction and purpose. He hesitated near a mossy tree stump, its longer broken trunk covered in shelf mushrooms. The scent of something rusty met my nose.

"What is it?" I asked, positive at this point that I wouldn't want to know the answer.

The Seer knelt and pulled aside an array of large ferns that had been concealing a body.

A very dead, very mangled, and very bloody body.

36

SILAS

I SMELLED THE BLOOD before I saw it.

Sharp and metallic.

Leander waited to receive us, his milky eyes watching me without seeing. Caroline, Markus, Eden, and Nash had come with me. After Eden had burst into the room out of breath, we'd learned that someone had been killed and a Seer waited for assistance.

"My king." Leander, the Seer, bowed. "Thank you for coming."

"Lead me." I turned to Eden who had one hand pressed against her chest. "Do you need to sit down?"

She shook her head but didn't speak.

"Eden." Caroline placed a hand on her shoulder. "It's okay."

Eden's chin began to quiver. I turned my eyes to Nash.

If she cries, I won't know how to help her. I have duties as a king.

But Nash shook his head. "Go on. We'll stay."

I motioned for Markus to follow, and we tracked after Leander off the path. He bent low near a moss-covered oak stump. The scent of iron consumed my senses as Leander brushed aside the ferns covering the body.

The wolf's tawny fur had tangles of blood and dirt matted around his neck.

"Holy *silva*," I cursed.

Markus only raised an eyebrow.

"Did you know him?" Leander asked, eyes pointed to me. "He doesn't smell familiar to me, though the blood makes that a bit difficult."

"No, I don't know him. Probably an ambassador from Lukosan if I had to guess." I ran a hand through my hair. "They probably caught wind about my engagement and wanted to extend invitations to visit *Kahtentah*."

"We'll need to temporarily bury him." Markus maneuvered for closer inspection. "Most of him is present. Shall I take care of it, my king?"

I nodded. "Leander, would you mind retrieving the Elder? I'll stay here with the ambassador's body."

Leander bowed his head and disappeared into the trees.

"Oh, Lycaon." I rubbed my hands over my eyes. "I'll have to send a messenger."

"My king." Markus had knelt next to the body, digging in the bloodied ferns next to the body. "I found something."

I moved to him when he stood, passing me what seemed like an official letter. The seal had been broken. Unfurling it, I inhaled. The small print of the letter was practically blotted out by the letters in crimson.

Beware. Arcadia is shifting. History will repeat itself.

I clenched my teeth, exhaling.

"My king?" Markus had gotten the message. "What should we do?"

Taking a fortifying breath, I observed the dead *virlukos*. "Have the

Elder and Leander assist you in a temporary burial for the ambassador. I'll send word to Lukosan."

Markus bowed.

I retraced my steps. Caroline hugged Eden, a soothing hand on the girl's shoulders.

"Nash." I cleared my throat. "I need you to copy out what you can of this letter. The small print. I need to know what they want before I respond and break the news."

He grabbed the letter. Unrolling it, he tensed. "Si?"

I nodded. "I know. Please."

He bowed and disappeared down the path.

"Caroline?"

Eden stepped away from my sister, face emotionless.

"I need you to find Rusna, the *micc*. Bring him to Guardian's Glade. Offer him food and drink as well as a new hat from the Tailors. I need a favor from him."

She raised an eyebrow but left Eden and I alone, heading the opposite direction of Nash. The scent of iron still hung in the air. How many atrocities had Arcadia seen in its stretching history? How many murders had occurred on her soil?

I held Eden's hands in mine, gazing at our fingers intertwined. Nothing about this was conventional. Nothing in me wanted things to be this way. But knowing she would be by my side alleviated part of the stress.

"He was an ambassador from Lukosan, the other pack of *virlukos* I told you about." I rubbed my thumbs over the tops of her hands. "He had a letter, but Nyx intercepted him."

She tensed, hands tightening around my own.

I swallowed before continuing. "I thought we had a little more time, but I'm not so sure."

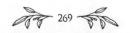

She tilted her head to meet my gaze, eyes overflowing with worry. "What do you mean a little more time?"

I dipped my chin, shifting my weight to the side. "I thought he might try something during the winter solstice, but we can't keep waiting like this. He's growing impatient."

"Impatient for what?"

I met her eyes, swallowing the fear ever present since the day Eden had tumbled into my life. I had wanted to tell her at the meeting with Markus present, explain what I'd discussed with Elder Macon. It would've been the ideal moment, but Nyx had the worst timing.

"Eden, there's something I need to tell you. I–"

"There's a vision," Eden blurted, covering her lips.

Blinking, I shook my head more to reset my thoughts than anything. "Come again?"

She rubbed her hands over her eyes and then her eyebrows, finally resting her hands on her flushed cheeks. "There's a vision in the Compendium. I wasn't sure what to think, and I didn't know if I should tell you. It's about–"

I held a hand up to stop her. "I've read it. I'm well aware that I have to die to reset the balance in Arcadia."

Eden's jaw dropped. "What?"

My eyebrows pulled together. "What?"

"What you just said."

"I've read it."

She balled her hands into fists. "No! After that."

"I'm well aware that I have to die to reset the balance in Arcadia?" It slipped out more like a question than a statement this time, but she wasn't making sense.

"You... you *have* to die?" Her breath hitched.

"What vision did you see?"

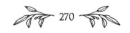

She turned her eyes away, seeming way more confused than heartbroken at the prospect of my death. "There was a page with your birthday, the last day of July. The meanings of your names and then the paw print with blood."

"So you do know."

She shook her head. "Elder Macon didn't really explain much. Only that a lot could change. I didn't think it would be a sure thing. I thought maybe…"

I held her shoulders, rubbing them. "Eden, you have been so understanding, patient, and caring through all of this. It's been torture trying to navigate this… this *thing* between you and me. And I don't expect you to hang around after–" I swallowed and then cleared my throat. "After I meet Nyx. But you always have a home in Arcadia whether I'm here or not."

"Silas–"

"I'm not finished. I'm leaving. Soon. I need to end this. I don't want any more blood on my hands or on Arcadian soil. And I need a favor from you. I need you to help stack my stones because I don't know that Nash and Caroline will be able to do it. And when you bury me, be sure to–"

"Silas!" Eden fisted the fabric of my robe near my waist. "I love you. And I'm not leaving. And I won't let you face this on your own. Whatever I have to do, I will do."

My entire being relaxed at those first three words.

My chest ached with the weight of them.

"Eden," I breathed.

"Kiss me," she whispered.

I closed the space between us, sliding my hands to the back of her neck and lacing my hands in her hair. Her eyes sparkled from underneath her eyelashes.

Those eyes.

This beautiful human.

"Eden, I don't want to hurt you."

"You won't." One hand remained at my waist while the other brushed my hair out of my eyes.

Leaning in, I paused a breath away. "*Je feru kunin.*"

She smiled, her eyes closing. "My wild king."

I brought my lips to hers, soft and careful. If this would be our last kiss, I wanted her to know. I needed her to have no doubt how deep my affection ran for her. It ran wild, sprinting towards the horizon, taking off with my heart and all of my dreams.

My impossible future.

And I would hold her until death parted us.

37

EDEN

THE FUNERAL FOR THE ambassador was unlike anything I had ever witnessed.

Silas slipped out of our room before I woke, leaving me to find his side of the bed cold in his absence.

The previous evening, we'd waited until Elder Macon arrived to head back to Guardian's Glade. There, we found Nash with a translated letter and Caroline with Rusna, the small forest tender who sported a new hat.

I watched Silas be a king, dictating a response to Lukosan and an invitation to Arcadia to retrieve their man's body. The response also included an update on the state of Arcadia regarding Nyx and his looming presence as well as the burial.

Silas had sealed the letter and entrusted it to Rusna for safe delivery. *Micca* were apparently well known for being secretive and hidden, which I'd had the pleasure of witnessing firsthand.

We'd then eaten in silence before retiring to Silas's room.

There, he and I had spoken about the vision, their names, Silas's nightshade vision, as well as his glimpse into the past from Ransom, and even Caroline and Markus's soon-to-be wedding. They had to wait, of course, until after our wedding, but Silas had brushed that off by saying that our wedding would be a difficult one to plan and might take the rest of his life to accomplish.

I had cried at that thought, and he'd pulled me into his arms, holding my hand and combing through my hair until I fell asleep.

If I had one wish, I would have frozen time in that room to live in that moment for the rest of my meaningless life. It might have been enough to fill in the cracks.

For the funeral, Caroline lent me an iridescent white robe. She walked me to the outskirts of Aisle of Kings in silence, our footfalls the only noise present. We arrived early, only a handful of people waiting for us. Silas and Markus were in conversation with Elder Macon. Leander stood nearby with Nash and the guard, Kane, who had been assigned to me upon my arrival to Arcadia. They all, too, wore white.

"*Rauha*, ladies." Nash bowed his head. "How are you doing?"

I shrugged. "Completely unrested."

He pulled me into a hug.

I had never had siblings. Never had a sister to share clothes with or a brother to annoy me or stand up for me. But it felt nice, comforting even, to know I had someone to share in my pain.

With a slight squeeze, Nash pulled me out of my thoughts and back to reality as he stepped back.

Silas strode over, wrapping his arms around me. "If this is my last day, I want to hold you as long as I can."

I leaned into his touch, tucking my head under his chin. "You disappeared this morning," I murmured, voice muffled in his robe.

"I needed to collect the stones for the funeral." He rubbed a thumb across my shoulders and spine. "You looked so peaceful, and I didn't want to wake you."

Pulling back, I tilted my head. "How are you?"

He shrugged, his dark hair falling down into his eyes, slipping from underneath a crown of willow. "A little disjointed, if I'm being honest. Arcadia feels..."

"Wrong?" Nash offered.

Silas nodded. "Uneasy."

"I'm glad I'm not the only one who noticed." Caroline folded her arms over her chest. "Is it because he's from Lukosan?"

"No." Silas pulled back from me but held my hand tight. "I think it knows that something is shifting. It's almost like Arcadia is warning us."

"About Nyx?" I furrowed my eyebrows.

"Not necessarily."

"What are you thinking?" Caroline's body visibly tensed.

"I think it's a mix of everything. My engagement with Eden, now yours and Markus's, Nyx, the death of a Lukosan ambassador. I think it's all tilting the balance Arcadia has held for so long."

"Tilting?" I questioned.

"What about the standing stones?" Nash asked.

"What do you mean?" Silas scratched his chin, watching Nash with sharp eyes.

"The stones have a certain way that they balance on their own, right? They flop over and stay that way until something moves it."

"What's your point?" Caroline asked.

"Silas is about to balance stones for this funeral. It's not the natural balance for the stones, but they *find* balance again. A creative balance or a new perspective. It takes a lot of shifting and maneuvering, but eventually the stones find peace again."

I glanced around, turning to Silas and Caroline to explain.

"Am I wrong?" Nash glanced at his brother and sister. "Arcadia is finding its new balance after so many things have shifted."

Silas shrugged. "It makes more sense the more I think about it. That's a good point, Nash."

"So who's going to balance the stones?" Caroline unfolded her arms. "Us or Nyx?"

"Us." Nash shook his head. "Definitely us."

Elder Macon cleared his throat as he approached. "I am sorry to interrupt, but we must start soon. Are you ready, my king?"

Silas nodded, dropping my hand.

"If everyone would gather around, please!" Elder Macon called.

I noticed then that many people had emerged from the forest around us without me knowing, like ghosts in the misty morning.

Markus stood on the opposite side of the burial spot outside of the Aisle of Kings. Elder Macon stood on the other.

Silas cleared his throat. "Thank you for coming with such short notice." He smiled at the crowd, his eyes flicking over their heads. "Yesterday, our longstanding enemy threatened Arcadia. He's coming closer to home, so today I will call a council to address our plans as a people. But now, we mourn the loss of a brother. Though we do not know his name, he lives with us in Spirit."

Silas bowed his head, the crowd following suit. I bowed my head, closing my eyes. The memory of discovering the wolf's body with Leander haunted my thoughts, the stench of blood and flesh so vivid in my memories.

A haunting call shocked my eyes open.

Markus's hands cupped around his mouth as he called out an eerie and echoing tune, dissonant and unfinished and aching from grief. Then Elder Macon took up the call, his kulning reverberating in the surrounding trees.

Two Guardians lowered the figure wrapped in brown cloth into the grave, covering it with the recently removed soil. Silas knelt next to the mound, laying the first large stone at the head. He had four more stones near him, choosing an oval-shaped stone next and balancing it on its very tip. A few moments passed, but the onlookers stood still like they'd been frozen by Elder Macon and Markus's calls.

Silas then picked up a long stone, balancing it perpendicular to the ground and the next long stone the same way. He then placed a small round stone on the far end of the first long stone for a counterbalance and finished the stack with another oval-shaped stone.

The effect was magical.

Silas stood, careful not to disturb the newly balanced stones. He retraced his steps back to my side, his hand reaching for mine.

Elder Macon muttered something in the Ancient Tongue.

Markus called out again in that same dissonant echo, leaving me off-kilter and somewhat hollow. As his last note melted into the sounds of the forest, Silas squeezed my hand before slipping my fingers through his. He stepped forward again.

"My friends, *rauha ussen*. Peace to us all. I will see you all tonight at Guardian's Glade."

He bowed, dismissing them to their normal daily tasks, and they all dispersed with quiet murmurs and whispers between themselves.

Silas turned to face me. "I have to tell them tonight."

"Tonight? But–"

"I need to end this before any of our people die."

Our people.

"Silas, I don't–"

"My King."

We turned to face Markus and Elder Macon.

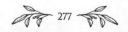

"May I suggest an established plan before we tell the kingdom?" Elder Macon held his staff with both hands. The blue glow from his staff shone bright in the dim morning.

Silas nodded. "We need to discuss what happens if–" He swallowed, but didn't finish his thought.

"After you." Elder Macon motioned down the path leading back to the Yard.

Without another word, Silas started down the path, and I followed. Nash filed in behind me, followed by Markus, Caroline, and Elder Macon.

Silas led us back to Guardian's Glade without so much as a backwards glance at me or anyone else. Inside the private space of Guardian's Glade, Elder Macon closed the door behind us.

"Eden, if you will collect the Compendium."

I did as instructed. The table that had been set for dinner the night before was still there, though no longer decorated for a meal. I placed the heavy book onto the wood surface, dragging it open and flipping through the pages until I found the page with the second vision.

"The next few days are full of much difficulty," the Elder began, "and I'm not positive how things will turn out. My king? If you will..."

Silas stood at the head of the table, pulling the book to rest in front of him. "If you'll all take a seat. I have an important matter to discuss."

While we all shuffled to sit, Silas continued. "I meant to elucidate last night, but we were interrupted. So, today will have to do." He thumbed the pages, licking his lips. "As you all are aware, I asked Ransom to oversee a vision session with nightshade. This was after Ransom had shared with me a vision from the past, Lycaon's past. And his brother, Nyx."

Caroline tensed beside me.

"During the vision induced from the nightshade, Lycaon gave me

His blessing. And I am to stand in place of our kingdom against Nyx."
Silas's eyes flickered to Nash for a brief moment. "And I don't expect
I'll return. I had planned on waiting as long as possible, maybe until
the winter solstice; however, in light of recent events, I fear it will have
to be tomorrow."

Nash bowed his head but said nothing. Markus's face had turned
an ashen color.

"Given that I have no successor, I believe that my throne will pass
to Caroline and Markus." He turned to face them.

Markus shook his head.

"Elder Macon is aware of this, and Nash has agreed that it's the
best option." He turned to me. "And Eden will be welcome in Arcadia
until the end of her days. That will be my final act as King of Arcadia,
giving her safe haven in this place."

I tried to reassure him with a smile.

"I won't accept any pity. This is my fate. This is my job as King of
Arcadia. I hope you all will understand. Eden will stack my stones in
the Aisle of Kings alongside Nash and Caroline. And the next Autumn
Equinox, I'll return in Spirit along with our mother and father."

"Silas," Caroline breathed, "I can't. How could I?"

Silas moved over to his sister, bending to wrap his arms around her
shoulders. "It's in your blood. You'll do fine."

"Si." Nash stood, joining their hug.

Elder Macon moved to stand next to Markus who still stared
forward, eyes glazed over. And I sat staring at my intertwined fingers,
eyes moving from focused to unfocused.

I hadn't expected it to be this difficult. Elder Macon had said that
their mother had chosen me.

And she will laugh, at ease with her fate.

She is wise, though she does not know it.

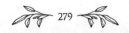

And she will treat our people with kindness.

All sound fell away aside from my sputtering heart.

This was where I belonged: I would be the Princess bound to the rock. I would be the wolf spirit standing in the gap. I would be the fourth shape in the flames, a human brought to Arcadia for this moment.

Eden: a place of delight. Arcadia would once again be a place of rest, a paradise.

I would take Silas's place.

The decision seemed almost natural, like it had always been a part of me. Like destiny. Like Ellie and Iain chose me, saved me from that river for this moment—so I could save their children.

I watched the siblings for a moment longer, trusting they'd have much more to worry about than where the human had disappeared to. I stood, slipping out the door into the dim light of early afternoon, marching into the Sage Brush.

38

EDEN

I DIDN'T MEET A single soul.

Not a bird.

Not a *micc*.

Not a squirrel.

Not a *kuslar*.

Not a deer.

Not an *ugal*.

My feet froze at the entry to the Sage Brush and a chill seeped into my bones. It felt extraordinary, like stepping into the underworld. The darkness shifted, clawing to claim me as its own. The lanterns flickered like this monumental moment didn't affect them.

I took a step, and the darkness swallowed me.

It occurred to me that I hadn't thought about what I would say to him.

Ransom had known, of course, from the beginning. He had tried to tell me in secret ways without alerting anyone to the coming future.

He had tried to be gentle, and I had taken it for malice, for unsettling Seer ways.

What a fool I am.

I didn't come across a single Seer while I walked.

The supernatural blue fire that burned in the center of the ceremonial grounds crackled. I stopped at the threshold, waiting for someone, *anyone.*

But I was alone.

When I stepped over the entryway, the flames from the pit grew higher, an image of myself swirling amongst honeysuckle vines. The phantom seemed somber, a doleful expression taking over her blurry features.

Books lay haphazardly, bundles of plants hung to dry, and star charts had been left pinned to tables with heavy objects on their corners. I perused the items one at a time, glancing over scribbled words in a mix of Ancient and English.

The fire behind me sparked, pulling my attention. A lone figure stood behind it.

I hadn't heard him approach.

"Ar vaara innu lo feru, je kunin."

There is danger in the wild, my queen.

"Ja feru."

I am wild.

He shook his head. "My answer is no."

"Panni, Ransom. Please."

With a flash of movement, his hood fell back, revealing dark ashy circles around his eyes. He regarded me assiduously. "What made the matter clear to you?"

I breathed a sigh. "Silas gathered us together after the funeral. When he spoke, something Elder Macon had told me about... about–" I wasn't sure I had the right to say, but I was past the point of no return.

"*Lo sain*? The legend?" He clasped his hands together as he walked over to the star charts.

"The second vision the Elder made."

Ransom dusted off the sheets, rolling them up and storing them in a clay pot with other rolls of paper. He moved to the books next, closing them and starting a stack.

"I know all about the second prediction. I also know the Legend of the Wild in addition to its epilogue."

"Lycaon's story?"

Didn't Silas say something about Lycaon and his brother—Nyx?

Ransom heaved the stack of thick books into his arms. "If you will follow me, my queen. I can explain a bit more. Stay close."

He turned down the path we had traversed in total darkness when Silas had taken nightshade. I couldn't see even inches in front of me, but the swish of Ransom's robe on the leafy growth below told me I followed in the right direction.

The path stretched longer this time around, and I wondered if there were other corridors or if Ransom could bend the trees like Elder Macon. The Elder was a Seer, after all.

Something hit me.

Or rather, I ran into something thick and hard.

This can't be Ransom. Is it a door?

I stretched my hands. My fingertips touched something rough and almost flaky, nothing like the doors I had seen in Arcadia, worn smooth from decades of use. I'd run into a tree, meaning I had lost my guide.

"Ransom?" I whispered.

The forest around me made no sound in reply.

Lycaon, this can't be happening.

"Ransom!" I hissed.

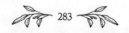

"Is the dark unsettling to you?" A disembodied voice spoke from behind me.

I whirled around but couldn't see a thing. I pressed my back against the tree. "Quite a bit, yes. And I think you're twisted for finding it amusing."

"Who said it amused me? I'm curious to see if you had the Sight in you. The Sight is a gift, but certain things are sacrificed for such a gift. For instance, darkness."

A shocking flare of blue sprang up to the right, a small flame nestled in Ransom's cupped hands. His face fell as he studied the flames.

"This place, the Sage Brush, is supposed to feel sacred for those who enter, needing the Sight to guide their way through the dark and winding paths. But for me..." With a flourish of his hand, blue light flew to lanterns hidden in the dark. "For me, the darkness is day. The darkness means nothing."

The path illuminated, and my body relaxed.

"For me," Ransom continued, folding his hands again, "this is just another day." He smiled, motioning to a door. "Please, come in. Aubrey is making breakfast."

His words jarred me even as I stepped through a doorway into a small living area, furnished with normal Arcadian things, bones and plants and a wardrobe identical to the one in my old room. Then there were Seer things, odd plants hanging above the doorway and symbols decorating the stones around the bed. A bench rested in the center of the room in front of a small fire where Aubrey knelt over a pan.

She glanced up when we entered. "Eden, please, make yourself at home."

Ransom held a hand out to the bench. He took a seat at the far end, rubbing the ash markings off of the skin around his eyes.

Aubrey laughed to herself. "I knew you'd be here. I sent Ransom

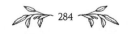

284

out to find you."

I turned to Ransom. He had such an expression of love on his face for his wife that it almost hurt. He seemed so proud to be her husband.

Silas would never look at me like that. He wouldn't have the chance.

"So, I gather you know then?" She pulled the pan away from the fire, the aroma of cooked meat filling the room. "What is your decision?"

"I think it's a bit obvious." Ransom furrowed his brow.

Aubrey rolled her eyes, carrying the pan to their table, where she pushed aside a pair of books. "It may be obvious to us, but she still has to decide. It is her life."

"What is your decision then?" Ransom turned to me, eyes dark with focus.

"I want to take Silas's place. Is that something I can do?" I turned to Aubrey for reassurance.

"It's not unheard of." She shrugged, dishing out meat onto three plates with bread already waiting. "That is what Lycaon did, taking the place of the rest of Arcadia. All Nyx ever wanted was the throne. He felt passed over when Lycaon assumed responsibility after their father passed. The only issue being that, of course, Nyx killed their father. The Branches deemed him unworthy, and so the people of Arcadia cut him out of the pack. And that made him unworthy of the title of Alpha."

"He killed his own father?" I blinked, trying to wrap my head around the morbid history.

"Elder Macon feared that Nash would repeat the past," Ransom began, massaging the palms of his hands. "He's been keeping tabs on Nash ever since he started disappearing when we were all still children."

"You grew up with them?" I rubbed the space between my eyebrows.

Ransom chuckled. "Quite possibly why Silas doesn't prefer my company. I always bet on Nash when they wrestled."

"You are such a pest." Aubrey rolled her eyes. "Eden, would you

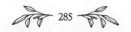

like coffee?"

That caught my attention. "You have coffee? What kind of magic is this?"

Aubrey and Ransom both laughed.

"We're Seers, not magicians." Aubrey brought mugs over for Ransom and me. "But it's something I always ask for when they send people into town. Only for special occasions, of course."

The aroma itself was intoxicating.

"Anyway," Ransom started again, inhaling the steam from his cup. "Elder Macon knew Nash's whereabouts for most of his absences, but this last one..." Ransom rubbed his jaw. "Nash had been in *Kahtentah*, living in and around the Lukosan pack. He'd written to Iain often, sending messages with *micca* and *ugals* or any creature he could convince to help him."

I lowered my mug in surprise. "He'd written to Iain?"

Ransom nodded as Aubrey brought our plates and sat between us. "I don't know how much Iain knew. But Elder Macon said Iain had grown worried after not hearing from Nash. His last message said that he would return before *Joulo* and he'd be coming through *Washita*. But he never arrived."

"He had been gone for a month, though." I turned to Aubrey. "Why didn't he return? And why did he return now?"

Ransom shook his head. "I'd been trying for months to find him with the Sight before he returned. A gaping hole stood in place of the usual visions. I caught glimpses of his eyes, his tracks, his surroundings, but nothing helped me find a firm location, and the glimpses were few and far between. And then..."

He met my gaze.

"What, me?"

"I saw you from Nash's perspective."

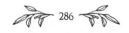

I bit the edge of my lip to keep from interrupting. Questions burned inside of me.

"I saw you start your hike the morning Silas found you. Nash bolted, but that was the first long moment I saw from him. I wasn't surprised to see him the next day, only I hadn't had the chance to warn Silas." He ran a hand through his thin hair.

"We think Nyx worked through Nash to find a loophole in his banishment," Aubrey started. "That somehow he blocked out interference through the Sight. We've been attempting to understand how that would be possible."

"And so *Nash* brought him here?" My voice came out much smaller than I intended. But I couldn't bring myself to speak any louder.

"It's all speculation," Ransom offered. "But Nyx must have caught him between here and *Kahtentah*. Or somewhere in *Washita*."

"Like the messenger." I shook my head, vision blurry.

"Maybe." Aubrey lay a cold hand on my knee. "But if that's the case, he's more powerful than we thought. And..." She shifted.

"And," Ransom took up the sentence, "it could complicate things *if* you decide to go."

The thought of being out of control of my body and mind unsettled me. The idea that I could end up a puppet to such a brutal creature turned my stomach.

I set the plate of uneaten breakfast aside. "As much as I would hate that, I would rather risk it than watch Silas lose everything he loves and has lived for."

Aubrey nodded. "We don't have much time if Silas plans to act tomorrow. We'll need to do this today."

"What do I do?"

Ransom stood, picking up one of the books on the table. "I think it would be best to meet Nyx at the Little River this afternoon. End this

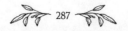

where it began."

"How do we know he'll be there?" I questioned.

"He will be."

Chills ran down my arms and up my spine, reaching as far as the top of my head. The thought of those dark waters still haunted me.

"Since it's rained, the handful of rapids will be a bit unpredictable. That can work for you or against you. And then there's the option of attempting to trick him. Maybe you face him head-on, offering a trade."

"What would he be interested in?"

Aubrey flashed a reproachful glare at Ransom.

Ransom blushed. "Well, he wants the throne. He wants Arcadia. And what better way to edge his way in than pair with a lady of Arcadia?"

"Me? You want me to propose to him?" My words sounded distant to my ears.

"Offer a trade. It'll be like a contract or a covenant that he has to uphold: he'll get a mate if he swears to keep the peace. And if he thinks you're already Queen, maybe he'd be willing to listen. Marrying the Queen means instant access to the throne."

I stood, beginning to pace on the other side of the fire. "Is there an option where I don't have to marry the immortal demon wolf?"

Aubrey set her breakfast aside. "You wouldn't *ever* marry him. We'll have Guardians nearby, close enough to attack at the right time. If we can catch him off guard for a moment, we might have enough of an upper hand to end this for good."

I shook my head. "I don't think I can do this."

"You don't have to." Ransom closed the book in his hands, tucking it under his arm. "You don't have to do anything."

"But Silas–" I threw my arm towards the door leading back to the Sage Brush.

"Is the King of Arcadia," Ransom snapped. "We will be committing

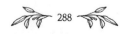

TO LIVE AMONG WOLVES

treason on the highest level by disobeying him."

He hissed the word *treason* so sharply that it cut my spirit. Silence filled the room.

Ransom clasped his hands. "But we are willing to go against him because we believe in you. I believe you will succeed."

"I'm scared," I breathed.

Aubrey stood and reached to hold my hand. "We'll be with you the entire time. And I have a plan."

Ransom made his way to the plants hanging over the door, pulling a small bundle down. He held it out for me to take.

"What's this?"

"Honeysuckle." He smiled. "It's always been yours. Built for the sweetest passion of love as well as the devotion to love lost."

"Does that make me the love lost?" I held the bundle in my hand. It smelled sweet.

"*Veime, myt, dumahn.* Past, present, future... Only time will tell."

My memory flickered with the thought of four-year-old me with Iain asking if I would see him again.

Past, present, future... Only time will tell.

He had insight I hadn't.

There is life after death.

And I would see him again.

39

SILAS

THE BIRDS ALERTED ME to the storm before the thunder did. The crows had been circling, and the songbirds foraged before disappearing to hunker in their nests. Not long after, the first crackle and echo of rolling thunder ensued.

I loved the rain, but electrical storms had always put me on edge. Power lurked in those clouds. Danger and flood followed in its wake. And yet, the rainy season had only begun.

I leaned back from my position between Nash and Caroline, where we sat at Rauha. I lay down between them, gazing up at the tree branches stretching over the edge of the outcrop past our bare feet. The black clouds on the horizon couldn't be seen if I looked straight up.

Caroline lay down, turning her eyes to meet mine.

Nash laid down, sighing as he did so.

"What now?" Caroline whispered.

I smiled at her. "I'm taking this day a moment at a time."

I was grateful Eden had been aware enough to give us space. It's not often you have a whole day to spend with your family before you die.

My mother hadn't gotten that luxury.

My father hadn't been given it either.

I needed this.

If I'd taken my stand tomorrow amidst secrets and lies, attempting to soften the blow to my family, I would've been a coward. If I were to hold my ground against Nyx and protect my kingdom and my people without saying a proper goodbye to my siblings, I would've been restless as a Spirit.

I wanted to do this right. Or at least as right as I could. This seemed like the best option.

After another warning rumble of thunder, Caroline started to hum a tune that Elder Macon once taught us. Nash joined in, humming along, taking breaths during the pauses. The nostalgia sent aches through my chest as I let my eyes fall closed.

We used to spend hours up here, hiding from training or bathtime or lessons. Mother would hike up to us and drag us back down with threats if we didn't behave well.

But it had been a refuge during hard seasons or when there were altercations with local human populations. It had been my safe haven when Mother passed on. We'd always had a place to go where we knew who we were.

We weren't royalty for once.

We were siblings.

But that part had disappeared along with Nash after our mother passed on, leaving me and Caroline to pick up the pieces and try to make our family whole again.

I'd started coming up to Rauha alone. It felt empty back then, but it was supposed to be this way. Us three together forever.

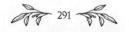

"My king?"

Forever apparently didn't last forever.

I opened my eyes. "Markus."

Caroline scrambled to her feet, dusting off her robe in seconds.

Nash and I shared a bemused expression as we pulled ourselves to our feet. Caroline had only ever been like this with Markus. Never anyone else. And gratitude rushed through me, realizing that she had found someone.

Markus bowed. He seemed anxious.

Maybe this whole engagement and then becoming king thing has severed his nerve.

"Markus, loosen up a bit. You're in good company here." I shouldered Nash.

"It's Ransom," Markus said.

"What about him?" I raised an eyebrow, peace slipping from my grasp like it always did with Ransom.

Markus scratched at the back of his neck. "He's gone. And he's taken Eden."

Wind be with me.

I sprinted down the path towards my mother's garden where the sacred ruins lay waiting.

He has to be there.

Most of Arcadia avoided the place, superstition thinking it haunted. But my mother saw it as a place of beauty, not ashes.

Nash and Caroline tumbled behind me, Markus somewhere behind us.

I shoved branches aside, groaning with every bite and burn. I didn't

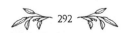

have much of a need for my skin and bones after tomorrow.

But Ransom wasn't the type to disappear.

Something was wrong. Arcadia felt it.

Wind, be behind me.

I tripped onto the path between the Yard and the heart of Arcadia. I turned left, farther into the forest.

"Wait!"

Nearly colliding with Nash and Caroline who were right behind me, I spun to find Leander gliding towards us. His unseeing eyes stared at me, an unusual ashy substance covering his lids and surrounding skin, something I'd never seen him do before. But maybe it was some Seer ritual.

"You're going in the wrong direction."

"No offense, Leander," Nash started with labored breaths, "but how do you know which direction is right when you can't see?"

Leander blinked, turning his head to Nash. "You never change, Nash." With a quiet chuckle, he turned and set off at a brisk pace towards the Yard. "Follow me. I know what he's planning."

Caroline huffed in disbelief. "Leander has never been wrong before, but now is not the best time to test that."

I shook my head. "We need to follow him."

"He's blind." Nash threw a hand out after the Seer. "Isn't there a proverb about that?"

"I can still hear, you know!" Leander called. "We're going to miss him if you all don't hurry up! *Nu, panni!*"

I didn't need another command. I jogged to catch up with Leander.

"I apologize for my brother." I shook my head, matching the Seer's pace. "I've been apologizing for him for years, and it seems I won't be stopping anytime soon."

Leander cracked a smile. "You know what they say, better to be

blind than to see but not have vision."

Leander led us to the depths of the Sage Brush, Markus finally catching up to our small party as we turned down the path we'd taken when I'd ingested nightshade. But the path grew longer and darker.

Suddenly, a small blue flame appeared in the palm of Leander's hand. He blew on it, and the embers flickered and flew around us, lighting lanterns that had been immersed in darkness.

I turned to see Leander open a door and freeze.

"What is it?" I placed a hand on his shoulder.

He took a deep breath and backed up. "We are too late."

Nash groaned. "I told you! We should've kept to our original–"

"Like you're one to talk," Caroline cut him off. "You've always been the one to–"

They continued bickering and talking over each other when I turned back to Markus. He watched Leander, eyebrows low over his eyes.

"Leander," he murmured, pushing past Nash and Caroline's argument. "Face me."

I glanced between them as Leander shifted to face us.

"*Silva,*" Markus cursed. He stepped forward, taking the Seer's face in his hands. "I could bite Ransom right now," Markus growled, wiping the strange, ashy substance off of Leander's face. "He's learned this ancient way of Sight. It's a little like a parasite. He and Aubrey have been experimenting for quite some time."

"What do you mean by experimenting?" I barked. "What's going on?"

Markus stepped back, giving Leander room. Nash and Caroline had shut up and watched the Seers. Leander shook his head as if to clear his thoughts.

"Better?" Markus asked, holding his friend's shoulder.

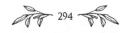

"Ransom?" Leander murmured.

"Who else?" Markus threw his hands up, sighing when he turned around.

"Does someone want to explain what happened with the eyes and the–" Nash motioned circles around his eyes.

Leander bowed his head. "My sincerest apologies. We have all been deceived."

Markus ran a hand through his hair. "There are old texts—centuries old—that discuss this parasitic practice of Sight. It's almost like it puts the host's conscious mind to sleep, and the parasite can walk, talk, live, breathe, see, and speak through the host."

"That's terrifying," Caroline said.

"I can't remember the space between now and when I bumped into Ransom when he headed out." Leander held his hands to his temples. "It's like the memory disappeared and there's a hole where it had been before."

"A hole?" I turned to Markus.

"Like a gap in memories." Nash nodded. "It's like everything is gray between then and now, right?"

Leander and Markus looked at Nash but stayed silent. I let the information sink in, worried that being with Ransom put Eden in danger.

Was he on our side? Had he ever been?

"What do we do now?" Caroline asked, turning to Markus.

"I should find the Elder," I said. "He would know what to do. With everything going on–"

"That's just it, Silas," Markus interrupted. "You bolted before I could explain everything, and I've been trying to catch up to you. Ransom and Eden are gone. So is Elder Macon. I couldn't find Aubrey either."

"You could've started with that," Caroline said, throwing up her arms.

"I tried!" Markus growled. "Silas took off before I could say more."

"Do you think they're seeking a vision of her future?" Nash turned to Caroline.

"Here's what's going to happen," I snapped. I had enough of bickering and differing opinions. "Markus, you'll take Caroline and Leander and search for them wherever you think they'd do the vision ceremony." I pointed at Nash. "You and I are going to Mother's garden."

"The ruins?" Leander asked.

"I have a hunch."

"A hunch," Nash repeated, eyebrows raised. "We're trusting a hunch?"

"Do you have a better idea?" I shoved past him. "You're the Omega here. You listen to me whether you like it or not."

I threw my robe on the ground. With barely a backwards glance, I shifted and ran back down the lit path and through the Sage Brush until I reached the light of day. I didn't stop to wait for Nash and took off towards the heart of Arcadia.

The storm had grown restless in our absence, clouds hanging low. Purple streaks of hot lighting streaked through the cloud. A moment passed before an ear-splitting crash shook the trees around me. The forest aged while I ran, the trees becoming older and denser. Moss coated the floor instead of pine needles and leaf litter. The roots of trees reached out in a hesitant greeting as I approached the edge of the garden.

The stones of the ruins rose out of a light fog, wildflowers mingling with ferns, quaking in the wind of the storm. I shifted in a stumble, bare feet hitting the forest floor. The breeze picked up speed, tearing through my hair while I threw myself to the ground in front of the ruins.

I was alone.

They weren't there. My hunch had been wrong.

I thought for sure that Ransom would have brought her here, like a mirror of the vision he had shown me with Lycaon and Nyx. I thought maybe he would bring her here and Nyx would come in, like two lines of a circle meeting over space and time.

But I was wrong.

My knees hit the grassy earth in front of the bloodroot and daffodils. My heart ached at the sight of them, thinking of my mother and father.

"I want things to be as they were before. I want to go home," I choked.

But you are home.

A harsh breeze rustled the petals of the Solomon's Seal and echinacea flowers, throwing my hair into my eyes. I could almost hear my mother saying I needed a trim, teasing me for my un-royal appearance. I hadn't had the energy to keep up with it. Between the nightmares I'd had since taking the blasted nightshade, the growing tension with Eden, and deciding to die tomorrow, I hadn't even thought about my hair.

When I moved to sit against the ruins, heavy breathing and approaching footfalls reached my ears followed by my brother's exhausted features, shifting to his human body as he stumbled into the clearing. Thunder rolled, echoing in my ribcage.

"Not used to long-distance running." Nash panted, planting his hands on his knees. His chest rose and fell in a rush to suck air back into his lungs.

"Can't keep up with the Alpha?" I raised an eyebrow.

The dig didn't feel as rewarding as I'd hoped. The disappointment of not finding Eden had far too much control over my emotions.

"Nash," I started, unsure how I would ask. "Where were you? All

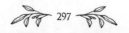

those times you disappeared, where did you go? You left us after we'd already lost so much."

He straightened, brows pinched while he tried to balance his breathing. "I went everywhere. Anywhere. I needed to get away from this place." He shook his head. "I needed away from all those expressions of pity people gave us. I couldn't answer their questions or comfort them. I hurt too much to console *their* sorrow for Mother's death."

"I couldn't give them answers either, but you left me alone."

I heard the bitterness in my voice and hated it, but my filter had disappeared with the arguing in the Sage Brush and the panic of the unknown. My nerves were fried.

"I didn't leave you alone," Nash shook his head. "You had Caroline and Father. *I* was alone. And I know, I chose it for myself. I made my decision, and I'm dealing with the consequences."

"I'll never understand you, Nash." I leaned my head back, gazing up at the dark storm clouds above, casting the clearing in a muggy gray. The ground rumbled another warning and a bolt of lightning crashed somewhere east of us.

Nash slumped against the stone near me, one arm dangling over his knee. "I sent letters to Father, you know, when I..."

The sentence hung there, unfinished in words but complete with meaning.

"Letters?" I asked, heart twisting. "He never said."

"Every week away. Told him what I did, who I met. Even the bad parts." He swallowed. "When I went hungry or got rejected by some other wolf pack, and my rough encounters with humans."

"Nash." I shook my head. "Why didn't you come home sooner?"

He shook his head. "That's just it. I told you. Months of my life are gone. I sent a letter to him, saying I would return home before the

Joulo feast. I knew I'd been gone too long, and it had been a difficult month. But the next thing I remember is being back in our neck of the woods just before *Sarva*."

"But..." I started, blinking a few times. "That would mean–"

"I lost almost an entire year of my life." Nash's jaw ticked.

Thunder rumbled under us, shaking the trees.

"After seeing Leander like that with his eyes all..." Nash clenched his fists. "I'm wondering now if Nyx found me in a low moment and–" He waved the thought away, biting his lower lip.

"Nash," I reached out, placing my hand on his shoulder. "I am so sorry."

He shrugged, sending my hand sliding back to the earth. "Nothing we can do about it now. Just have to move on."

"Do you think Elder Macon would know?" I glanced up at the angry sky. "You saw how he moved the trees. Maybe he knows something we don't?"

Nash shook his head. "You're caught up on the tree thing? We studied it during part of our lessons with Father."

I straightened. "What?"

Nash's eyes met mine, raising an eyebrow. "Did you miss all of that? We talked about it for a week."

Incredulous, I pushed to my feet. "If you paid attention to those lessons, can *you* bend the trees?"

Nash frowned. "Never had the knack. You have to be pretty dedicated to it. Something about a gift from Lycaon or something like that."

"You knew how to gain the ability to move trees and manipulate the wind, and you didn't care enough to attempt?"

He shrugged. "I wasn't the one who didn't pay attention to Father's lessons."

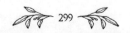

"Unbelievable." I shook my head at him.

He sighed, standing. "Well, I guess we keep looking. Do you have any idea of where you're going?"

"Not a clue." I rubbed my jaw, my mind still on the trees.

"All right, we'll meet back up at Guardian's Glade in an hour, yeah?" He backpedaled towards the path to the Yard.

"See you then. Howl if you find anything."

With a single nod, he phased and disappeared around a bend in the path, leaving me alone once again.

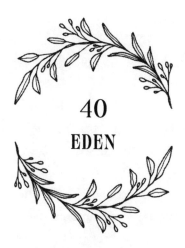

40

EDEN

"**H**URRY. THIS WAY." RANSOM led us through the stony corridor, a faint roar up ahead. Aubrey stayed close behind me. "Markus pulled Leander out of my grasp."

"What about the Guardians?" I craned my neck around to see if they were following Elder Macon, who limped a few paces behind Aubrey.

"They have been alerted and will follow." Elder Macon glanced behind. "They will come."

"I'm beginning to question our planning skills." I rubbed my arms, trying to slow the quaking of my hands and warm myself in the stony corridor. Adrenaline rushed through my veins.

Light gradually filled the stone hall and water roared in front of us. The back of a waterfall barred the way forward, light still gray in the misty afternoon, and Ransom motioned for me to stand next to him.

"This is the gateway, Feru Falls." He had to shout over the pounding water. "We'll climb down the slow way for you to stay dry, but you'll have to ride with someone if we want to evade Silas and reach the river before someone finds us."

Turning right, he started to climb down, sometimes using his hands to lower himself.

This, I was used to. Hiking, climbing, knowing where to step. The water sprayed from the falls, but I picked my way down the path and caught up to Ransom with ease.

It seemed strange to be leaving Arcadia. Something shifted in me, like my body knew the crossing of the invisible borders.

Ransom brushed his damp hair out of his eyes. "It'll be colder from here on out."

I exhaled, leaning against a knotted tree and gazing back at the waterfall. It wasn't tall, but it made up for its height with its thundering sound. It echoed around the grotto while the water flowed further downstream.

"It's beautiful!" I shouted to no one in particular.

Aubrey gazed back at it. "It is, isn't it?"

Ransom unbuttoned his robe. "We're expecting it to freeze by the solstice, but I hope it's not a repeat of last year."

He shared a meaningful glance with Aubrey as she removed her robe.

Iain had been killed last year. The waterfall had frozen. Silas had become king. So much had happened to this resilient little kingdom. If I could help it, I didn't want to add to their woes.

I gazed up at the waterfall, its roar drowning out the rumble of thunder from the black clouds above us. Suddenly, a massive white form burst through the waterfall at full speed. The white wolf plunged into the river and swam onto the bank where we waited. Its eyes were level with my shoulders as it shook its coat free of water.

"Elder, do you want to carry Eden?" Ransom asked, tucking his and Aubrey's robes in a crevice near the entrance of Arcadia.

"It's best if she rides with you." The Elder pawed at his nose. "I'm afraid I'm getting on in years."

Ransom rolled his shoulders, phasing when he bent over. His form, thinner and lighter than I expected, was recognizably him. Aubrey phased next, her coat a glossy gray.

"Do we wait for the Guardians?" I asked, gazing up at the Gateway again, expecting more wolves.

"They'll be a bit more discreet. They'll cross the border elsewhere and spread out." Ransom stretched. "Climb on. We have a long ride ahead of us, and this storm is rolling in fast."

I stepped forward, running my hand through Ransom's fur. I glanced back at Aubrey. She lowered her head, her tail wagging.

"I'm not fragile." Ransom huffed out a laugh.

With a deep breath, I hauled myself up and over Ransom's shoulders, settling myself like I rode bareback on a horse and not a gigantic wolf. His body radiated heat, and I buried my hands around his shoulder blades hoping my fingers wouldn't freeze. It had to be below fifty degrees, and the spray from the waterfall didn't help.

"Hold on tight. And keep a low profile." Ransom glanced back. "I don't want you getting knocked out by a branch before you make yourself dinner for Nyx."

A nervous laugh escaped my lips, my doubts thundering loud like the falls behind us. The plan had too many contingencies. I said a quick prayer, hoping that I'd have enough time to distract Nyx for the others to have an advantage.

With a small yip at the Elder and Aubrey, Ransom took off. Air whipped through my hair, breath rushing out of my lungs. Bending low over Ransom's form, I watched the trees pass in a blur. A louder rumble rippled through my chest, the hair on my arms standing in response. I craned my head backwards, catching sight of a few more wolves in pursuit. I tightened my grip on Ransom's fur, lowering my shoulders.

"*Relax!*" Aubrey barked, running alongside Ransom. "*They're only Guardians.*"

I glanced at them again, watching their movements. I had put in hours of research, wanting to see *this* in action, feet pounding against the earth and muscles flexing with every motion. Power thrived in them.

Ransom ducked to the right, pulling my attention back to holding on for dear life.

I hadn't thought much about it yet, but I could be riding to my death, riding to pain and torture. Riding straight towards mind control or whatever had happened to Nash. I hadn't thought about it at all.

I shifted my grip on Ransom's fur.

"Ransom," I started, "if this goes south..." The air had dried my mouth, making words difficult to form. I swallowed, trying to spit it out. "If this doesn't work, will you tell him?"

He tilted his head and pushed further into the depths of the forest. "*Tell him what, je kunin?*"

I swallowed again, trying to quell the fear rising from my gut. "That all of this is for him. That I want him to be happy and weightless again, no matter what it takes."

He stayed silent aside from small pants of air.

"Ransom?" I called out, bending lower over his shoulders.

"*I'll tell him.*"

While my fear climbed higher into my throat, the heavens opened.

41

SILAS

I CLOSED MY EYES, feeling foolish as I stood under the rippling sky next to the ruins.

Talk to Lycaon. He said that He would be with you.

"Where is Eden?" I asked aloud.

The air around me rumbled with thunder.

I opened my eyes. "Lycaon, where is Eden?"

The clouds above opened, rain starting slow and picking up to a torrential downpour.

"Lycaon!" I screamed, anger controlling my entire body, pulling it taut. "Speak to me! Show yourself!"

My throat felt raw and rough. My stomach turned.

"Sen aun atsta alla."

A voice.

I pushed the wet hair out of my eyes, searching for the whisper in the storm. I hadn't heard anyone approaching.

You cannot protect everyone.

"But I have to try!" I shouted, voice cracking. "Please."

Wind picked up, shaking the tree branches in a wave of movement. It circled the ruins, faster and faster, whipping my hair around my ears.

"I don't understand!"

The wind swirled up, ripping leaves free from their branches.

"Do you toy with me now in my hour of need?" I shouted at the gusts of wind.

Eddies of leaves whipped around me as I shielded my face.

Please. Panni.

If only I could speak to Lycaon. I would give anything, absolutely everything.

A torrent of leaves flew past me and the trees groaned, forging a path through a thick wood. The trees bent and creaked.

"Sen sun lo lukos kunan. Sen sun lo dumahn e lo feru."

Wolf King, future of the wild.

"Thank you. Lycaon, thank you," I whispered, throwing myself down the new trail that shouldn't have existed.

The trees ended at the bank of the Great River, an eddy of leaves leading the way. The rolling water roared, attempting to escape its boundaries after the rain from the past two days. The gust of leaves stayed ten steps ahead, guiding me downstream.

I felt it when I crossed the boundary of Arcadia. The magic rippled, leaving me exposed and vulnerable.

The forest around me had been tinted in a deep green only moments ago, but now the deciduous trees held every shade of yellow, orange, red, and brown. A painter's palette of autumn leaves littered the muddy river to my left.

I phased as I ran, struggling to keep up with the wind. The thought ripped a laugh from my lungs.

Like I could keep up with the wind.

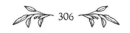

I howled low, hoping it might carry its way back to someone at Arcadia.

Yes, I was king. Yes, I should have stayed behind and been more organized with my search. But Lycaon had shown me where to go. Eden had left Arcadia.

And Ransom had gone with her, along with the Elder and Aubrey.

What did she need with three Seers?

I didn't want to admit how much it stung me. But her words—she had finally said she loved me, but what did I know? This whole time, maybe she had been waiting for the right moment to make her escape, to work her way out of this arranged marriage. Maybe she asked Ransom to guide her out. And how I acted now, bounding after her, wasn't that the action of a lovesick fool?

My heart couldn't take it.

If she rejects you, what will you tell your people?

Your family?

Your father?

Will it even matter come tomorrow?

The rain fell so hard now that it blinded me. I slowed to a stop, searching for the eddy of leaves or the wind to guide me to Eden.

I can't lose her now.

Please.

A low howl downstream caught my attention.

Ransom.

42

EDEN

WE SLID TO A stop in front of the bank I remembered all too well. This time the storm unleashed its torrents of rain without remorse. Rain pelted my skin, causing my limbs to shake without restraint.

The rushing water drowned the sandy shore of the river, seeping past its normal banks.

Aubrey's nose nuzzled my hand. *"Calm down."*

"I am calm," I lied.

"I can hear your heartbeat, Eden." She sniffed. *"I can tell that you're lying. And I can tell that you're freaking out."*

"Way to help calm my nerves," I grumbled, rubbing my arms.

Her shoulder blades moved in a wolfish shrug. *"There's not much I can say to make this any easier on you."*

I nodded without conviction, stumbling when I dismounted from Ransom's back. My feet landed in the freezing cold mountain water. I stepped back onto the bank.

Elder Macon sniffed the air as the Guardians appeared from the shadows.

"What do we do now?" I asked, turning to Ransom. He had the most detailed plan out of all of us.

"*Now?*" He flung the water off his coat despite being in the middle of the storm. "*We wait. There's nothing else to do.*"

"*That's not entirely true.*" Elder Macon stretched. "*We could alert him to our presence. He might not be expecting any sort of action.*"

"*Shall I then?*" Ransom turned to the Guardians.

They bowed their heads in response before melting into the shadows.

A chill ran down me, and I realized how cold I was. My bare feet grew numb on the stony bank of the river.

Throwing his head back, eyes closed and facing the sky, Ransom let out a mournful bellow. It cut through the rumbles of thunder, the pounding of rain, and rushing of river.

I turned in a slow circle, watching the shadows. Would he approach from our bank or the other? Would he be in human form or in wolf form? Would he come at all?

After several long moments of silence, I turned to the Elder, opening my mouth to ask what we should do next. But my words were cut off by a louder and deeper howl from across the river, sending chills through my spirit.

He's here.

43

SILAS

A SINGLE RESPONDING HOWL called back to Ransom's.

It chilled my bones more than the ice of winter, more than the bite of the rain on my fur.

A fog rolled in faster than natural.

Nyx.

44

EDEN

I SAW A WEREWOLF for the first time when I was four years old.

No one believed me. I don't blame them.

I was an imaginative girl living amongst the mountains, studying them, befriending them. A girl who screamed in the wind, unruly dark curls flying behind her.

And I was about to be killed by a shapeshifter. A werewolf. A *virlukos*.

I had searched for this, searched for belonging. And I found it. But at what cost?

Around me, a dense fog swallowed everything in its path. Trees, stones, friends—all were blanketed in mystery. It disoriented me.

He's messing with your mind.

Stand your ground.

There's no backing down now.

Above me, the clouds rumbled in their unease, a storm fighting in their depths, rain making it difficult to keep my eyes open. The Little

River rushed before me as I stood on that same shore where Iain had rescued me all those years ago. I thought I could face this place and that memory without a problem, but my entire body shook with fear and cold.

I had come here to trick a beast.

What a fool I am.

My death was inevitable.

But Silas.

I prayed that he'd find the resolve to forgive me for leaving. I prayed that he'd find the strength to not blame himself if I died.

I thought of our would-be wedding.

Until death do us part.

Death would've been the only reason to leave him. But it came much earlier than I expected.

My veins filled with ice at the sound of that sickening growl. Nyx emerged from the dense fog like a ship on the ocean, slipping into existence with ease. The times I had dreamt of him, he had been half wolf and half smoke, difficult to see. But reality was much worse. His face had been scarred, ugly gashes visible despite his fur growing back in places. And those reddish amber eyes bore down on me, unrelenting in their hate.

I had thought he'd be scrawny like the regular wolves that roam without a pack. Instead, his shoulders shifted while he walked, his strength evident in his tensed muscles. He loomed powerful and larger than life.

And the terror of it rooted my feet to the ground.

"Has the little king attempted to send a message?" The wolf huffed. *"He thought a human could stand against me?"*

I swallowed, my words spilling out before I thought better of it. "He thought the Queen of Arcadia could."

Nyx shifted where he stood on the opposite bank. "*Queen?*" The word rattled in his throat. He swished his tail, snarling. "*He's made you—a human—his queen?*"

I straightened my shoulders, wanting to appear strong.

"*Folly of the youth.*" He sighed. "*Go back to your cities and your tame life.*"

My shoulders dropped. "What?"

He turned like he didn't plan to stay.

"I am the Queen of Arcadia. I demand your respect." One of my allies moved behind me. True, I wasn't a queen yet, but semantics didn't matter today.

Nyx angled his head at me. "*You, a human, demand my respect? You, a human, thought it wise to stand before me?*"

I said nothing, willing myself not to turn away from his eyes despite the intensity of his hellish gaze.

He faced me now with hackles raised. "*You, a human, are willing to die for Arcadia? To atone for its deceit and abandonment of its own?*"

My resolve faltered at the sight of his anger, and I attempted to keep my voice unwavering. "I came to negotiate." I lowered my head to peer at him through my lashes. "I think I can offer something you might desire."

45

SILAS

"**W**HAT COULD A HUMAN *offer me?*" I could hear him.

Silva, I could hear him.

I couldn't breathe. I pushed harder despite the sharp pains in my lungs. I needed to catch my breath and shake the rain off, but I couldn't stop.

I'm coming, Eden.

"Me." Eden's voice sounded definitive.

I faltered, skidding to a stop.

"*You?*" The monster of a wolf laughed.

"You want the throne, do you not?" Her voice didn't sound afraid.

"*You've done your research, little Historian.*" He sounded impressed.

The fog rolled in thick, making it hard to see. I followed the sounds of their voices, and it grew more difficult to see in the dense cloud layer that blanketed the forest.

"It is my Branch, after all."

"It will be advantageous to have you on my side."

"I do have conditions."

"I would be disappointed if you didn't."

Trees loomed like twisted shadows, and the two voices grew louder by the second.

Straining my ears, I heard not one, not two, but eight separate hearts beating over the roar of the river. Friend or foe, I wasn't sure. And they were guaranteed to hear mine.

I let out a low, short howl.

46

EDEN

"*THE LITTLE KING?*"

I swear I saw Nyx arch an eyebrow.

I turned to the sound of the howl, shaking my head. "I have several Guardians with me. I didn't think you should be trusted."

"*Good girl,*" he rumbled.

The sound of his voice in my head sent new chills down my spine.

"I try to be prepared." I tucked my wet hair behind my ears when Ransom stepped forward, brushing his fur against my right side. He leaned against me.

Something must have caused him to second-guess our plan.

"*So these conditions. What do you stand to gain out of this?*" He moved his weight, tail flicking.

"No more bloodshed. There must be peace in Arcadia. And I retain my freedom."

He snarled, flashing his teeth at me. "*And if I disagree?*"

I eyed Ransom. "*Je kunin–*"

I held my hand out. *"Rauha,* Ransom."

Nyx's shoulders relaxed. *"You've learned the Ancient Tongue."*

It made me sick that he sounded impressed.

"A fitting thing to do as the Queen of Arcadia."

Something moved behind Nyx. I arched my eyebrows, trying to watch without alerting him. We hadn't discussed much of a plan with the Guardians before leaving, so I couldn't be sure if it was one of Nyx's allies or one of mine.

"While I appreciate the attempt at diplomacy," The beast sighed. *"I deny your conditions. And I reject you. Humans are pointless and nothing without virlukos."*

With a single leap, he crashed into me, throwing me to the ground. I slipped down the bank and sank under the river's current like a stone.

47

SILAS

IT HAPPENED SO FAST that I had no time to register before my legs launched me from the river's shore after Nyx.

He's going to kill her.

My head broke the surface, and somewhere she gasped for breath. Lightning crackled nearby.

"*Eden!*" I paddled with the current, praying for speed.

Aubrey, Ransom, Elder Macon, Kane, and two other Guardians sprinted past me on the opposite bank, baying and barking. Ransom hesitated for a moment before launching himself into the fray in the river.

Coughing cut through growls and snarls.

If I could see her.

Aubrey paced along the left bank, watching the water.

"*Where is she?*" I barked.

She glanced at me. "*Under.*"

I dove into the murky waters, swimming with the current. Sticks and debris from the storm scratched against my fur. I pulled myself out of the water, aggressive snarling assaulting my ears.

A third wolf had joined the fight, though I couldn't tell who from my position in the river. They dipped under the surface, bumped into stones, and tumbled over each other while they fought.

"*Silas!*" Aubrey threw herself into the water several feet down the river.

She emerged holding the back of Eden's robe between her teeth. Eden sputtered as Aubrey struggled to keep them both above the water. I ducked under, supporting Eden's full weight on my shoulders. As soon as Aubrey noticed the shift in weight, she released Eden.

I pushed out of the water onto the bank, rolling Eden onto the earth. I glanced back at the fight in the water, spilling over the rapids. The other Guardians were swimming now, paddling around the fight, joining in when they saw the chance.

Aubrey pulled herself out of the river, shaking the water from her fur as another crack of lightning sounded nearby.

Rolling my shoulders, I phased back into my skin, cupping my hand over Eden's cheek. "Are you hurt?"

Eden, still coughing, shook her head. "I think– I think I'm all right."

"What were you thinking?" I hated how angry I sounded, but I was furious and terrified.

She shook her head, body shaking from the chill of the water. "C-couldn't let you do anything stupid." Her lips were tinted blue.

A laugh escaped me. I leaned over, kissing her forehead. "Aubrey, stay with her. Keep her warm."

The Seer nodded, curling herself next to Eden.

With a growl from my core, I bolted down the river and past the fight, phasing as I went. I watched the tussle for a moment before Nyx pulled away, clawing himself onto the bank near me. A low, rumbling snarl rippled through my body, causing him to turn my way.

"*Little king.*" He huffed, shaking out his soaked fur.

"*Menace,*" I snapped.

He had old scars, but someone had landed quite the blow to his face, one eye mangled and blind and a tear through one of his ears.

"*You look terrible.*" I bared my teeth.

"*You look like a wet field mouse.*" His ears flattened, and he lowered his head. "*But I'm glad you're talking to me yourself instead of being a coward and allowing the human to handle it.*"

I snapped at the air. "*Enough. This is between you and me now.*"

"*You want to play, little king?*" Nyx growled. "*Let's play.*"

And then it was teeth and claws, ground and sky, river and thunder.

I had trained my whole life for this moment. I pictured all the times Nash had bested me, the times he'd kicked up the dirt around me while celebrating his victories. He wasn't a terrible brother, but he had always fought like we were enemies.

This would be no different.

Only Nyx aimed to kill.

My teeth met Nyx's shoulder first and he tried to sling me off. We tumbled over each other, a pile of gray and black on the bank of the river. I released Nyx's shoulder when he bit at my ears and neck.

The nervous whining yaps from the Guardians pulled my attention away, causing me to lose my footing on the uneven bank. Scrambling for purchase, I clawed back up until I had sure footing for my backfeet.

Sharp pain rippled through my body as Nyx's teeth clamped onto my throat. It burned as he threw my body at his feet, knocking all the air from my lungs.

"*Weak and worthless.*" He snarled.

Gasping for air, I lifted my head from my tangled position on the ground to see him turning his head and one good eye to my people.

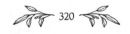

I failed them.

"*Gather around to watch the death of your king.*" He laughed. "*May his spirit find peace among trees.*"

He bent closer to me, lip quivering over bared teeth. I could smell his rusty breath.

This is when I die.

"*Wait,*" an old voice croaked.

Turning my head, I spotted Elder Macon limping towards us. His limp seemed more pronounced than usual. He must have been injured from the fight in the river.

"*What sort of mutt is this?*" Nyx snapped.

Elder Macon lowered his head, unusual for him. "*Macon, sir.*"

Nyx's tongue ran over his teeth. "*I appreciate your respect, Macon. But I'm in the middle of something here.*"

I shifted my weight, pushing up on my front legs, which turned out to be a mistake. Shockwaves of pain radiated from below the joint. I had been injured, and I ground my teeth together to keep my groaning at bay.

Elder Macon shifted on his feet, staring Nyx down. "*No matter what you say or do in this moment, you will never be King of Arcadia. And you will never be more than smoke, a vapor in the stretching history of time.*"

Anger rippled over Nyx's shoulders. "*You dare–*" His whole body began to shake with rage. He stepped over my body towards the Elder.

With a growl of pain, I pushed myself to my haunches.

"*No!*" I screamed, forcing myself up.

But my voice drowned in the howling sound of wind, roaring of water, and rumbling of thunder. Leaves ripped off trees with the force that circled around Elder Macon. He braced his back feet against the earth before throwing his head back in a haunting howl.

The ground trembled under my feet, and everyone tried to regain their balance. The torrent ripped up loose sticks and stones, causing a grayish cloud of dirt and dust to circle us. Elder Macon had somehow harnessed the earth.

"Silas!" Eden's voice called, but I couldn't see her through the chaos.

Nyx let out a terrible bark, spinning towards me. Behind him, the Elder met my gaze.

It was all or nothing.

With a growl, I placed myself in front of the beast. His eyes were filled with such rage.

This was history in the making.

The birth of a Legend.

With as much warning as it began, the torrent disappeared, and the Elder launched himself at Nyx's back legs, pushing our enemy right towards me.

"*Now!*" Ransom led the charge with four Guardians he'd brought along, Elder Macon already fighting, tooth and claw.

A frenzy of fur encapsulated my vision. Seven to one with Nyx holding his ground in the center of the skirmish.

I aimed for his neck this time, gripping with all the strength I had left in me. Nyx swung his head, trying to turn around to fight the attacker behind him. The Guardians in the back pulled at his legs. His teeth snapped near my eyes, and I ducked to avoid the blow.

Ransom shoved into the throng near me, biting into Nyx's jaw. I followed his lead, biting down hard on the opposite side. Nyx howled in pain, attempting to back up towards the river. The others herded him back up the bank towards the treeline with Ransom and I still attached.

I pulled away, backing out of the cluster of wolves. I watched as Nyx shook his head, throwing Ransom's body against a tree.

The Seer didn't stir.

Nyx spun around and bit Elder Macon's flank, tossing his head back and forth.

One of the Guardians leapt over the others, taking hold of Nyx's hackles and sending both of them tumbling to the right. Nyx released the Elder in surprise.

The other Guardians were on the enemy in seconds, snarls and barks filling the air. I watched from a few paces behind, struggling to see beyond the wall of gray fur.

I caught sight of Nyx's tail spinning as he tried to force his way to the top again, but it was no use. He whined and whimpered while the yaps and barks continued from the Guardians.

We outnumbered him.

He had been bested.

I moved forward gingerly, leaning my weight to the right. The Guardians held Nyx down.

Nyx snarled and licked blood away from his jaw, tongue lolling to the side. "*Come to offer me mercy?*"

"*You had your chance once. Your own brother gave that to you and you squandered it.*"

Nyx's body jerked as he attempted to attack, but the Guardians handled him well, holding him down once more.

I stepped forward, gazing down at his prone form. "*I am the King of Arcadia. My job is to uphold our laws and keep my people safe.*"

"*You will never fill his tracks. You will never be enough.*"

His words were poison in my thoughts, but I'd already come to terms with it. "*I will never be Iain. But at least I get the chance to be Silas.*"

I launched myself at him, teeth sinking into flesh. The scent of iron filled my senses, and I felt Nyx squirm under me. The Guardians backed off, leaving Nyx in my grasp. He cried out, trying to pull himself away, but he had lost too much blood. I pulled on his throat until I severed the artery.

My jaw locked until Nyx's body went still. The beast wouldn't breathe again.

I stepped back, his blood lingering on my fur and under my tongue. The Guardians and Aubrey crowded me, licking my fur and nudging me in celebration. But not everyone had joined me.

Panting, I limped over to Ransom's form. I could still hear his heartbeat.

"*Aubrey,*" I whimpered.

In a moment, Aubrey and Eden joined me. The former sat at her husband's side, nudging and licking his muzzle.

He lifted his nose, offering a small whine.

"*We need to carry him within Arcadia's border.*" I turned to the three Guardians. "*Can you carry him?*"

Phasing from fur to skin, the Guardians bowed their heads. "Of course, *je kunan.*"

With careful movements, they hoisted Ransom's lanky wolf body into their arms, beginning the trek back to Arcadia.

"*Go.*" I nodded to Aubrey. "*Be with him.*"

After a bow, Aubrey took off straight after the Guardians, tail disappearing into the undergrowth.

"Where's the Elder?" Eden turned on the spot, watching the forest for his shape, the fog dissipating. "Did you see where he went?"

I turned around, staring at Nyx's body for a breath before scouring the treeline.

I howled. The sky met my howl with its own softening rumble.

"There!" Eden breathed.

I could hear a faint cry not far off. With eyes peeled, I limped

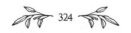

forward up the river where I'd come from, Eden following behind me. We found him upstream.

He dragged his back foot behind him, hanging crookedly now, paw turned to the side. He stumbled, phasing between man and wolf while he regained his balance. His breath came in short wheezes as he turned to face us, his ears folding back and tail tucked between his legs.

"*Do not worry. I am old, je kunan.*" He took labored breaths between sentences. "*I am not afraid to die.*"

"*Elder.*" I circled him, rubbing my head along his shoulder. "*I can carry you back to Arcadia. Asa will–*"

"*–already be tending to Ransom who needs it more than I do. Ransom has a longer life ahead of him.*"

"Edler Macon." Eden rested a hand on the side of his face. "What can we do?"

He whined again before glancing up at the river and the Great Mountain beyond it. "*I think I am in good company. Time shifts, and life moves on. Tell Markus he will make a wonderful Elder. It's all there for him to discover.*"

With a whimper, he dragged himself to the base of a tree, curling up into a broken ball.

"*Please don't leave me,*" I begged.

The Elder lifted his head. "*I'll see you again soon. When you stack my stones, face me east. I always loved the sun in the morning.*"

48

EDEN

I SHOULD'VE BEEN NERVOUS to stack burial stones for the first time. But it felt right.

He would have supported it.

The minor notes of Markus's lilting call echoed between the trees of the Aisles. The scratch of his voice matched the stone in my hands, weighty and difficult to bear. Silas, with tears streaming down his face, took the stone from my hands and placed it over the freshly turned earth that covered the late Elder's wolf form.

My chest ached, spirit hollow.

We'd won the war but lost a warrior.

The days following the death of Nyx were filled with celebration and mourning. We'd lost the Elder and nearly lost Ransom. Asa had gone to work with everything in his arsenal as soon as Ransom crossed the Arcadian border. With rest, Asa claimed Ransom would be almost as good as new, minus a few aches and pains from time to time.

The Elder passed soon after he laid himself down by the river.

Racking sobs overcame Silas's scratched up body, and I held him, not knowing what else to do. I knew my words wouldn't comfort him.

After some time, when Silas had calmed down to sniffles and steady breaths, Nash and Caroline arrived with an entourage of Guardians robed in their light blue. I stood, but Silas didn't move from his seat on the ground. Some of the Guardians lifted Elder Macon's body with ease, and others lifted the body of Nyx following the first group back to Arcadia. I watched as Silas's siblings sat by him.

Silas's bloodstained shoulders shook once more, and he leaned into his sister. Any words he tried speaking were so garbled I couldn't understand a thing.

Nash moved over, hugging me. "I would say you were stupid, but now's not the time."

Despite myself and the yawning hole in my spirit, I chuckled.

"But even if it was stupid, I'm glad you were here." Nash pulled back enough to glance at Silas. "Who knows what he would've done if he'd been alone. The Elder has always been there, kind of like a grandfather figure."

"I'm so sorry, Nash."

He smiled at me, a soft, sad kind of smile. "I'm starting to realize a part of growing up means coming to terms with change. I may not like it, but I can't really fix it either. I simply have to let things be and process them when they come at me."

Caroline had placed a hand on Nash's shoulder. Silas stood facing the river, rubbing away tears with the backs of his thumbs.

"Talk to him, please." She nodded her head towards Silas.

Nash stepped over, words drowned out by the distant rumble of thunder and the rushing of the river.

"I think Silas's arm is injured." Caroline sighed, running a hand through her long hair. "And he has a lot of deep gauges and scrapes.

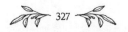

Are you hurt at all?"

I shook my head. "Not that I'm aware. Aside from coughing up river water and uncontrollable shaking, I think I came out unscathed. A few scratches and bruises."

After Nash talked to Silas, they started walking back home, and we followed. The preparations were made, a plot of land dug for the Elder's body, and stones gathered for his memorial. And the people of Arcadia mourned even while they celebrated the death of their enemy.

The Hunters skinned Nyx's body, reserving the fur for the evening of Elder Macon's funeral. The head and tail had been removed to make a ceremonial robe for Silas, and the rest of the thick fur had been used to wrap the Edler before burial.

And now, watching Silas balance the next stone, it amazed me how collected he could be while grieving. Tears streamed down his face, but his hands held the stones steady as he found each balance point. His eyebrows pinched together through the balancing.

I held out the last stone, a pyramid-like rock with round edges.

Silas looked up at me, eyes swollen. "I want you to balance the last stone."

"Silas, I don't think that's a good idea," I whispered.

The eyes of the people of Arcadia dressed in white—standing, kneeling, sitting—watched while Silas balanced the stones. And they would all watch me send the entire stack tumbling.

"I'll help you."

Inhaling, I held the stone to my chest. With movements like a sloth, I held the stone over the stack.

"No. You have to be brave." Silas placed his hands on the rock, rotating it to where one of the points faced down.

"I'll never get it to balance." I glanced at him, then back at the stone with a dubious glare.

"Trust yourself. Trust me." Silas moved his hands to cover mine, his injured one wrapped in cloth. "You have to feel the stone, listen to it through your hands. Allow your thoughts to disappear into the wind."

Heart pounding, I lowered the stone until it touched the stack Silas had already balanced. Eyes open and head straight, I shifted the stone by millimeters, attempting to find whatever frequency Silas talked about.

I started to move my hands, but Silas pushed them back. "Not yet."

Markus called out again, a melancholy howl rustling against the leaves.

Silas pushed his hands against mine, turning the stone to the left. "Start here." He closed his eyes, hands over mine.

I turned my attention back to the stone and repositioned it again. I started to find the off-balance moments. I thought the stone would never balance, but specific stones had been chosen. Surely they would pick stones that would balance with the right touch.

"Stop," Silas murmured, hands stiffening.

My entire body froze at his command. "What did I do now?"

His eyes opened, that brilliant green glistening when he smiled. "You did it."

Wary of collapse, I pulled my fingers off the stone, letting my hands fall away. The pyramid stone commanded respect at the top of the stack, looking impossible.

And I realized that Arcadia was like that, too.

Entirely impossible.

Yet absolutely real.

49

SILAS

I slouched in my throne, letting my head hit the woven branches behind me.

"You did well." Caroline hugged Eden while they started talking about the stone balancing ceremony.

I was glad it had finally ended.

Between the confrontation at the river, the Elder's passing, worrying about mine and Ransom's injuries, and the blurry days since then, my body ached for solitude and simplicity.

In a way, it was a blessing that tradition had the King of Arcadia balancing the stones for each death. I could channel my grief that way, by focusing on each of the stones.

Arcadia had been righted, and I didn't think Nyx's death alone caused the change. Something else had tilted back into place, like balancing two round stones at an angle. That balancing point where they no longer tipped had been found and stabilized.

Has it always been a life for a life?

Or something related to the Spirit that righted the wrongs?

"Si?" Nash snapped his fingers in front of my face. "Arcadia to Silas."

"What?" I blinked.

"You have a response from Lukosan." He nodded towards Rusna, the *micc*, who shuffled behind Nash. "He won't give it to me. Says he'll only give it to you."

"*Onni*, Rusna." I sat up, my smile turning to a wince when I put pressure on my injured arm.

He pulled his new hat off his stone-colored hair and bowed. "*Rauha, je kunan. Ar ussen.*"

I took the letter from his small, calloused hands. "*Bene.*"

He straightened, donned his hat, and disappeared out of the double doors of Guardian's Glade.

"What does it say?" Eden asked, stepping over to lean against the armrest of my throne.

Such audacity from a human.

My human.

My Eden.

In all my days as a king, I had never expected this. In all my years, I could never have prepared for losing my mother, losing my father, losing my brother for a while, becoming king, and on top of it all, marrying a human.

When I glanced up at Eden, she ran her thumb down my cheek. "Are you going to open it?"

I broke the wide-leafed seal depicting sassafras leaves. The letter had been dated only two days previous. They responded immediately.

"*Rauha*, King Silas," I read aloud. "We are heartbroken over our messenger's fate. In a week's time, we will send two of our Guardians to reclaim his body and his stones. Thank you for honoring him."

I swallowed, tasting the iron and blood in the air of my memories. "We are sorry for your war with Nyx. We will send aid if you ask. But we first respect Arcadia's boundaries. Since we also respect you as an Alpha in your own right, we invite you and your mate to join us in Lukosan whenever you desire."

I met Eden's eyes. Her eyebrows bent low over her eyelids.

"What is it?" I questioned.

"It's a pity they didn't send aid *with* Rusna. Maybe they could've managed Nyx for us." She swallowed. "Maybe we wouldn't have lost Elder Macon."

I pulled her closer to sit on the armrest, my arm wrapped around her waist. "What's done is done."

She sighed, resting against me while I continued.

"If you desire, your family may visit with you. Say hello to Caroline and Nash for us. We hope you will accept our invitation, and congratulations again on finding your mate. Much love, A."

"A?" Eden asked.

"Andra." Nash waggled his eyebrows.

"Who is Andra?" Eden bent over the letter.

I passed it to her. "The Alpha of the Lukosan tribe."

Memories of childhood flooded back as I recalled the days long past when we met with the nomadic tribe. Andra and Archer were our playmates, born the same summer as my siblings and me.

"They've grown up a lot." Nash folded his arms over his chest. "They asked about you both a lot while I stayed with them."

"I forgot that you said you were there." I pushed to my feet, favoring my injured arm. "How are they?"

Nash shrugged, frowning. "Don't know. I haven't seen them in a year, remember?"

I shook my head. "As soon as Ransom is better, I need him to

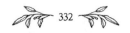

explain the Sight thing they did on Leander. I'm hoping it can help explain what happened to you while you were..." My voice trailed off.

Nash sighed. "Or at least unlock some of those memories. I have no idea what I did during that time."

"So are we going to go?" Eden stood, folding the letter. "To Lukosan?"

I exhaled. I'd never traveled long distances with a human. It was bound to be different and more difficult. But a part of me yearned to leave Arcadia for a while, to escape the painful memories. And I wanted to see Archer and Andra, catch up with them, and see how they were running their kingdom.

I turned to Caroline. "Would it be too soon to visit in a few weeks? Is that irresponsible of me?"

She pursed her lips, eyebrows wrinkled. "I don't think so, considering the death of their messenger and your betrothal. Markus and I can keep the kingdom under control while you're absent. But I wouldn't stay too long. You do have a wedding to plan."

She smiled, giving Eden a knowing look.

"I am absolutely going with you." Nash patted my shoulder.

I nodded then tugged Eden into a hug. "You wanted to see all the magic in the world, right?"

She pulled away enough to meet my eyes. "I do."

"Let's go find it."

THE LEGENDS CONTINUE...

FIND EDEN, SILAS, AND
THE WOLVES OF LUKOSAN IN

TO
BREATHE
BENEATH
STARS

 DECEMBER 2024

Acknowledgements

To my readers: Thank you for making this possible. Every book read is another opportunity for me to continue this wild dream of being an author.

To my betas, Jamie, Jordan, McKenzie, and Reagan: You gave this story the breath its lungs needed to sing. You are the reason that the ending changed and the reason that Nash already has a fan club. I hope you'll continue to champion this funny little wolf pack through the next two books.

To Caitlin, my editor: You refined this story when it was in rough shape and full of passive voice. Forgive me for telling (or not telling enough) rather than showing. And thank you for telling me about your favorite lines and the ones that reminded you of Noah Kahan songs.

To Maria, my cover designer: You did it again, and I will never stop saying that you're a cover wizard. You make magic.

To my husband, Cody: You have been so patient with me. I'm sorry for forgetting I meant to cook dinner. But I'm grateful you're so supportive of this crazy career I've chosen. Here's to more nights of me talking for an hour about plot holes and character arcs that most readers will never see.

And to God: Thank you for blessing me with this gift and the resources to pursue this dream. I hope my words bring people a little more hope and a step closer to you. May they meet you in my stories, somewhere in the trees. You are Lycaon. Ja rakassen, je kunan.

ABOUT THE AUTHOR

A story lover at heart, Morgan has always been crafting stories. Growing up in East Tennessee in the Great Smoky Mountains, their mystery and beauty have inspired many of her tales. She's a big fan of rain, stargazing, coffee, and taking the long way home.

Currently residing in East Tennessee, Morgan lives with her husband, writing books and exploring the mountains. When she's not reading or writing, you'll find Morgan outside foraging among the plants or trying new coffee shops.

Keep in touch with Morgan at
WWW.MORGANHUBBARDAUTHOR.COM
and on Facebook or Instagram @morganhubbardauthor

Made in the USA
Columbia, SC
20 July 2024

39063063R00212